The Marquesa

Heroines of the Golden West
BOOK TWO

THE MARQUESA

STEPHEN BLY

CROSSWAY BOOKS • WHEATON, ILLINOIS
A DIVISION OF GOOD NEWS PUBLISHERS

The Marquesa

Copyright © 1998 by Stephen Bly

Published by Crossway Books
        a division of Good News Publishers
        1300 Crescent Street
        Wheaton, Illinois 60187

Cover design: Cindy Kiple

Cover illustration: Dan Brown

First printing, 1998

Printed in the United States of America

Library of Congress Cataloging-in-Publication Data
Bly, Stephen A., 1944-
   The marquesa / Stephen Bly.
     p.   cm. -- (Heroines of the golden west : bk. 2)
   ISBN 1-58134-025-7 (alk. paper)
   I. Title. II. Series: Bly, Stephen A., 1944- Heroines of the golden
west: bk. 2.
PS3552.L93M37 1998
813'.54—dc21   98-33717

11	10	09	08	07	06	05	04	03	02	01	00	99	98
15	14	13	12	11	10	9	8	7	6	5	4	3	2	1

For
Kathy Jacobs

"If we confess our sins,
he is faithful and just to forgive us our sins,
and to cleanse us from all unrighteousness."

1 JOHN 1:9 (KJV)

— One —

HE WAS A MILITARY MAN.

Isabel Leon could tell that much.

Neatly trimmed hair, clean-shaven except for mustache and straight sideburns . . . stands tall . . . shoulders back . . . West Point, no doubt. Gun worn high at the waist. Cavalry. With all that gray hair, he's either a colonel or a general.

Or used to be.

The crowd inside the Cantrell Mercantile, Montana Territory, packed most of the aisles three deep. Smooth-faced, blue-eyed July Johnson scurried across the store directing both clerks and customers. Very little of the mild April breeze that drifted up from the Yellowstone River and through the budding cottonwood trees made it into the large, stuffy building. Absolutely none of the cool air made it to the loft where Isabel Leon gazed out at the mass of goods-needy gold seekers below. Her dark green knit shawl was now folded neatly on the supply shelf beside her. She shoved the black lace sleeves of her dress halfway up her forearms. Then she tugged at the cramped collar of her dress and tried to fan herself.

His tie is too tight.

But a nicely tanned face.

Civilian suit.

Clean but worn.

Kind of like the man himself.

Obviously, he wants to make an impression on someone.

Well, sweet Carolina Parks, you and Ranahan picked a busy time to go to Maryland and have that baby of yours. July looks fifteen going

*on forty. If you don't get home soon, he'll wear himself out. Perhaps Ran
can rebuild these loft windows so that they open. We need air up here.
Summer will be intolerable with the store crowded. That's why we're
having a full veranda on both stories of the hotel.*

She watched the man with the narrow eyes and square, well-
defined chin resolutely pick his way through the crowd and say
something to July. They talked for several minutes. Finally young
Mr. Johnson nodded his head and pointed to the loft.

He's coming up here? I wasn't planning on having male visitors!

She snatched up the shawl and placed it back on her shoulders.
She brushed her hair straggles behind her ears with her fingers and
hunted for a mirror.

*This is silly. Isabel, there is no man in this room you have to impress.
You are the only woman in this entire store at the moment, so just why
do you think you have to enchant this military man with the confident
air? You are who you are. Who cares what this man thinks? Who cares
what any man thinks? Especially one who looks old enough to be your
father! He probably wants to purchase some supplies in bulk. Where's
Carolina's inventory? Let's see, it's 10 percent off for orders over $200
and 25 percent off on orders over $500.*

I think.

Her dress suddenly felt terribly constraining. *I don't know why
I let Carolina talk me into wearing these high-collar dresses. I'm an
actress, not a schoolteacher.*

She carried the heavy green ledger to the rail of the loft and
tilted it at an angle to catch more light.

*Mr. McGuire brings in his shipment on Thursday. July and I will
have to go over the inventory tonight after we close.*

With the harmonious dull roar of a dozen masculine conversations filling the store, she couldn't hear the march of footsteps on
the rough wooden staircase. But she knew they were coming. She
refolded the shawl and then sat at the oak table and began to flip
through the ledgers in front of her. Out of the corner of her eye,
she caught a glimpse of the man with the round, wide-brimmed hat
and the black stovepipe boots worn on the outside of his charcoal
gray wool trouser legs.

"Excuse me, ma'am, are you the Marquesa?"

It was a deep voice.

With a pleasant tone.

But not a lot of patience.

She turned to face the man but remained seated. For the first time all morning Isabel wondered if she had remembered to put on any lipstick. She wanted to tug on her green and silver dangling earrings but didn't.

"I'm Isabel Leon. Most people seem to enjoy calling me the Marquesa."

"My name is Dawson Mandara. Most often I'm just called—"

"Colonel or General?"

A slight smile flashed across the man's leather-tough face and quickly faded. "Only a captain, I'm afraid. But that was a few years ago."

"'It is a gift from heaven. Something you leave the womb with. An officer always looks like an officer,'" she replied. *From* The Last Battle, *Act I, Scene 1 . . . opening line.*

"So I've been told." He pulled off his hat and ran his fingers through thick gray hair.

"What can I do for you, Captain?" *I imagine that in dress uniform in your prime you turned many a young lady's head.*

"I would like to speak to the owners who are building that hotel across the street. I understand you have some connection with that venture?"

She folded her small, thin hands and rested them on top of the table. "Yes, what can I do for you?"

"Actually I do need to speak to the men in charge. Do they live here in town?"

Isabel rapped her thin fingers on the oak tabletop and narrowed her full, dark eyebrows. "Captain Mandara, *I* am in charge of the hotel. What do you want?" *Some men are much more interesting at a distance.*

"I reckon I'm not expressing myself very well. My apologies, ma'am." He glanced over the loft railing as if trying to spy someone in the store below. "Let me start all over. I understand the men originally hired to construct the hotel have all left for the goldfields at Devil's Canyon, leaving a partially built hotel. In fact, the whole town seems partially built."

Captain, this conversation is going nowhere. "Last summer this building was the only one here. This is a boomtown. I still don't know what you are asking."

He pulled out a gold watch from his vest pocket, opened it, glanced down, then closed it. "What I'm asking is to speak to the owners of that hotel. If you'd just point me in their direction, I'll get out of your hair."

My hair! It's a mess, isn't it? I knew it wouldn't stay in these pearl combs. "I told you, I'm in charge of the hotel."

His brown eyes widened. The permanent creases in their corners spoke of victories and losses. "You own it?"

She rested her elbow on the edge of the table and held her chin in her palm. "You find that hard to believe?"

He stared straight into her eyes as if attempting to pry out the truth with a glance. "I was told different."

She narrowed her eyes and didn't flinch or turn away. "Oh, what was it that you were told?"

"That three men who struck it rich down in the Big Horn Mountains are building the hotel."

"That's only partially true. While Mr. McCallister, Mr. Diggs, and Mr. Conley do own a gold mine, the four of us are in a partnership arrangement on the hotel project."

"Thank you, ma'am." He put his hat back on his head. "Now where can I find these three men?"

"They are either at the Little Canyon Mine or in San Francisco, I would speculate. Perhaps they sailed for Europe. I really don't know."

He rocked back on the heels of his boots and looped his thumbs into his worn black belt. "Well, no wonder that project is half-done. It slows down construction when all the bosses are gone, doesn't it? Well, thanks, anyway. Good day, Marquesa." He turned to leave.

"Captain, what is the nature of your business with my partners? Perhaps I can relay it to them when I contact them again."

There was a split-second flash in his eyes that made Isabel

flinch. "Tell them I can finish building that hotel of theirs in six weeks." He turned back and marched down the stairs.

Isabel leaped up and scooted to the top of the staircase. "Captain! What did you say?"

He stood straight and tall. The big crowd in the store below, like an army in battle, stretched out before him. "I've built hotels before. I can finish the construction for them."

Isabel's borrowed dress felt extremely constraining. Her arms were now crossed. "If you'll come back up, I'd like to discuss that with you."

"I need to talk to the men in charge."

"Oh, that I could find a man among men . . . or at least a man among the women." The Lady Pirate's Last Voyage, Act II, Scene 2. Isabel's otherwise wide, full lips lost any hint of a smile. "I'm in charge."

His baritone voice boomed above the crowd noise. It sounded condescending. "Of the construction?"

"Of everything to do with The Hotel Marquesa," she snapped. *And I am much too busy to waste time like this!*

"That's what they're going to name it? The Hotel Marquesa?" He laced his thumbs into his vest pockets. He seemed to be staring past her at some heavenly vision.

"That's what I named it. After all, it is my hotel."

Even from a distance, his brown eyes locked onto Isabel's. "Yours?"

Must you always stare into my eyes? It's like you're undressing my soul. She glanced down at the store full of activity but spoke a little louder. "Does that surprise you, Captain Mandara?"

"I wouldn't say I'm surprised. Perhaps unconvinced."

Unconvinced of what? You think I'm lying? "Oh, that your egotistical superiority might be subject to your own scorn." From The Maid's Revenge, Act I, Scene 2. "You don't think a woman has the ability to run a hotel."

"I didn't say that." His bronzed face revealed absolutely no emotion.

"My partners have given control of the entire construction and operation of the hotel to me. They wanted a place to spend some of their recent fortune. I gave them an opportunity. They have unconditionally nothing to do with its construction."

He brushed his thick graying mustache with the back of his hand. Then he loosened his tie and unfastened the top button of his shirt. "I wish you luck. But by the looks of the number of half-built buildings in this town, not many jobs are ever completed here." Then he tramped on down the stairs.

She held up her long green dress above the ankles of her lace-up black shoes and traipsed after him. "Captain!" She knew it was her "Cora-of-Connecticut" voice. "Do you mean to tell me you are not interested in building the hotel if you have to work for me?"

He whipped around. She was two steps higher, but their eyes were now even. "Yes, ma'am. That's exactly what I mean. It is not personal. I don't know you at all. I don't work for women. I hope you don't find that offensive."

Captain, you are talking to the wrong lady. I won't curtsy and giggle you out of this. "I find it extremely offensive and degrading. Are you saying that because I'm a woman, I am not capable of supervising the construction and operation of a hotel?"

She thought she saw his eyes soften, although the rest of him seemed to be permanently at attention.

"No, ma'am. You got me wrong. What I'm saying is that I don't work well with women. Except for my wife, Claire, I have a habit of quickly making women irritated and angry with me. In a matter of days, you would be ready to dismiss me."

"I'm ready to dismiss you now, and I haven't even hired you."

"Then you see my point. Good day, Marquesa."

He took two more steps down.

Insult me and leave? You are tangling with the Queen of Insults! "Captain Mandara!"

"Marquesa?"

He sounds perturbed. Good. He deserves it. "Let's be candid. You need a job, or you wouldn't have come here."

"There are other jobs available in this town."

"Yes, there are. But none as grand as my hotel. This will be a landmark building. And I need a builder. No matter how disagreeable we may find each other, I believe we should at least discuss this project."

He stepped up toward her. He was now closer and taller. "I told you, it won't work."

Isabel backed up a step and drew her eyes even with his. "Captain, if you work only five days, you will have five days' pay, and I will be five days closer to completion of my hotel."

Mandara pursued her one step and looked down at her again. "It's not that simple."

This time she scooted two steps up the stairway and looked down at him. "Is it possible to discuss this up here rather than shout above the noise of the crowd?"

He pulled off his suit coat and folded it neatly across his arm. "Kind of warm in here. I was going to the cafe for some dinner. Would you like to join me? We can discuss things there."

The last thing on earth I want to do is have a meal with you! This is the first time I've been insulted and then asked to dinner. Usually they wait until later in the evening to insult me. Your audacity is unsurpassed. "I will meet you there in a few minutes. I have some business to finish." *Actually, that's mostly a lie, but you need some time to sit and wonder if I'm really coming.* "Which restaurant are you going to?"

"The one across the street called Quincys'. At least it has a canvas roof."

Isabel returned to the large table and shuffled through a stack of invoices and retrieved a three-foot-long roll of papers. She set an ink bottle on one edge and a thick ledger on the other and then unrolled the paper and studied the construction plans for the hotel.

You don't like working for women? Isn't that too bad, Captain! I intend to have my hotel finished by June 1. And you just might be the one to do it. If not, I'm sure I'll enjoy dismissing you. You don't think I can run a business? I'll give you the business!

Isabel fiddled with one of Carolina's hats for several minutes. She succeeded in knocking half of her coal black hair out of the combs. It sprawled wildly across her shoulder.

Proper ladies wear hats in public.

I can never find one that looks decent.

But then I've not often been called a proper lady.

What would you do, Captain Mandara, if I wore one of my low-

*cut stage dresses and combed my hair down over my shoulders? You'd
stumble all over yourself just to sit at my table. You would, like many
before you, soon forget all about your poor wife . . . what's her name?*

The total silence in the crowded store was more alarming
than a shout. Isabel hurried to the railing and gazed down as a
dozen customers backed away from the front door, leaving a
knife-wielding man facing fifteen-year-old July Johnson. The
young store manager held his ground.

"You cheated me!" the dirt-caked man with the heavy canvas
coat screamed.

Even from the loft she could see the back of July's neck redden.
"You gave me two double eagles, and you know it."

Circling around the white-aproned Johnson, the wild-eyed
man continued to scream and wave his knife. "I get sixty dollars'
worth of supplies!"

"You drank up your other twenty dollars. Forty dollars is all you
have left, and that's all you get. Hudson, you tried the same thing
last trip to town."

Hudson curled his dirty fingers around the fat-handled, dull-
finished knife, waving it at Johnson's perspiring forehead. "But
Ranahan ain't here this time to protect you!"

July stood his ground. "Put the knife down. I don't have time
for this. I have a store to run. Go over to the livery and sleep it off."

Isabel rushed back to the table and picked up a double-barreled
shotgun propped against the back wall. *Maybe I can bluff him.*

"You just step back, boy, and give me all my goods."

"Hudson," July barked, "I've got customers to attend. There's
your forty dollars' worth of goods. Now get out of here!" He pointed
to several brown-paper-wrapped bundles near the door.

Hudson wiped the sleeve of his filthy canvas jacket across his
mouth. He spat tobacco on the floor near the bundles. "No kid can
tell me what to do!" He stalked closer to Johnson.

The crowd cowered back even farther.

July didn't budge.

Isabel leaned over the railing and pointed the shotgun at the
man with the knife. "'Maybe you'd like to talk to Mr. Greener here!'"
She nodded at the gun barrel. *From* Little Daisy Goes West, *Act III.*

"Who . . . who are you?" Hudson stammered, his knife now hanging at his side.

"The bouncer."

"You cain't bluff me," he screamed and pointed the knife back at July Johnson.

"I'm not." She noticed how stale and dusty the air felt in the loft. "You would not be the first man I've shot."

"I'm takin' all sixty dollars' worth of goods," he declared.

July tossed two gold coins on the floor in front of the man. "Hudson, you aren't buyin' nothin' here. Pick up your money and get out. We've got too many good customers to mess with the likes of you. Don't come back."

"You heard him, Hudson!" Isabel waited until he looked up at her and then cocked both hammers.

"I ain't never been run out by a kid and a woman."

Isabel lifted the shotgun to her shoulder. The customers plastered themselves against the distant wall. "I don't suppose this will be your last time either. Pick up your coins and get out."

"No, ma'am . . . I won't. . . . I'm takin' my goods. All sixty dollars' worth. Now if you want to pull those triggers and cut down me and the boy, then go right ahead. I'll jist take my chance."

Isabel's shoulders slumped. *Why does a girl always have a shotgun when she needs a carbine?*

The man at the open doorway caught everyone's attention.

He was a military man.

Isabel could tell that much.

Again.

"Get out of here!" Hudson screamed at the intruder, threatening with his knife. "Or I'll kill you, too."

Captain Dawson Mandara marched straight up to the man. "Give me the knife!"

"Yeah, I'll let you have it—in your belly!"

Hudson lunged at the captain, who stepped aside and grabbed the man's wrist with his right hand. One violent squeeze and a twist, and the knife dropped to the floor.

Hudson cried out in pain.

Mandara cranked the man's arm behind his back and then

placed one of the polished black boots on his backside. A powerful kick sent Hudson straight out the doorway. Isabel leaned low
and watched the man stagger off the porch and crash facedown
into the hard-packed dirt of Main Street.

He didn't move.

All eyes were focused on Mandara. He bowed to Isabel Leon.
"I wanted to remind you to bring the hotel plans with you. I've figured out several areas where the construction can be improved!"

She lowered the shotgun. "We had everything under control
here, Captain Mandara. You could have gotten yourself hurt taking a chance like that."

He looked around at the customers who once again scooted
into the aisles of merchandise. "Sure, you were in control. Provided
you didn't mind filling half your customers with buckshot." He
turned to July Johnson. "I'll tie this hombre to the hitchin' post.
When he sobers up, you can give him his goods."

"Thanks, Captain!" July beamed.

Mandara waved his hand. "That kind's not worth shootin' anyway. He's just angry at himself for his obvious lack of moral restraint
and Christian virtue."

"I do believe that's a nice way of sayin' he's next to worthless
when he's drunk." July scooped up the two coins. "Now come on,
folks, let's fill your orders and get you up to the goldfields."

Isabel watched Mandara leave.

*Mr. Mandara, your opinion of a woman's ability to take care of
things is extremely low. I do believe you need to learn a few things that
the military forgot to teach you. Fortunately, I'm a very capable
instructor.*

I pity your poor wife.

Your poor, dominated wife.

The sun was bright yellow and straight up in the southern sky
when Isabel Leon stepped out on the newly covered front porch
of the Cantrell Mercantile and Mining Supply Company. The
cloudless sky was a pale pastel blue. The breeze coming up from
the Yellowstone felt cool. The river could be seen through the
trees, which were still a few weeks from leafing out.

She paused to gawk up and down the busy street.

Wagons, mule pack trains, coaches, and single riders on horses milled through town. Next to the Mercantile, there was a line of customers at the Assay Office and Bank. The only other solid wooden commercial building was Ranahan's Blacksmith Shop. Isabel could see the hired man, Rawbone Porter, working the forge, but the noise from the street drowned out the pounding of the sledge on the anvil.

At least fourteen commercial buildings were in partial stages of completion. Most had white canvas upper walls and roofs. Most waited not for wood but for workers.

Straight across from the store was Quincys' Cafe. Next to it, a large sign on a tent proclaimed, "Granger and Sons, Fresh Groceries." And next to it on the corner of what people were calling First Street and Main was the half-completed wood-frame skeleton of The Hotel Marquesa.

Behind the hotel, on lower ground near a grove of cottonwoods, was a street with seven tent saloons lined up in a row. She was still looking at them when July Johnson walked out the doorway and stepped up beside her. He was a couple of inches taller and at least fifteen hard years younger.

"Ain't it something!"

"Cantrell?"

"Yeah. Last year when I rode in here with Mr. McGuire, all we found was one broken-down building with a half-empty store at one end and a near-deserted saloon at the other. Look at this, Marquesa, we've got streets, houses, businesses, people . . . and everything. It's startin' to look like a city, ain't it?"

"You're right, July."

"Did you ever wonder if we'll someday be old-timers sitting on rocking chairs out on the front porch of our houses telling little kids about the old days when Cantrell just got started?"

A slight breeze refreshed her face and calmed her spirit. "No, I don't believe I've ever considered that."

July shrugged. "Yeah, me neither. Is that captain fella going to finish building your hotel?"

"I'm going over to talk to him now. I hope he can. We need to get it ready. Mr. and Mrs. Parks will be bringing that baby home in a few weeks. I promised them a suite in the corner of the hotel."

"And you promised me the room nearest Quincys'."

"How are you and Molly Mae doing?"

"We ain't seen near enough of each other, if you get my drift. They're still tryin' to run the cafe with just the family, and with Ran and Miss Carolina gone . . . I'm as busy as a weasel in a henhouse."

Isabel brushed down the skirt of her dress. It felt a little snug about the waist.

"When I get through talking to the captain, I'll come back and spell you some, July. Then you can go eat. Would you like me to say hello to a certain young lady for you?"

"I reckon I would, Marquesa." His grin seemed to be tied to his ears and yanked hard.

The simple, unashamed enthusiasm of a fifteen-year-old. I wonder where they lose that?

Standing beside him, she slipped her arm around his waist and rested her hand on the handle of his sheathed hunting knife. "July, it is very respectful for you to call me the Marquesa. That was my stage name. Please call me Isabel."

"I reckon I cain't ever do that." His grin now revealed nearly perfect straight teeth. "In my whole life, I've never known anyone with a title. I like the way it sounds. 'Howdy, I'm July Johnson . . . and this is my good friend, the Marquesa.' So if it ain't offendin' you none, I aim to keep on callin' you that."

July dropped his chin to his chest and rubbed his forehead. "Can I be honest, Marquesa?"

"By all means." She left her arm around his waist.

"It makes a man feel good down deep in his bones to have a purdy gal for a friend. You know what I mean?"

"I think I know what you're saying."

"I really like having you for a friend." He glanced at her eyes and then quickly looked away. "Now don't you ever tell Molly Mae this, but you're without question the most beautiful woman I've ever been around in my whole life. Even if you are old enough to be my mama!"

Isabel dropped her arm.

A blushing July Johnson hastened back into the crowded Mercantile.

Old enough to be his mama! I'm only twenty-eight years old! It says so right on my . . . phony birth certificate. Okay, I'll be thirty-one in May, but that's certainly not old enough . . . Of course, if I had had a child when I was sixteen . . . Other women have children at that age.

Other women have children.

A tear slipped down her cheek. She pulled out a lace-edged handkerchief from her sleeve and dabbed the corner of her eyes.

The street dust is horrible.

You can go to Hades, Jacob Hardisty. As long as I live, I will never forgive you for what you allowed that New York doctor to do to me!

She dabbed her eyes again and started across the busy street.

We must do something about this street dust. Perhaps we can put cobblestones or brick along Main Street.

The two outside tables at Quincys' were already full. Isabel poked her head inside the tent flap door and finally spotted Captain Mandara sitting next to a wooden barrel that had several planks nailed to it to form a crude table. He sat on a bench. The other end formed seating for a neighboring table. Across from him stood an empty straight-backed faded blue wooden chair.

The voices were varied, but the tone was the same as it was every day—teasing respect. She smiled her way through the 90 percent male crowd.

"Marquesa! Sit down and let me buy you dinner!"

"Achy, first it would be dinner. Then you'd just be wanting to buy me something else, wouldn't you?"

"You lookin' for some company, Marquesa?"

"I hope you strike gold, Blackie, and can buy some teeth. I just don't feel like chewing your steak for you tonight!"

"Marquesa, say hello to a man who's about to become a millionaire."

"Chad, you and every other man within a 100-mile radius of Devil's Canyon are planning on becoming millionaires. One of these days we'll all be so rich money will be worthless!"

"Marry me, Marquesa, and move to my claim with me. I guarantee you won't regret it!"

"Why, Dub? Do you plan on dying soon?"

"Hey, Marquesa, didn't I see your smile on the stage in Chicago?"

"You might have seen a lot more than a smile, Earl."

"It would be a great honor, Marquesa, if you'd join me at the Hair-of-the-Dog Saloon fer a drink."

"Oh, why's that, Grady? Would I be their first female customer?"

"Would you save the next dance for me, sweet Marquesa?"

"The way you stepped on my toes last time, Flynn? I wouldn't save you a buffalo chip!"

She made it to the barrel table and laid the rolled-up hotel plans on the table as she scooted into the blue chair. A clean white linen tablecloth covered the rough-sawn wooden planks. A small blue glass medicine bottle held a permanently dried yellow cornflower.

"You're quite the popular lady," Mandara began.

"These boys are lonely and democratic."

"Democratic?"

"They'll make a pass at anything wearing a skirt. Actually it's a little game we play every night. Have you ordered?" she asked.

"Yes, and I ordered for you."

"You did what?" Isabel choked. "Captain, let's get one thing clear. I order my own food, and I pay for my own food."

His tanned face and narrow brown eyes showed no hint of emotion. "Fair enough. The young lady in the green gingham dress said you always ordered the corned beef and cabbage on Tuesdays. Since we intend to go over some business matters, I assumed it would expedite matters to order for you."

"You were wrong!" Isabel raised her thin, fair-skinned hand and then called out above the roar of the crowded restaurant, "Molly Mae!"

The young blonde girl scurried to their table. Her round cheeks seemed to be permanently poised to release a giggle. "Hello, Marquesa! How's July today?"

Isabel Leon tilted her head and raised her thick black eyebrows. "Pining."

"Really?" Miss Quincy's eyes widened in a sweep of delight.

"He said to tell you hello."

"Tell July I'll meet him tonight if I don't see him before."

"What time?"

Molly Mae Quincy exploded in a giggle. "He knows."

"Where?"

"He knows that, too!" She put her hand over her mouth to suppress the laughter and then cleared her throat. "I'll have your orders out in just a minute."

"I need to discuss that with you. I'm afraid you'll have to cancel what Captain Mandara ordered for me."

"It seems I acted presumptuously," he admitted.

"You did?" Molly Mae gasped.

"What he means is, I like to order my own food."

"What would you like then?" Molly Mae asked.

"What's the special today?"

"Corned beef and cabbage. It's not pickled cabbage either. It's fresh cabbage all the way from Old Mexico."

Isabel scowled at the captain and then turned to Molly Mae. "Well, good. I'll have the corned beef and cabbage."

The young waitress's perfectly round mouth dropped open. "But that's what the captain ordered for you!"

"Yes, well, I chose not to have what he ordered. I'll have what I ordered."

Molly Mae glanced over at Captain Mandara and rolled her eyes to the ceiling. Then she scooted behind a framed, canvas-covered wall that separated the kitchen from the dining area.

The captain watched the young waitress until she ducked out of sight. When he turned back, his mind seemed focused on a vision beyond the room.

The Marquesa tilted her head and leaned forward. "She's a cute girl."

"Oh . . ." the startled captain replied. "I guess I miss my daughter."

Captain Mandara, I wonder how old you really are? "You have a daughter her age?"

"Nellie is fifteen. She's quite the young lady. A lot like her mother, of course."

Isabel's fingers traced the edge of the empty china coffee cup beside her. "And you have other children?"

"Georgia is thirteen. Philip is eleven. Grant is seven. Children grow up so quickly. It doesn't seem that long ago when the baby was born."

"I take it your family is not here with you."

"They're all in St. Louis visiting Claire's parents." Isabel noticed that the captain's face grew rigid. "But I'm not here to discuss personal matters."

For a moment, Captain Dawson Mandara, you almost sounded warm and vulnerable.

"Well, here are the plans for the hotel. Were you serious about being able to finish the job by June 1?"

He took a small black tally book from his suit coat pocket and retrieved something that had been written in pencil. "I'll need three men to work with me."

"You'll be lucky to hire one. No one wants to be left out of the gold claims."

He rapped his finger on the little notebook. "If I choose to take the job, I'll find the men."

She rapped her fingers on the rough board that formed a tabletop. "If I choose to give you the job, I'll expect that June completion."

Mandara rubbed the bridge of his narrow nose and brushed back his thick, graying mustache. "We'll need to modify the plans of course."

Isabel felt any remnants of a smile drain from her lips. "You haven't even looked at the plans." She pointed at the documents rolled up in front of her.

"I've looked at the building. That veranda has to go. At least on the east and north sides."

It did not sound like a suggestion but an order. She sat straight up and folded her hands on her lap. "Why?"

"Because it will fill up with snow and create extra weight and work in the winter. And because it robs you of floor space. You are building a hotel that intends to make money, aren't you? A veranda on the north and east sides is a waste. In fact the entire veranda

idea is a vast misuse of space. Who in the world designed this building anyway?"

With a professional scowl that had often silenced entire theater audiences, Isabel reacted. "I did."

"Oh," the captain replied with the steely nonchalance of a professional gambler or a seasoned Indian fighter.

The young girl in green gingham buzzed out of the kitchen
with a tray full of food for the men at the table behind them.

Isabel turned around in the chair. "Molly Mae, cancel my meal.
I've decided to skip dinner." She stood and snatched up the hotel
plans. "Good day, Captain."

He took a slow sip of coffee from a thick beige porcelain cup.
His voice reflected indifference. "I take it you're angry with me?"

"What a delightfully quick mind you have!" She waved the
rolled-up hotel plans at him like a sword. A lock of her hair pulled
free from her comb and flopped across her ear. "You insulted my
plans, my hotel, and my intelligence. Obviously you don't want to
build my hotel. Therefore, to continue this charade would be a
waste of your time as well as mine." Isabel stormed through the sea
of chairs, tables, and diners.

An explosion of gunfire behind her caused all conversation in
the cafe to cease. Isabel spun around. Captain Mandara stood on
the bench, a smoking army revolver in his right hand pointed
toward the canvas ceiling.

"Boys, the Marquesa has got to get her hotel built by June first.
Now I think you all will agree that Cantrell needs a hotel. But in
order for that to happen, I need three men willing to work with me
sixty hours a week for thirty dollars."

"Thirty dollars a month or a week?" a deep voice boomed.

"A week."

"Them's good wages, mister."

"You'll earn ever' penny. You'll get room and board until the
project is done, and then the lump sum balance on the first of June.
It will make a nice grubstake for prospecting."

"I'll take one of them jobs!" a man in tattered duckings and a
worn bowler hollered.

"Me, too!" echoed a thin man wearing chaps and spurs.

A black-bearded man called out from the front doorway, "Save me one of them jobs, partner!"

"I'm a cabinetmaker by trade," called a man who was almost as wide as he was tall. "Could you use four men?"

Mandara waved his hand toward the front door. "I'll meet with any of you who are interested on that big porch in front of the Mercantile in an hour. Pass the word around town."

The captain sat down.

The conversations continued as if on cue.

Isabel stared at Captain Mandara, now occupied with his meal that steamed off a blue-enameled tin plate.

Of all the arrogance!

She lunged back through the crowd, waving the hotel plans in the air over his table. "I did not hire you to build my hotel. Nor did I approve of the wages you want to pay these men," she fumed.

He dissected the corned beef and stabbed a forkful. "Let's be straightforward, Marquesa. I'm the only one in this town who can get a hotel built by June first. You don't need to like me. But you do have to decide if you want a hotel built."

"I don't want 'a hotel.' I want *my* hotel!" She lowered the plans to her side.

He dipped a biscuit into cabbage juice and then bit off a large piece. "That's what I meant."

"Verandas included?"

Captain Mandara wiped cabbage juice off his chin with a white cloth napkin. "Verandas included."

"Exactly according to plans?" she demanded.

"As per plans unless I can convince you of an improvement."

"You won't," she snapped.

He took another bite of corned beef and sipped his coffee while she waited by the table. "I'll keep the plans this afternoon and give you an estimate on the cost of completion by night. How far do you have to go for sawn boards?"

"Billings. They'll ship them downriver at this time of the year. But I have all the materials purchased." She felt the tension in her neck relax.

"You're missing four doors and three windows," he announced.

The neck tension returned. "How do you know? You haven't looked at the plans."

"I've looked at the building."

"Well, by all means, we want enough doors and windows."

"Good. We'll go to Billings tomorrow and order the rest of the supplies needed. I presume you have the furnishings ordered."

She reached up and rubbed the back of her neck. "If you mean stoves, furniture, and such, those will come in from Chicago and be delivered here by Mr. McGuire around the first week in June. But I am not going to Billings with you. I do not *ever* go to Billings!"

He stared at her long enough to make her feel uncomfortable. "You dislike civilization? Or is there someone there you'd like to avoid?"

"Neither." She paused long enough for him to blink. "I was run out of town by the sheriff. If I return, I'll be thrown in jail."

"For what reason may I ask?"

"For attempted murder."

"Murder? Who did you try to kill?"

"The previous builder!"

For the first time since she had met him, a wide, relaxed, pleasant smile broke across his sun-hardened face. Isabel thought it made him look ten years younger.

"Sit down, Marquesa, and join me for dinner. Let me tell you what my fee will be."

Isabel slumped once again into the blue chair.

Molly Mae scurried by with a platter. "I have an extra corned beef and cabbage here. I don't suppose you'd be—"

"Yes, I believe that is what I ordered," Isabel Leon demurred.

Young Miss Quincy left the heaping plate of steaming food in front of the Marquesa and mumbled on her way back into the kitchen.

"Now, Captain Mandara, what is your fee?"

"Room and board until the job is finished and enough lumber to build myself a three-bedroom house."

She lowered her cabbage-laden fork. "What?"

"Lumber, Marquesa. I want lumber to build my family a house . . . so we can move here."

Across the noisy room someone shrieked for more coffee.

"You want to live in Cantrell?"

"Can you think of a site with more opportunities for a builder?"

The cabbage was only lukewarm but sweet to her taste. "I'll need to know the approximate cost of those supplies."

"I'll bring that back with me from Billings after I price it out."

She held the bite of corned beef in her mouth. It had a rich, deep salty taste. "That will be fine."

"We have an agreement then?" He waited for her eyes to glance up at his.

"Not until I know what it will cost me," she asserted.

He seemed eager to stab the corned beef again. "You can afford it."

"How do you know I can afford it?"

"If you have enough money to waste space on wraparound verandas, you have enough to buy a few extra boards for me."

"No agreement until I hear your estimate."

"That's fair enough." He spoke with his fork in his left hand and his knife in his right. "Now did you really try to kill your last builder?"

"No."

"I didn't think so."

"I shot an old boyfriend."

He stared at her eyes so intently she glanced away.

"That doesn't surprise me," he finally added.

"I only wounded him. He's still alive."

"Now that surprises me." The captain motioned toward the plans. "Roll those out and tell me all about your hotel."

When Carolina Cantrell Parks inherited the Mercantile, it occupied only half of the present building. Within weeks she purchased the saloon at the other end of the building. After their short honeymoon, Ranahan and Carolina Parks had opened up and expanded the entire building to include a covered porch, a long, narrow storeroom across the back, and small living quarters at one end.

Isabel now stayed in the Parkses' tiny apartment while they

waited in Maryland for the birth of their child and she waited for the birth of her hotel.

Carolina had installed a large mirror over the dresser, and Isabel now sat combing her hair and staring at the reflection.

The store was closed.

It was dark outside.

And most of the noise came from the saloons on Second Street.

July Johnson had slipped out at a certain time to a certain place known only to him and a smiling young lady with perfectly smooth skin under slightly freckled cheeks and the yellowest hair seen within 100 miles.

"Well, Marquesa, what would young Mr. Johnson say if he saw you without makeup, jewelry, and fancy clothes? Would he be impressed if you didn't dye your hair and some gray began to show?"

She turned her head and glanced at her profile from side to side. "Not bad. At a distance. Still able to impress them when up on the stage. I'll put a huge mirror in my suite at the hotel, floor to ceiling, in the corner . . . so I can see both sides at once."

Perhaps I should continue to act. Maybe someone will build a theater and . . . maybe I will build a theater. I could direct and star.

She leaned closer and inspected the hardened crow's feet in the corners of her eyes. *Or perhaps I shouldn't put in a mirror at all. Mirrors are not nearly as forgiving as our memories.*

Perhaps last winter's season in San Francisco is your last, Marquesa.

"And what does the Marquesa do now?" she mimicked to the mirror.

"Oh, haven't you heard, she's banished to running a hotel out on the wild frontier of Montana."

"A boarding house?"

"No, a hotel. A small but elegant hotel."

"Oh my, what a shame, and she had such potential when she was young!"

"Did you catch her in *The Pharaoh's Woman* in Philadelphia? It might have been her best work."

"Oh, yes, I was there the night the young man with the bouquet of flowers ran out on the stage and kissed her right in the middle of her . . . soliloquy."

"My, what happened to that lad?"

"He lived."

A loud banging on the door caused her to stand up, but she didn't bother going out to the door.

Let them knock. We're closed.

She sat back down and nonchalantly ran the comb through her nearly waist-length hair. *Sixteen . . . seventeen . . . eighteen. Fifty strokes in each place takes a long time.*

She shook her head back and forth and let her hair flop. It felt softer, more relaxed. The banging continued.

Come back tomorrow. It can't be Mr. July Johnson. He'd let himself in with his key. Besides, it's much too early for him to come home.

"Marquesa!" a muffled voice shouted from the porch. "This is Dawson Mandara! I can see your lamp on. I know you're in there. We have some business to discuss."

Isabel pulled a long green silk robe over her faded flannel gown and walked barefoot through the store lit only by the kerosene lamp she carried. The wood floor, though cleanly swept, carried scattered traces of sawdust, which stuck to the bottom of her size five feet.

The knocking continued. "Marquesa!"

She parked herself beside the door but left it locked. "Captain Mandara, would you please stop battering the door?"

"I need to talk to you."

"It's much too late for a social call."

"This is no social call, I assure you. I have to talk to you about the hotel plans."

"I have on my bedclothes."

"Good. Then you can open the door and let me in."

I can what? Does your sweet, subservient wife, Claire, know you make the rounds like this on single women?

"Captain Mandara, whatever you want to discuss can wait until morning!"

"I'll be leaving by 4:00 A.M. Would you like me to stop by about 3:30?"

"I most certainly would not!" she fumed. "What is so urgent that can't wait?"

"I studied the plans. If you took the veranda off the east end where it touches up against the grocery, you could add a parlor for the upstairs guests and a stage to the dining room/ballroom below."

She felt a tingling in her throat. "Add a what?"

"A small stage . . . so you could host some dramatic productions."

Isabel unlocked the door and opened it a few inches. Her lamp-reflected face peeked out into the darkness. "How did you know I wanted a stage?"

Standing in the shadows as if at attention and drilling his troops on a parade ground was Captain Dawson Mandara. "Young Mr. Johnson told me you were an actress, and when I had a chance to ponder the plans, the idea came to me that you might like to have a stage in the ballroom. Would you like me to show you my idea?"

"I only have my gown on, and it's late . . . well, yes, of course, come in."

Mandara pushed open the door and marched into the dimly lit store. He wore the same clothes he had on earlier. Only now the top two buttons of his shirt were unfastened, and in the darkness none of his gray hair could be seen peeking out from under his hat. He unrolled the plan on top of a stack of white canvas tarps.

"Hold the light over here, would you please, Marquesa?"

In case you haven't noticed, Captain Mandara, I am barefoot and wearing a dressing robe. I am not accustomed to entertaining gentlemen so attired. Especially with no makeup and jewelry!

"That's it . . . a little more over this way. Can you lean toward me a little?"

I've heard more subtle come-on lines from drunken drovers on a Saturday night tear.

Her foot-to-neck flannel gown was buttoned under her chin, as was her green silk robe. Still, Isabel held both tight at her neck with her right hand and the lantern with her left. Her right shoulder rubbed up against his strong left arm.

"As you can see," he circled a callused hand over the map, "the ballroom/dining room is on the east end here. It will be a beautiful room, I might add. If the veranda were discarded on this end, you could put a small stage here." His short, straight-cut clean finger-nails pounded the plans.

"How small?"

"Fifteen by twenty-five feet."

"That's adequate for most performances." Isabel noticed in the shadows that her bare toes peeked out from under the gown and robe. She scooted them back out of sight. *Captain Mandara, I have no idea on earth why you bring out modesty in me. It's never been my greatest virtue.*

"I built a theater in Dodge City a few years back. . . . We had less room than that. I figured the spare room on each side could be dressing rooms for the performers. They're not large, but it would be something."

"That's extremely thoughtful of you, Captain Mandara." Isabel stepped back from the stack of canvas. "I like your plans, but I did have my heart set on a veranda all the way around."

The captain took a deep breath and let it out slowly.

I suppose this touches off another tirade. You are a difficult man to work with, Captain Dawson Mandara!

"Marquesa, let me be quite frank. I believe a veranda that faces the side of a grocery store wall is nothing more than a cramped, crowded alley. They do intend to finish the walls of the store, don't they?"

"Yes, they do." Isabel set the lamp on top of the plans and released the neck of her robe. She interlaced her fingers and rested her hands against her stomach. "It will only be one story."

Mandara rubbed his forehead. "Well, I don't understand why—"

She held up her hand to silence him. "Captain Mandara, did you ever promenade with your wife at twilight in the summer when the sun dips down and the air is beginning to cool?"

"What? What does that have to do with . . ."

Again her small hand muzzled his words. "Captain, did you and your wife ever dress for supper and then after a fine meal go for a slow leisurely walk around the fort . . . or wherever you were?"

Mandara stared across the still blackness of the store.

Has it been that long since you've seen her?

This time his voice was soft and melancholy. "Yes . . . yes, of course. Promenade. I understand."

She reached over and laid her hand on the sleeve of his suit coat. "I want a promenade balcony somewhere off the dust and dirt of Cantrell, Montana Territory, where a man and a woman can stroll or talk or just watch the sunset. It's a luxury, no doubt, but a luxury I desire. I do not expect ever in my life to again have so much freedom in designing a building. I don't want regrets over this one."

He stood straight up. Although Isabel guessed him to be a little under six feet tall, his military posture made him seem to tower over any surroundings. "Yes, well, Marquesa, I see your point. I was thinking pragmatically of how to put more rooms in the hotel. I wanted to generate the most income from your investment. I had forgotten the joys of a simple promenade."

"I take it you've been away from your family for a while?"

"Eight months and twenty-one days, to be exact."

Oh, the precision of a military mind. "Then you will be looking forward to constructing your home with as much anticipation as I am to completing the hotel."

He ran his fingers across the corners of his tired brown eyes. "You're right about that. Now, Marquesa, what about the stage? It is *your* hotel."

I believe, Captain Mandara, that's the first time you acknowledged that fact. This is progress. "Let's take out the east end veranda on the ground floor but leave it upstairs. Will that make the building uneven looking?"

"To some degree," he admitted. "We could always delete the west side veranda on the ground floor and thereby—"

"Don't waste your breath, Captain. I would never agree to that."

He stared her straight in the eyes. "I didn't think so."

Isabel glanced down at the hotel plans. As she did, she lifted her thick black hair off her shoulders and pushed it to her back. *I've spent the last fifteen years of my life getting used to men staring at me.*

Normally they don't stare at my eyes. "Are there any other details we need to go over?"

"Finances. How do I pay for the supplies?"

"You can bill my line of credit at the bank next door. I assure you, the funds are sufficient."

"I never doubted that."

"So I do get a full veranda upstairs?"

"That you do, Marquesa." He cleared his throat, then became silent.

She stood awkwardly waiting in the shadows. "Is our business concluded, Captain Mandara?"

"Marquesa." He pushed his round, wide-brimmed hat to the back of his head. He brushed his thick mustache with the tips of his fingers. "I have a rather delicate matter to discuss."

You also have a wife in St. Louis, remember? Don't do something dumb and ruin this business deal! "Yes, Captain Mandara?"

Once again he stared her in the eyes. She fought the urge to turn away. Instead, she stared right back. "Before I say anything else, I need to explain something. I'm a Christian man."

"Yes, well, we do live in a Christian country. So that sort of includes all of us, doesn't it?"

"Eh, that's not exactly what I mean. For me, my allegiance to Christ is of primary concern in my life, and I feel a burden to live my life in obedience to the Bible's teaching."

"Captain Mandara, that's very commendable. You will enjoy becoming friends with Mr. and Mrs. Parks who own this store. They have similar convictions. But I'm building a hotel, not a church. I fail to see the connection."

"I do not mean this statement personally. And it is no aspersion on your virtue. There are just some kinds of buildings that I refuse to construct. It's not my place to judge others. The Lord will take care of that. But there are standards I have set for myself."

"Captain Mandara, beating around the bush does not become you."

For the second time since they met, a slight smile stole across his face, then disappeared into the darkness. "Yes, I suppose I should come right to the point. Marquesa, I cannot be a part of building a saloon or a brothel."

Isabel Leon once played Queen Elizabeth in a play that ran fourteen weeks in Baltimore. She felt herself slip into that role. "It is obvious these plans are not for a saloon."

"Yes, quite so," he admitted.

"Then what you are really asking is, do I intend to run a brothel in this building?"

"Yes, that is the real question. Marquesa, please don't take it personally."

"Of course I take it personally! I am not accustomed to having men . . . of any persuasion . . . tell me I look like a madam or a . . . a soiled dove!"

"But you misinterpreted what I—"

"Oh, I did?" she ranted. Her voice echoed off the glass gun case on the distant side of the store. "Do you mean to tell me if I wore a bonnet and flour sack dresses, curtsied every time I spoke, and laced my conversation with 'yes, sir', 'whatever you say, sir,' you would have asked me that same question?"

He looked her in the eyes once more. "I would have to ask you that question if you were ninety, toothless, and in a wheelchair. I would have asked it if young Mr. Johnson were building a hotel . . . or anyone else."

"I doubt that!" she fumed. *Actually I halfway believe you, but I'm not about to let you know that.*

"It was a question I had to ask. I apologize that I am not good at being tactful or sensitive."

"That's a vast understatement."

"However it came across, Marquesa, it was not personal. I don't even know you."

"You bet your Springfield musket you don't know me. You don't know anything about me!"

"And you know little about me," he returned. "But shall we work together to build The Hotel Marquesa, or would you prefer that I seek other projects?"

What I would prefer is that you and all the other men in this town would treat me with half the respect you give a woman like Carolina Parks!

"Captain Mandara, I want my hotel built. At the moment you are my best, if not my most charming, hope. Build the hotel. But I believe the fewer conversations we have with each other, the better."

"I suppose you are right about that. I warned you that I don't work well with women. Too many years in the army, I suppose."

"Frankly, Captain Mandara, I am surprised that you ever wanted to leave the military."

"I never said I wanted to leave. As I mentioned, Marquesa, you know very little about me. I will return late tomorrow night or perhaps the next morning."

"That will be fine."

"Would you like some sort of written agreement on this construction project?" he asked.

"Is your word good?"

"Yes, Marquesa, it is."

"So is mine, Captain Mandara."

"That is something I knew the very first time I met you."

That is probably, Captain, the first compliment you have given me. "Then, I presume, our business meeting is over?"

"You will have your hotel by June first. I will settle for nothing less."

"Nor will I, Captain Mandara."

She walked with him back to the front door of the darkened store. The kerosene lamp, still setting on the stack of canvas, cast wild shadows around the large room.

"Good night, Marquesa."

"Good night, Captain."

In the doorway he turned to stare into her eyes once more. "I'd be negligent if I failed to mention that your hair looks quite attractive combed down like that."

Her mouth opened to reply.

No words came out.

The door closed.

The room was silent.

And lonely . . . in a cinnamon and fresh-leather-smelling sort of way.

She shuffled slowly back to her room, carrying the kerosene

lamp in her hand. Closing the door behind her, she set the lamp on the nightstand and then returned to the mirror.

"Your hair looks quite attractive." What does that mean, Captain? That it looked simply horrid all day long? Did you feel guilty that you had been so abrupt and were driven to find a compliment?

She laid her silk robe on the straight-backed chair and scooted across the hooked throw rug toward the waiting bed. With the cotton sheets and thick comforter tucked under her arms, she reached over to turn off the lamp.

Instead she picked up Carolina's black Bible and opened it to the ribbon bookmark.

— Two —

ISABEL LEON STROLLED THOUGH a collection of boisterous men lounging on the porch of the Mercantile. Like suitors at the court of a queen, each tipped his hat to acknowledge her presence. She waited for two freight wagons and six horseback riders to pass before crossing Main Street. Then she breezed over to a small congregation of men who stood watching the hotel construction.

"Mornin', Marquesa. Handsome mornin', ain't it?"

"It's springtime in Montana, Harlan. It's a glorious season."

"Marquesa, did you see that new horse ol' Ivy bought?"

"Not yet, Kindel. What does it look like?"

"Long-legged, wide at the back, and plenty of decoration. She is one beautiful animal."

"Marquesa, is your hotel going to have big old oak front doors with cut-glass inserts?"

"That's the plan, Liddon. We have the doors already."

"It will look fine. Plumb fine."

"Things must be going choice for you, Marquesa. You're sportin' a mighty snappy smile."

"Shoot, the Marquesa always has that there purdy smile."

"Thank you, boys."

It's a beautiful day, horse, front door, and smile. Not one mention of how I look. That's different. I'm glad they moved beyond the flash of a skirt.

You lie, Marquesa!

This is absolutely the most boring dress I have ever worn in my life! "Please, don't hesitate to wear any of my things," you told me, sweet Carolina. What you didn't tell me is that I'd look like a serving girl from

Omaha. When you wore these, you always had that royal look. Which, of course, has nothing whatsoever to do with your clothing.

Well, it's time for me to rise in stature, and Cantrell is the place for it to happen. I am not merely an opera house Marquesa. I'm Isabel Leon, business lady. I expect to be treated as such! And if I need to wear boring clothes, I'll wear boring clothes!

I'll decide.

And I just decided. I don't want to wear boring clothes!

"Marquesa, is that you?"

Unable to find any of Carolina's hats that would fit over her billows of thick, stacked hair, Isabel had no protection from the bright spring sunshine. She shaded her eyes with her hand and stared up at the man on the tall, black horse.

"Logan?"

The broad-shouldered man with a two-week beard swung his leg over his horse's head and looped it around the saddle horn. "Seeing you standing there is about the nicest thing that has happened to me all spring."

"How have you been, Logan? How's Sally?"

"I've been fine. Sally's dead."

"I'm sorry to hear that. Was it an accident?"

"I reckon. They said it was probably something she ate." He pushed his hat to the back of his sandy blond head and stared at her from toe to head. "I'm surprised to find you in the middle of Montana dressed like a bank clerk's wife." Two deep dimples set off his easy grin.

"And I'm surprised to find out you're still alive. I thought by now you'd be dangling from a rope or have some girl's dagger in your midsection."

"Ain't it something? Who would have thought I'd have lived this long? Especially after that fracas in Savannah."

"Savannah? I was thinking about Cincinnati."

"Oh, yeah, that one, too." He loosened his tie and unfastened the top button of his once-white shirt.

Isabel tilted her head and raised one thick eyebrow. "What was her name?"

"Eh, I forget."

"You lie." She scowled. It was a pleasant, teasing scowl.

He slapped a cloud of road dust off his knee. "That's what keeps me alive."

"Now, tell me, what is the world-famous daredevil scout of the plains and expert animal trainer, Logan Henry Phillips, doing in Cantrell, Montana Territory?" She stepped up to the horse and rubbed its neck.

"Looking for a poker game."

"L. H. Phillips is a little short on funds, I take it?"

"Boomtowns always have some extra."

"I haven't heard of any big games, but if there is one, you're one street off. You want Second Street. But I can't tell you which place is best. So far, I've avoided going in any of them."

"Yeah, well, it looks like we could paint this town with a thimbleful of paint." He looked down at her and shook his head.

"I hope those are good memories you're dreaming about."

"The best I ever had. Seeing you here is probably the best thing that's happened to me in three years."

"It's almost like finding family, isn't it, Logan?"

He put both hands on the saddle horn and leaned forward, gazing down the street. "I reckon it is. Now it's your turn, Miss Isabel Leon. The last I heard some rich guy named Hardisty was pouring money at your feet. What is the pride of Baltimore, the songbird of Philadelphia, the queen of Chicago—the lovely and talented Marquesa—doing buried out in the uncivilized frontier?"

"I'm building a hotel, Logan." She stepped up on the boardwalk and swooped her hands in both directions. "This is my hotel."

"No foolin'?" Logan swung his left leg back into the stirrup and stood up. "I do have to hear the whole story on this. Can I buy you supper after a while?"

Isabel brushed a tassel of dark hair off her ear. "I'd enjoy that."

He sat down in the saddle and picked up the braided rawhide reins. "Where can I find you about sundown?"

"I'm staying at the Mercantile down the street. I'm helping some friends with their store until they return. Why don't we meet at Quincys' Cafe?"

"At sundown?"

"That would be fine."

He slowly studied the building on the skyline. "This really is your hotel?"

"Yes, it is. Amazing, isn't it?"

"I don't know. Somehow it fits you. It doesn't surprise me. Darlin', you never were just some opera house singer. You always thought too poorly of yourself."

"You've grown kind in your old age!"

"Old! Why, there's not one gray hair in my head!"

"Mine either. What does that prove?" She grinned. "Besides, if I had thought more highly of myself, I might never have chummed around with you."

"That's the truth, Marquesa. How long until you're done building?"

"About five more weeks. They should finish the roof today or tomorrow."

"Do you know anything about building a hotel?"

"More than I did two months ago. I have a very good builder now."

He began to laugh.

"What is it?" she prodded.

"Who would have thought I would ride off to the edge of the world and find the Marquesa building herself a hotel? Write a few tunes and make a musical out of it. It's glorious! Save me an upstairs room with a door to the balcony."

"All the upstairs rooms have exits to the veranda."

"I should have known. You always did like to step out for fresh air. Well, I'd better go win us some supper money." He grinned. It was a patented grin that usually caused all the young ladies in the front two rows of an eastern theater to swoon.

"Marquesa, excuse me, but I need to show you something."

She turned around to see Captain Mandara standing beside her on the edge of the boardwalk. His white shirt sleeves were rolled up to his elbows. A soiled white canvas nail apron hung around his waist.

She glanced up at the mounted rider. "Captain Dawson Mandara, this is an old friend of mine, Logan Henry Phillips."

"The one that scouted for General Miles?"

Logan nodded. "For a season."

"Good work, Mr. Phillips. I heard all about that trek. Very good work."

Logan reached over and patted his horse's neck. "Thank you, Captain. I haven't seen the general for going on ten years."

Mandara pulled off his hat and wiped the sweat off his forehead. "You looking for work, Phillips?"

"Nope. I ain't much of a hotel builder, Captain." Logan rested his hands on the tarnished silver-plated saddle horn. "Me and Sally tore up a hotel or two, but I've never built one back."

Mandara glanced at the Marquesa and wiped his hand across his mustache.

"Logan had a Wild West act in the East that included a partially trained bear named Sally," Isabel explained.

Mandara pulled out a sixteen-penny nail tucked behind his ear and tossed it into the apron pocket. "Well, if you get low on funds and want to learn a trade, I could use some more help. Phillips, you got a job with me anytime."

"Thanks, Captain. Nice to know someone remembers those scoutin' days. I will certainly keep that in mind. Good day, Marquesa." He tipped his hat and rode down the street.

The captain turned toward Isabel. "A partially trained bear?"

"It made the show exciting."

"I'll bet it did. Now if you'd step in here," the captain motioned toward the building, "we're framing out the stage area, and I need to know how much room you will need for the curtains."

Isabel Leon traipsed after the hat-in-hand Dawson Mandara as they hiked through a forest of two-by-four-framed rooms and hallways. Without any siding or coverings to distinguish walls, the hotel was no more than two stories of vertical sticks with a shake roof on top.

"The roof will be finished by dark," the captain reported.

"That's wonderful! What will be next?"

"The siding. I figure we better get that up before a wind comes along and blows the whole thing down."

"That's possible?"

"Oh, yeah. Now here's another thing that I wanted to show you." He pointed down at a series of short one-by-six boards lying on the floor. "How about using this pattern for the railing around the upper veranda?"

"That's very attractive, Captain. Where did you come across it?"

"It's what we used on the enlisted men's quarters at Fort Laramie."

"Well, I like it!" She turned to him and grinned. "And, besides, the men will feel at home when they come to stay at my hotel."

"This isn't a hotel for enlisted men," he reported.

"It isn't?" There was a teasing lilt in her voice.

"It's an officers' hotel. Trust me."

"I do, Captain Mandara." She looked around at the building. "You've got a lot done in just a week."

"Not as much as I had hoped. Some of the previous work had to be corrected. I'm a rather precise builder."

Captain Mandara, you are rather precise in everything you do. "Was there anything else you needed to show me?"

"Just this." He pointed to a small nail keg perched in the middle of the large room.

"The barrel?"

"Yes. I told the boys to leave it right there and not move it until the hotel's done."

"Why on earth did you tell them that?"

"It's for you."

"Me?"

"Marquesa, that's for you to sit on while you're contemplating."

"I don't understand."

"See that raised floor down there?"

"Yes."

"That's your stage."

"Then this is my ballroom, isn't it?"

"Ballroom, dining room, theater. You should get plenty of use from it." He used a claw hammer to point out special features. "The windows will be over there . . . the entry from the parlor over there. The chandelier should hang above the barrel. Every evening when we're all done, I like to sit in a room and contemplate all we have to do the next day. I stare at the walls and review what it will look like when we're done.

"I figured you'd like to do the same thing. If you sit still on that keg long enough, Marquesa, you'll see velvet curtains, bouquets of fresh flowers, ladies dressed in silks, and gentlemen in long coats. Stare up at that stage, and you might envision a beautiful dark-haired singer, soliloquies from Shakespeare, dancing bears, or whatever. I figure a person needs a little time to sit and dream."

Isabel was surprised to find the Captain looking down at his hands rather than straight into her eyes. *You have any particular beautiful dark-haired singer in mind?* "Captain Mandara, I'm amazed. That is very thoughtful of you."

"Yes, well, I suppose I do have a lapse into thoughtfulness every now and then."

"That's not what I meant!"

"Marquesa, I take pride in my work. And I enjoy it. I want a building I can look at every day and say to myself, 'My, what a fine building!' The Bible says to work as unto the Lord, and I am always aware that everything I build stands under heaven's gaze."

"I like that. We are all under heaven's gaze, aren't we?"

"Yep. Now, Marquesa, I have one more question for you. As you know, me and the boys have been renting cots in Ransford's tent. We'd like permission to bunk out here at the hotel until it's completed. That would save us $3.50 a week for each man. I'd tack it onto their wages."

She glanced around the open building. "That's fine with me, but it won't be very warm or comfortable."

"We can build a scrap fire every morning, and frankly where we are staying now with twelve men in a small tent is not the height of comfort."

"Yes, by all means, help yourself."

"Thank you. Now watch your step on your way out. I'd better get back up there and help them finish that roof. Once we get it done, I won't be so worried about a storm blowing in."

"A storm? There's not a cloud in the sky."

"Good things don't last forever, Marquesa."

His brown eyes looked strained. *Is that a prediction or a reflection from the past, Captain Mandara? The more we visit, the less I know about you.*

While two aproned clerks in their early twenties scattered sawdust and swept the floor, July Johnson and Isabel Leon lounged at a round table near the woodstove to review the day's ledger and tally up their income.

When they had the accounts balanced, July walked over to the stove and picked up the coffeepot. "You want to try some more tea, or are you going to stick with coffee?"

"July, you know I can't stand the taste of tea. I know it's much more refined for a woman to drink tea, but I just can't stomach it."

"I ain't much on it either." He sat back down next to her with two cups of coffee and scooted over three stacked wooden cigar boxes. "Looks like we did a lot of cash business today."

"Yes, let's get some of this deposited in the bank."

"We need a safe."

"That's up to Mr. and Mrs. Parks to decide."

"I sure am anxious to get them home. Aren't you?"

"Yes, I am. It's one thing to run your own business. But it's a little nerve-wracking to run someone else's."

"It seems strange for them to take off and leave us in control, don't it?"

"Well, July, you've been a faithful employee and an honest worker. On the other hand, Carolina and I haven't always seen eye to eye. Ten months ago I came in here, and she was so sure I was going to steal her twenty-six dollars in the cash box that she kicked me out of the store. Now look at this." She pointed to the cigar boxes. "There's several hundred dollars right here."

"Marquesa, when Miss Carolina and Ranahan take a likin' to you, they purtneer adopt you."

She sipped the steaming coffee in the dark blue porcelain mug and glanced around the room. "I don't really deserve to be treated this well."

July shrugged. "Who does? Kind of the way the good Lord

treats all of us, ain't it? Generous-like, in spite of the fix we get ourselves into."

She studied his face and the wispy outline of an extremely thin mustache. "July, have you ever read much in the Bible?"

"Been readin' it near ever' day since Ranahan gave me one for Christmas."

"Tell me something." She set her coffee down and gazed at his mostly clean face. "Do you understand what you read?"

"Not all of it. No, ma'am. Some confuses me sorely."

"What do you do when you read part of it you don't understand?"

"I just go on to the next part."

"Doesn't it bother you that you can't figure some of it out?"

"Shoot, no, Marquesa. I'm havin' a hard enough time livin' up to the part I do understand. I figure if the Lord wants to hide some of it until I'm smarter, that's all right with me. Why do you ask about the Bible?"

"Oh, I've been reading the one Carolina left here, but I'm afraid I don't understand much."

"You know what Molly Mae heard someone say?"

"Eh, no, what did she hear?"

"That Mr. Kline's sister-in-law's brother is a Baptist preacher, and he might be coming out here to hold meetings."

"Mr. Kline?"

"He runs the bakery."

"What bakery?"

"The one next to the Chinese laundry."

"We have a bakery in town? How long has that been there?"

"Two or three days, I reckon."

"I need to get out more. All I seem to do is go from the store to the hotel and back."

"Shoot, you probably ain't even seen the photography studio."

"Here in Cantrell?"

"She pulled in yesterday mornin'. She's settin' up a tent at the top of the hill."

"A lady photographer?"

"Yep. Ain't that something? I heard she has yellow hair almost as purdy as Molly Mae's, but I don't rightly believe ever'thing I hear."

Isabel stood and strolled toward the open doorway. "Perhaps I'll take a walk before dark. Would you like to join me, Mr. Johnson?"

"No, ma'am. I mean, yes ma'am, I would like to, but I promised Molly Mae's daddy I'd help her patch up a table and some chairs that got busted up in that big fight last night."

"What fight?" she asked.

"When those buffalo skinners smellin' like spoiled meat came to town and tangled with Hudson, the man the captain tied to the hitching post last week."

"Hudson is still in town?"

"He was last night."

The Marquesa rubbed her pale hand across her forehead. *I can't believe I live in a little town like this and never know what's happening. It won't be that way when I'm running the hotel.* "Yes, well, July, you'd better go on and help Mr. Quincy."

"They sure are nice folks. Why, they treat me like I was family." July beamed.

Mr. July Johnson, I've seen her eyes when you walk into the room. You are family. There is no way that girl will ever let you go.

When Isabel Leon stepped out of the Assay Office and Bank, the sun was still hovering above the cliffs to the west of Cantrell. She stood for several moments at the intersection that had been rolling hillside only a few months before.

Maybe I should rent a rig and drive around town. But it wouldn't hurt me to walk! If I get tired, I can go to the hotel and sit on my nail keg and contemplate!

She hardly noticed the strangers sitting on a bench when she exited the bank. They lounged a good ten feet behind her, but she could hear their voices.

"She's a beaut, ain't she?"

I will not amplify their remarks by turning around and glaring at them.

"Purdiest one between Billings and Miles City, I reckon."

Only if Carolina Parks stays in Maryland.

"Built sturdy, too. I like 'em when they're sturdy."

Sturdy? I've been called lots of things over the years but never sturdy!

"I cain't wait to try 'er out myself."

Why didn't I put my revolver in my purse? I can't believe this. This land is too unsettled to go out alone without some protection.

"She'll be mighty fine to come home to at night, that's for sure."

If any of you lay a hand on me, I'll . . . I'll rip your eyes out. . . . I'll scream and 100 armed men will be here in seconds and riddle your body with lead balls. I've got friends in this town. Lots of friends. And they all carry guns! Don't mess with the Marquesa!

"I heard tell they're going to open her up by June first."

A chill slid down her back, and her hands started to quiver. *They are planning on doing what?*

"They got a name for her?"

She sucked up a deep breath in preparation to scream. *May the Lord have mercy on their souls . . . and mine.*

"The Duchess Hotel. That's what I heard. Next time we come in from the claim, we're staying in there."

Her left hand flew over her lips to silence her laughter. *Hotel? They've been talking about my hotel! Never mind about their souls, Lord.*

"Not unless we find more color than last week."

"That's for sure . . . that's for sure."

Just prospectors eyeing the new hotel. Isabel, you didn't used to be so suspicious and nervous.

"I thought I heard it was going to be called El Capitan."

Well, you heard wrong, boys.

"Nope, the captain is just buildin' it. But he don't own it."

"Excuse me, ma'am."

Isabel turned around slowly. Three men covered mostly with mud and duckings sat leaning their backs against the Assay Office wall. "Yes?"

The one who had a mustache that drooped well below his chin spoke up. "Hate to trouble you, ma'am, but do you know the name of that new hotel?"

"It's going to be called The Hotel Marquesa."

He turned to the heavier man on the far end of the bench. "See there, I told you!"

"You said it was The Duchess."

"Same difference."

She stepped out into the street feeling the heels of her shoes sink a little in the dust and dirt. *They are more impressed by my hotel than by me. That's good. That's what I want. I need to buy myself some dresses like Carolina's. Boring. Plain. In a conservative yet elegant sort of way.*

Isabel Leon, you liar.

You were disappointed they weren't talking about you.

No, I wasn't.

Yes, you were.

All right, perhaps just a little.

She waited in the middle of the street for a carriage to pass.

Instead it stopped right beside her. She glanced up to see Dawson Mandara tip his hat.

"Evening, Marquesa."

"Captain Mandara, are you leaving town?"

"Only until dark. I wanted to ride up on the mesa of that south mountain."

"Oh?"

"Have you ever been up there?"

"No, I've only been north from the store to the river."

"Well, it's quite a dramatic view of Cantrell up there."

"You've gone up there before?"

"Most every evening if it's not storming."

"Why?"

"Sometimes to pray. Sometimes to contemplate. Did you know that anyone coming to Cantrell from the Devil's Canyon goldfields will crest that mountain, and the first thing they see is The Hotel Marquesa?"

"Really! That's exciting."

"It's a nice view. That's how I decided which lot to buy for building my house."

"Which one is it?"

"The one up next to those cedars. But you don't get the lay of the land from down here. Up there you can tell that from my front porch, I'll be able to watch every one leave and enter town, as well as see the traffic along the river."

"That sounds delightful!"

"If you have an extra hour, hop in and ride along. I think you'll enjoy the view."

She stared up at his narrow brown eyes that were neither anxious nor peaceful.

I am suspicious of all men, Captain Mandara, even those who claim to be happily married. Such an attitude has undoubtedly kept me from some trouble.

Not often.

But every once in a while.

Isabel realized that he was waiting for a reply.

He tipped the front brim of his hat. "Sorry, Marquesa. If that invitation seemed improper, please disregard it. I didn't mean to suggest anything that might appear compromising to your honor."

"Oh, no. I'd like to ride up there with you, but I have a dinner engagement about dark and was just wondering if we would be back by then."

"I assure you, I'll get you back by dark."

"Captain Mandara, that was spoken with the tone of a man who keeps his word."

She lifted the hem of her beige dress several inches above the dirt and placed her left foot on the carriage step. The strong grip of a callused hand in hers gently tugged her up to the wide carriage seat.

"Do you always take a carriage to the top of the mountain?"

"I usually ride horseback, but I thought today that I might take some company along with me." He reached under the carriage seat and handed her a neatly folded charcoal gray blanket. "Would you like a lap robe, Marquesa?"

"Thank you, Captain Mandara. Do you always take a wool blanket for your guests?"

"Only when the guest is my charming lady employer."

She turned toward him and tilted her head. "Graciousness becomes you, Captain Mandara."

"I'll try not to let it become a habit."

She thought she noticed a slight smile, but she wasn't sure.

The spring air felt cool as they ascended up out of the Yellowstone River Valley. Several empty wagons and various men on horseback were traveling down the grade. Each one tipped his hat to Isabel as he passed.

A hatless man with a wild shock of gray hair led a string of a dozen empty mules. He waved for them to stop. He spat a wad of tobacco straight over the nose of the mule he rode and then wiped his mouth on the sleeve of a greasy canvas coat. "Pardon me, ma'am." He nodded his head at Isabel Leon and then turned to Mandara. "Are you a doctor?"

"I'm afraid not," Captain Mandara replied.

"Are you ill?" Isabel asked.

"No, ma'am. We had a cave-in on the claim, and I reckon my partner busted some ribs. I'm looking for a doctor. Is there one down in Cantrell?"

"Not that I'm aware of," she replied, "but we have new people moving in every day. You might ask around."

"Thank you, ma'am, I will." He turned back to Mandara. "Say, you don't happen to be a judge, do you?"

Mandara shook his head. "I'm afraid I can't help you there either."

"Well, that's too bad. We surely need a judge up in the canyon. The miners' court was workin' fine until this spring, but now we got more men up there than Lee had at Gettysburg, if you catch my drift. When I seen you two in that carriage, I said to myself, 'Here comes a handsome and distinguished couple. Must be a doctor or a judge.' Sure could use a judge."

"Captain Mandara is a builder now."

"You don't say?" The man let fly with another wad of tobacco over the mule's nose. "We could use a builder up in the canyon, too. In fact, we could use about anybody except for more prospectors, Injuns, and bluecoats. Sorry to hold you up."

"I hope your friend gets better," Isabel called out.

"He'll either get better or die. One way I get to keep a friend;

the other way I get to keep the claim all to myself. Either way I reckon I win."

He spurred the mule, and the whole string jolted their way down the mountain. Mandara waited until the last mule plodded by and then pulled the carriage back into the middle of the road.

He slapped the line on the brown horse's rump and kept his eye on the trail. "That's an interesting philosophy to live by."

"I suppose there isn't much time to mourn if you're in a race to strike it rich," she commented.

"Some never mourn. And some spend their whole life mourning." He slapped the line again, and the horse picked up his pace. "I don't think I've ever been mistaken for a doctor or a judge before."

"I don't know . . . I think you look the part."

"Which one."

"Judge."

"How about you, Marquesa? Do you fit the part?"

"I've played about every part there is at one time or another in the theater. Which one do you mean?"

"The wife of a judge or doctor."

"I like the part of a doctor's wife. I've had to doctor many broken bones, cuts, and illnesses over the years."

"Yes, I could see you as a doctor's wife. Although you might need a little gray hair to instill the confidence of age."

That wouldn't be all that hard to provide, Captain Mandara.

They continued the trip to the top of the first mesa without any more conversation. When they turned south and drove along the ridge, Isabel stared out over the river to the land on the other side.

A handsome, distinguished couple. One of the benefits of being an actress is that you can play any part. If you're good, you can convince your audience that's just what you are. At least, you can convince them for a while.

"Do you see that land on the other side of the river?" she quizzed.

"Yes, I hear it's all one large cattle ranch."

"It's the Slash-Bar-Four operated by Tap Andrews. Have you ever met him?"

"No."

"You will. He and his wife, Pepper, are good friends of Carolina and Ranahan Parks."

"Seems like the Parkses are friends with most everyone."

"They're a splendid couple who seem to bring out the best in others."

"That's a mighty good reputation to have. I surely am looking forward to meeting them."

Mandara drove the carriage to a clump of cedars and jumped down to the ground. "The best view is from those rocks!" He pointed to rimrock just beyond the cedar. "Would you care to hike out there?"

"Captain Mandara, if you were sixteen, I'd think for sure you were leading me on."

"Marquesa, I am neither leading you on nor sixteen."

"I was teasing, of course."

"Yes, well, teasing is not something I'm good at giving or receiving. However, I would like you to see your hotel at sunset."

"Certainly, Captain Mandara." She accepted the offer of his hand, and she descended from the carriage. *Does this man ever relax and joke a little?*

The breeze stiffened as they approached the rocks. "Please accept my apologies," Mandara offered. "I didn't know it would be so windy tonight. Let me step back and get the lap blanket for your shoulders."

"Oh, you don't have to—"

"I insist. Stand right here and watch the sun. Do you see that big-roofed building straight below the trees?"

"Is that my hotel?"

"That it is. Keep watching. When the sun gets just right, it will begin to look twice as big. Now let me get to the point of why I brought you out here."

I've been wondering that, Captain Mandara.

"With the dark shake roof, I think we should build a cupola in the middle of the roof, paint it white, and stick a flag up there. It would set off the hotel and make it the absolute hub of the whole area. Ponder that for a minute as I get the blanket."

She gazed down at Cantrell as she listened to the dirt-crushing heels of the boots fading back toward the carriage. The northern horizon was crowded with thick-timbered mountains. To the east were mainly rolling hills of natural grasslands. Somewhere east, a ride of a day or two, were the blood-soaked grasslands where Custer and his men had died eight years earlier. Unseen, but stretched out across the Wyoming border, were the massive Bighorn Mountains. For a split second, Isabel Leon felt that she was the only human on earth. Then she glanced back down at Cantrell.

He's right. A cupola would be spectacular from this angle.

I just can't believe that really is my hotel.

But then I can't believe I'd ever be invited to ride out into the wilderness with a handsome man just to contemplate cupolas.

The blanket around her shoulders felt good as they descended back into the narrow river valley. The downhill ride seemed more rocky, and Isabel kept sliding forward on the slick black leather carriage seat. The captain had what she considered an "out-to-sea look" on his face, and they hardly spoke all the way back to town.

They slowed down near several tents just south of town. He walked the horse on the rutted dirt street. "I'm afraid my mind has been elsewhere. I've not been much company," he admitted.

"It was a delightful ride, Captain. No apologies needed. I should get outside more often. I am looking forward to standing on the veranda and watching the sunset. There are times when I enjoy the silence."

"Yes, and believe it or not, there are times when I enjoy conversation. Someday when the hotel is finished, perhaps we will discuss something besides construction techniques."

"Captain Mandara, from the looks of this town, you will never be finished with construction."

"Shall I take you to the cafe, or shall I let you off at the store?"

"The store will be splendid. I should probably wash up and try to get my hair back into the combs."

He drove up beside the porch and parked the carriage.

"There is no reason to get down, Captain. I can take care of myself," she assured him.

"Yes, you can. But I cannot but do what I must do. No woman

should be required to walk to a dark building unescorted. I'll help you light a lamp."

Captain Mandara led her across the porch.

"Let me find my key."

He pushed the door open with the toe of his boot. "Oh, it's not locked. Perhaps young Mr. Johnson's here."

"He went to help the Quincys. He won't be home for hours." She peeked into the darkened room. "Oh . . . no! It was my fault. I left the door unlocked!"

"You did?"

"Yes, I was just going to step to the bank and return. Then I decided to take a walk, and you came by . . . and . . ."

"And I caused you to forget to come back and lock up! You'll have to check the shelves to see if anything was taken."

Captain Mandara held his nose, pointed into darkness, and mouthed something.

Isabel stood on her tiptoes and whispered into his ear, "What?"

His lips brushed her hair as his deep voice softened to a bare whisper, "The buffalo hunters are in there!"

A sharp pungent odor drifted out to the porch. Captain Mandara had his revolver pulled out of the military holster. This time he spoke loudly. "Just lock up, and we'll check the inventory later, Marquesa. We're late for our supper guests!"

He pointed her back to the carriage and then ducked down and crawled into the darkened storeroom.

"Oh, you're so right, Captain Mandara!" Her voice was at that level she used for a small theater and a boisterous crowd. Lines from *Long Island Neighbors* came to her mind. "'The Johnsons are not the most patient people in the world. Just the other day I said, "Sylvia, you have got to be more sublime and peaceful; you will fret yourself to an early grave."'"

She closed the door and fiddled with the key in the slot but didn't lock the door. "'But do you think she'd listen to me? I don't think she's heard a word I've said in the last five years.'"

Isabel noisily stomped across the deck to the carriage. "'You would think a woman her age . . .'" She let her voice fade out as she reached under the carriage seat.

Captain, you're a military man. There's got to be one under the seat.

Her hand gripped the handle of a heavy musket. She pulled it out and studied it in the evening shadows.

A Springfield trapdoor. Great. Why does he have to be a single-shot army man? I never did learn how to open it up. Using both hands, she cocked the hammer back. *Well, Captain Mandara, surely no officer carries an unloaded weapon under his carriage seat.*

Isabel crept back over to the darkened doorway and waited in the shadows. She held the .45-70 to her side. A freight wagon creaked its way down the street.

A cheerful voice came out of the near darkness. "Evenin', Marquesa."

A woman crouching at the door, gun in hand. Nothing unusual about that. Just a "howdy, ma'am" and continue on your way. And I used to think the frontier was settled twenty years ago.

She stood close to the building where she would be out of sight when and if the door swung open.

Captain, I'm not at all sure what it is you're planning on doing in the dark.

She leaned next to the wall and listened.

A loud crash shook the door.

"Lindsay, is that you?"

Then a long pause.

That sounded like someone dropped a shelf of goods . . . or a body.

"Lindsay? Where are you?"

Undoubtedly, the captain has Mr. Lindsay occupied.

"I got the bullets. You got them lever actions? Lindsay?"

You men are planning to pay for your goods, aren't you?

"Dad gum it, Lindsay, I cain't see ya. Don't light a lamp. They might still be out in the street. I'll meet you over by the gun case."

The Marquesa raised the heavy carbine to her shoulder and pointed it at the closed door. *Which is obviously a diversion. I can't believe you would think anyone on earth would believe that line.*

The heavy barrel of the four-foot-long musket began to sag in her arms. She tucked her elbows into her rib cage and propped the gun up.

The three-by-eight-foot solid pine door of Cantrell's

Mercantile swung open. For a moment all the Marquesa could see was darkness.

But she could smell a buffalo skinner.

And dirt.

And sweat.

And dried blood.

And a putrid stench.

Then she saw a huge man in a dark brown buckskin coat step toward the door and trip over a well-polished but slightly dusty black stovepipe military boot. Bullets rattled and scattered across the porch like marbles out of a coat with a ripped pocket.

Landing flat on his face, the big man rolled to his back, a foot-and-a-half skinning knife in his right hand and a scream on his lips.

The minute the Marquesa shoved the gun barrel straight into the man's open mouth, his knife dropped to the porch, and he lay still. From the fresh, pungent aroma, Isabel Leon figured he had broken out in a cold sweat, but it was too dark to tell for sure.

"Mister, if you wiggle your head, I'm going to pull this trigger, and there won't be enough of you left for your mama to identify, so lay real still until I calm down. I want you to know I'm a very nervous and fitful woman . . . and I don't know if I can keep from killing you or not. You've got to help me. Lay very still. I don't want to live the rest of my life with your death on my conscience."

The man on the porch lay rigid; even in the darkness she could see that his bulging eyes ceased blinking. Captain Mandara dragged an unconscious man out of the store and dropped him beside the one pinned under her gun barrel.

"Don't pull the trigger, Marquesa. You'll be scrubbing the porch for the next two weeks!" he growled. "Let me light a lantern and see what else we have in there." He kicked the boot of the man nursing her Springfield. "Mister, you aren't planning on moving, are you?"

The frightened man slightly shook his head back and forth.

"That's probably the smartest thing you've done all day," Mandara added.

He returned with a lit kerosene lamp. "Looks like everything's all right in there. They knocked over a few goods, trying to feel their way in the dark. Now ease the hammer down real slowly on that musket. I'll take it from here."

"Shall I take it out of his mouth before I let the hammer down?" she asked.

"Yeaath!" the man on the porch moaned.

Isabel stepped back but left the gun cocked. Captain Mandara motioned for the man to sit up. He kept his own solid-frame army Colt .45 at the man's head.

"She liked to have killed me!" the buffalo skinner thundered.

"You were stealing things from the store."

"That door wasn't locked. We went in there to purchase some items, that's all!"

"In the dark?"

"It wasn't that dark when we first went in. We was just shopping. Ask Lindsay. Did you kill him?"

"Not yet," Mandara informed him. "But since when does a door have to be locked to protect private property? However, if you are customers, then pay the Marquesa for your bullets."

"I ain't got no money!"

Captain Mandara stepped back and brushed off the front of his brown leather vest and then waved the pistol at the man. "Well, there's nothing left for us to do but shoot you."

"What? For takin' a few bullets?" the man cried. "You cain't do that! Good grief, man, have some mercy!"

The captain glanced over at Isabel. "Marquesa, do we have a judge in this town?"

"No, we don't."

"Do we have a jail?"

"Not yet."

"A marshal?"

"No."

"You see, mister, we can't arrest you or throw you in jail or try you for burglary. So all we have left is to shoot you and bury you. I suppose in a few months we'll have all those nice things in place, but in the meantime, if someone commits a crime in Cantrell, we just shoot them."

"But you cain't do that!"

The Marquesa stepped up. "Captain, what if we just let these men go if they promise to leave town and never come back? I really don't want a mess on the porch."

"But what if they do come back?"

"Well, of course, we'd have to gun them down like dogs."

"I don't know, Marquesa. I don't like to put things off that ought to be done today!"

"Listen to her, man! We'll leave right now!" the man pleaded. "We'll be out of town in two minutes! My mules are down at the livery."

"What do you think, Captain?"

He shook his head. Then he lowered the gun to his side. "I suppose we could give it a try."

"You're a very generous and sensitive Christian man, Captain Mandara." She bowed her head in the flickering light of the lantern.

"Very well. Carry your partner down there with you."

Mandara handed the lantern to Isabel Leon and then pulled his watch out of his vest pocket. "He did say they would be out of here in two minutes, didn't he?"

"I cain't. It'll take me ten minutes at least!" he pleaded.

"Seven," the captain conceded.

"Okay, seven!" The man struggled to lift his partner to his shoulder.

The captain studied his watch. "Ready? Go!"

"I'm goin'! . . . I'm goin'!"

The Marquesa and the captain continued to hold their guns as the man staggered into the darkness with the dead weight of his unconscious partner over his shoulder.

"Do those men have any idea how bad they smell?" she asked.

"I don't suppose so."

"Do you think they'll really leave town?"

"I don't know. But what choice did we have?"

"We could have bound them and taken them to Billings, I suppose."

"Only if we wanted to miss two days of construction," the captain reminded her.

"Perhaps we do need a lawman in Cantrell. Ranahan always kept things quiet before. But that was mostly by mutual agreement."

Mandara picked up the bullets strewn across the porch. "What I want to know is where did you get that line about being a nervous and fitful woman?"

Isabel began to laugh. "It was from a play called *Prussian Intrigue*, where a comely young French girl rescues her *amant* from the clutches of the evil Austrian prince."

"The lady rescues the man?"

"It could happen, you know." She held the lantern above his stooping shoulders.

"Well, if it did, I would imagine it would be someone like you." He raised up when the bullets were retrieved.

"Actually, I'm not very brave unless I'm angry."

Standing side by side, staring into the darkness, Captain Mandara reached his arm around her shoulder and gave her a brief hug. "I must say that was the most fun I've had in ten years. Seeing that man totally rigid, sucking on your barrel. Where did you get that trapdoor musket?" His hand dropped back down. "Forgive me, Marquesa, I had no business touching you. It was strictly fraternal, I assure you."

Captain, I do believe you need your wife and family to move here soon! How long has it been since someone hugged you . . . or you hugged them? "Don't worry, Captain, I received it as a slap on the back or a handshake, as congratulations among partners. But the musket— it's yours. I pulled it out from under the carriage seat."

"I didn't have a musket under the seat. That's an infantry gun. I'm strictly cavalry. We use carbines."

"Then I suppose it belongs to the livery."

Captain Mandara holstered his revolver and picked up the musket. "Hold the lantern over here. Look at this. It's almost rusted shut. The trapdoor hardly opens. There's no bullet. You are a great actress! But let me teach you a fundamental lesson of living in the West."

"What's that, Captain Mandara?"

"Never, ever, point an unloaded gun at someone! Either be well-armed or back away from the scene quickly."

"I shall remember that."

"'Course, you could have pulled out the bayonet and pinned him to the porch."

"Are you sure you don't tease just a little?"

"Never." He almost smiled. "Do you need some help straightening up the store?"

"No, I'm just going to lock the door. Logan will be growing impatient for me to join him for supper."

"And I had better return this carriage before they charge me for having it out overnight."

"Good evening, Captain Mandara."

"Good evening, Marquesa."

Logan Henry Phillips was more than a Wild West showman and professional gambler. He had twice sailed to Australia. Once he ran a target range in Scotland. He rode with the legendary Stuart Brannon as they tracked Limpy Doc Franklin in the Mojave Desert. He scouted for General Miles during the Nez Perce war. He published a newspaper in Wichita. And he fled across west Texas with two dozen Rangers on his trail. At one time, six years earlier, he and Isabel Leon had a very intense and turmoil-filled relationship that lasted eleven days and ended with him dumping a barrel of rainwater over her head during her finale of a musical review in Pittsburgh. She retaliated by pouring a pitcher of hot coffee down his trousers.

They had become very close friends after that. Each refused to discuss their past relationship. They might go months or years without seeing each other, but when they did meet, it was like a family reunion. He was in some ways more than a fellow pilgrim. He was a brother.

And there was one thing Logan Henry Phillips could do far better than anything else.

He could talk.

And talk.

And talk.

Any subject. Anyplace. Anytime.

It was a gift that made him the center of almost every group of people he came in contact with.

For over two hours he and Isabel occupied the small table in the southwest corner of Quincys' Cafe. By the time he scraped the apple cobbler off his plate and licked his fork clean, he had filled the Marquesa in on the present whereabouts plus the physical and emotional conditions of all of their mutual friends and a few she had never heard of. It was one of the most relaxing evenings she had spent in years.

Logan, you are probably the only person on the face of this earth who has seen me at my rotten worst and still likes me. I can't pretend any-thing with you—you know better. You can't begin to imagine how com-fortable it is to have you here!

The Marquesa spent most of the time picking at her food, smil-ing and nodding her head to Logan's wild stories. In addition, she shot secret glances at Captain Dawson Mandara who ate alone and seemed to be occupied writing letters.

Is he ordering material? Writing to friends in the army? One could be to his wife but not three or four. Or could they?

Logan signaled for Mrs. Quincy to refill their coffee cups and then waved his hand at Isabel. "Marquesa, you told me about Jacob Hardisty and about your run in San Francisco last winter, but I have no idea how you ended up with a hotel in Cantrell, Montana Territory."

"I call it being at the right place at the right time. Carolina calls it Providence."

"Carolina?"

"Carolina Cantrell Parks. The town is named for her brother. She and Ranahan own the Mercantile."

"And the Blacksmith's?"

"Yes. They're quite religious. They tend to see God's leading in almost everything."

Isabel saw the captain hold each page up and read it by the light of the kerosene lantern on the table. *Did he wipe his eye? Was that a tear? Or are his eyes just getting tired?*

"I don't suppose there's any problem in seeing God in the midst of things," Logan piped up.

"No, I'm sure you're right."

"But you still haven't told me the story."

"It all started last summer when I tried to kill Jacob Hardisty and got run out of Billings." The cafe air felt very warm, but the aroma was delightful.

"Yes, you told me that."

"I ended up out here staying with Carolina Cantrell. That was right before she and Ranahan got married." Isabel fussed with her collar. *I don't think I'll ever get used to high-collared dresses. These were not invented for a woman's comfort!*

"Let me get this straight." Logan leaned against the back of his chair. "She hated you for stealing Hardisty from her in the first place, and you hated her for shoving your arm and keeping you from killing him, but she allowed you to move in anyway, and you became dear friends?"

"Yes. It sounds strange, doesn't it?"

"It sounds like Providence, my dear Marquesa."

"But that's not the whole story. I went to San Francisco in November and found a role in a musical pageant that lasted until March. Actually it is probably still going on. But in March I received a letter from Carolina. It seems that three men that she had befriended the last summer struck a rich claim in Devil's Canyon. They had promised her if they found gold, they would come back and build a fancy hotel."

Near Captain Mandara, Mr. Quincy began to stack chairs on tables in the mostly deserted cafe. *Is he just going to sit over there all night? Doesn't he have something else to do?*

I suppose not.

"So the miners returned to fulfill their promise?" Logan prodded.

"Exactly. Only they couldn't be gone from the diggings long enough to oversee the construction. So they asked Carolina and Ran to become partners with them."

"They turned down a deal like that?" Logan bit the end of a narrow black cigar, glanced at the Marquesa, and then shoved it back into his vest pocket.

"They had other plans. He had promised that their first child would be born in Maryland. And they didn't think they wanted to be tied to operating a hotel."

Logan pulled out a gold double eagle coin and spun it like a top on the table. "Making money didn't appeal to them?"

"They're kind of strange that way. Anyway, I got a letter from Carolina in March saying I could design my own hotel and receive half the profit from it, becoming one quarter owner if I'd move back to Cantrell. They said they had prayed about it, and my name kept coming to their minds."

"Did you pray about it, Marquesa?"

She stared at Logan and then sighed. "I must admit I didn't. But I have several times since."

"How long did it take you to decide to leave the theater and come to Cantrell?"

"About two minutes. I left the next morning on a train east."

"You gave up the theater so easily?"

"How long would it take Logan Henry Phillips to do the same thing?"

"About two minutes."

"I met the partners one night. We visited until midnight, and they took off the next morning leaving me a $50,000 line of credit."

"And you didn't have to do anything to get that?"

Her smile was precise, straight white teeth gleaming. "I didn't even dance with them."

"It's Providence."

"It's crazy, Logan."

"Yes, well, but what's with this plain and prissy look?"

"I'm wearing some of Carolina's things."

She hadn't noticed before how old Logan's eyes looked. From a distance he would still look like a handsome leading man. But up close, the hard life was making its claim.

"You look mighty content," he acknowledged.

"It is different for me. It's almost like leading a normal life."

He waved his arm across the now-empty cafe. "I can't remember a time when the Marquesa wasn't surrounded by adoring men."

"Oh, I'm still surrounded by men. Most of them are extremely friendly but respectful. They tease but keep their distance. All except Mr. Johnson and the captain."

"Oh? Do I hear some romantic interests?"

"Hardly. One's my happily married builder, and the other's a fifteen-year-old friend who works for the Parkses. And, of course, now I have my good friend Logan Henry Phillips."

"And everyone knows we are merely friends."

"Logan, I have never in my life known two people who made better friends . . . and worse lovers . . . than you and me."

He tipped his hat. "Marquesa, I couldn't agree with you more. I take that as a compliment."

"I intended it as such."

One of the first lessons Isabel Leon had learned in Montana Territory was that barely half the people knew or cared what month it was. She also quickly discovered that very, very few people cared what day of the week it was. And absolutely nobody gave two hoots what time of the day it was. Time seemed to be divided only into yesterday, today, tomorrow, and next season.

It wasn't that people didn't carry watches. Most every man with a vest, which was over half, had a timepiece in the pocket. Most of these were wound and ticking. Many of the ladies, who made up not more than 25 percent of the population, had a delicate watch on a necklace or silver brooch.

They just didn't look at them much.

And never paid any attention if they did.

Not one of the more than two dozen businesses had their hours posted. As far as she knew, there were no Open or Closed signs either.

The saloons on Second Street stayed open twenty-four hours.

All the other stores closed . . . eventually.

Take the Mercantile. They opened every morning more or less half an hour after July Johnson got things straightened up and any new inventory stacked on the shelves. The rule for closing was "about an hour before sundown or whenever the business thins out."

In spring, summer, and fall, the only Open sign was a business's front door. An open door meant the establishment was obviously open.

Isabel had never enjoyed getting up early.

But she had never gone for weeks of retiring at 10:00 P.M. For several weeks she slept long hours, as if catching up on a lifetime of short sleep.

Then she settled into a routine.

Bed by 10:00 P.M.

Read until 11:00 P.M.

She slept until July hollered that coffee was on the stove and he was opening the store.

Which was normally about 7:00 A.M.

The two clerks reported in at 8:00 A.M.

It was getting to be a nice, predictable routine.

That's why she was surprised that it was sunlight through the lace curtains on the east wall window that woke her up. She sat on the edge of the thick-mattressed bed and fumbled with her jewelry on the nightstand. The tiny silver latch on the diamond-shaped silver locket avoided her long, carefully filed fingernails. Finally it popped open.

It's 2:15! It can't be! Oh, it's upside down . . . 7:45 A.M.? I didn't even hear July open up. The store's quiet . . . a slow morning.

Barefoot and clad in her neck-to-floor flannel gown, she meandered across the bare wooden floor and gripped the cold brass door handle. She opened the door only an inch and peeked straight out into the middle of Cantrell's Mercantile.

No one was there.

Neither of the clerks, Merwin and Bray.

Not even July.

She opened the door a little wider and stuck her head out.

"July?"

She could hear the big brass clock on the back wall tick. And horse traffic in the street.

Nothing more.

"July? Are you there?"

She stepped out into the storeroom and immediately noticed that the front door was still closed.

"Where did he go?"

With her arms folded across her chest, she stalked across the store to the far wall, and July's bunk.

Either he didn't come home last night . . . or he made his bed and went out early. Why isn't he here? Marquesa, you're fuming like a mother with a wayward child.

He's only fifteen.

But he can run the whole store by himself.

Yes, but you were fifteen once, Isabel Leon.

Well, don't worry, Isabel. He didn't stay out all night with Molly Mae.

If he had, her father would be over here . . .

The thunder of a strong hand slamming against the front door caused her to scamper back toward her room.

"Who is it? We're not open yet!"

"It's Drake Quincy. I want to know where my daughter is!" the deep voice bellowed.

Oh, July! What have you gone and done?

— *Three* —

"IS JOHNSON IN THERE?" Quincy roared with about as much patience as a mama bear separated from her cubs.

Isabel scooted over by the door. She unlocked it and opened it an inch. Six feet tall, 250 pounds, Drake Quincy paced the porch, his wide-brimmed hat jammed low on his graying head.

"Mr. Quincy, July is not here at the moment."

"You're darn right he's not there. He's been out all night with my daughter," the big man fumed. "If he's compromised her honor, I'll kill him with my own bare hands! Do you know where they went?"

"No, I don't." Isabel clutched at her gown and glanced back over toward July's cot.

"Are any of his things missing?"

"Things?"

Quincy leaned close to the crack in the door, his fiery brown eyes only inches from Isabel's. "I want to know if he packed his satchel and ran off with my daughter!"

"Oh, I'm sure he wouldn't . . ." Isabel thought about the gleam in young Johnson's eyes every time he mentioned Molly Mae. *Well, I'm not too sure*. "Mr. Quincy, I'm slow getting around this morning. Let me grab my robe."

"Eh, yes, I didn't mean to harass you." Suddenly the big man's voice and eyes softened.

Isabel held her flannel gown at the neck and swung the store door open about a foot. "July is a respectable young man, and Molly Mae is a well-mannered young lady. We both know that.

There must be some logical explanation. Let me pull on a robe. Would you like to wait inside the store?"

"I'll wait for two minutes, that's all." He stomped right past her and down a dry goods aisle. "After that, I'll get my shotgun and go looking for them."

Isabel scampered back to her room and pulled on her silk robe. She paused long enough by the mirror to brush her long, thick black hair over her shoulders and shudder.

Well, Marquesa, you do look lovely. Men calling on you before you get ready. Running around barefoot in your gown. This kind of thing won't happen when you have your own hotel.

Will it?

"Excuse me, sir, but the Marquesa is not taking visitors until 10:00 A.M. Would you care to wait in the parlor . . . with the others?"

Who am I kidding?

Still barefoot, she padded back into the store. Quincy paced in front of the woodstove. Alongside him the store clerks, Tiny Merwin and Adam Bray, who had just come in, gaped at her attire.

"Boys, you'll have to open up the store this morning. July isn't here at the moment. The cash box is on my dresser."

"I want to know if Johnson was here last night!" Quincy stormed.

"Shall we finish crating that big order for the Eureka Mine?" Merwin asked as he tied on his ducking apron.

"Eh . . . well . . . I think . . ." Isabel Leon stammered. *July runs this business, not me. What does he want them to do?*

Drake Quincy stepped between her and Merwin. "I demand to know if Johnson was here last night!"

The front door swung open, and two prospectors marched in, freshly shaved and smelling of tonic water. "Mornin', Marquesa," the shorter one greeted her. "Where's July? We need four pick handles, some carriage bolts, and a couple of new panniers."

"Mr. Bray can help you with that," she instructed. "Tiny, you go ahead and crate the Eureka Mine order."

"Yes, ma'am."

"Mind if we hep ourselves to a cup of Arbuckles?" one of the prospectors queried.

Quincy poked a stiff finger into her arm. "I want an answer. And I want it right now! Did Johnson come home last night or not?"

Isabel took a big deep breath and peered into Quincy's anxious and angry eyes. *I am not anyone's parent. Not July's. Not Molly Mae's. What am I doing here? I didn't have problems like this in San Francisco!*

She turned away from him and scanned the woodstove where the prospectors poured steaming coffee into blue-enameled tin cups.

Coffee?

Quincy grabbed her shoulder and spun her back around. "I demand to know—"

She slapped his arm off with such violent force that he jumped back. "Mr. Quincy, do not ever, ever lay your hand on me again! You barged in here with me still in my nightgown, shouted demands, and grabbed ahold of my shoulder. I hope you treat your daughter better than you treat me!"

"You need help, Marquesa?" one of the prospectors called out from the stove.

Drake Quincy dropped his head and sighed. Huge callused hands wiped the corners of his eyes.

She held up her hand. "No, boys, it's all right."

The voice now was low, apologetic. "You're right, Marquesa. I had no right. It was improper. I'm just scared. I'm truly scared for my girl."

"All I can say, Mr. Quincy, is that July was here this morning. He straightened up his cot, built a fire, and made that big pot of coffee."

"He did?"

"July makes the best coffee in town!" one of the miners piped up. "He sinks them grounds with brown eggshells. That's what does it, you know."

"He was really here last night?" Quincy's tightly drawn eyes began to relax.

"Yes, but I don't know what time he got in nor what time he left this morning. It must be an emergency. He has never been late opening the store."

Quincy looked to the ceiling and sighed, "Lord, help her!"

Several more customers wandered into the store and ogled Isabel in her green silk robe. "You open for business?" one shouted.

She glared back. "The store is open if that's what you're asking!"

They wandered among the goods.

"Mr. Quincy, I really must get dressed. Have a cup of coffee. Then I'll help you search for Molly Mae."

He wiped his eyes, then looped his thumbs into his suspenders. "I better keep lookin' around town."

"I know July and Molly Mae enjoy going down to the river. Do you suppose they went down there this morning?" Isabel suggested.

"I already rode down there."

"And you've checked around town?"

"Every place but the saloons."

"I'm sure they'll wander in soon."

Drake Quincy ran the back of his hand across a bolt of flower-print material. "She took her Sunday dress."

Isabel locked her hands in front of her. "She took what?"

"Mama says her Sunday dress is missin'. I think they run off." His voice was soft, broken.

"But why would July get up, build a fire, make coffee . . . and then run off?"

A familiar boot heel caused Isabel to glance at the doorway. Straight-backed and expressionless, Captain Mandara tramped in.

"Excuse me, Marquesa, I just need that keg of siding nails. Don't mean to interrupt your visit."

He glanced down at her bare toes.

"July can find the nails for me."

You're not even curious why I'm standing here in my night clothes? Isabel spoke through clenched teeth. "I'm afraid July's not here right now."

"He ran off with my girl," Quincy blurted out.

"He what?"

"Him and Molly Mae took off. You ain't seen them, have you?"

The captain's face flushed. "You need some help looking for them?"

Maybe the captain can calm Mr. Quincy down.

"I'd appreciate it, Captain. I'm worried sick. I reckon they ran off to Billings or Helena."

"Well, if he's in this town, we'll find 'em," the captain blustered. "And I'll personally help you bust every bone in his body!"

"What?" Marquesa stammered.

"If he laid one hand on Nellie . . . I mean Molly, he ought to be tied to a cottonwood and flogged!"

Isabel dropped her forehead into her hand. *Nellie? Of course! His fifteen-year-old daughter! The only thing more dangerous than an irate father is two irate fathers!*

"Wait until I get dressed. I'll come with you," she insisted.

"Marquesa?"

Everyone in the store turned to view the man in the dusty brown suit and the small, round hat. "Are you the Marquesa?"

She held her robe and gown tight under her chin. "What do you want?"

"I jist came down off that south hill. A boy named July flagged me down. Said there was a wagon wreck up there on the rim. Asked me to tell you to send up a carriage for them."

Isabel scooted over to the door. "A wagon wreck?"

"I think a girl got injured." The man surveyed her from head to bare toes.

"He had a girl with him?" Quincy cried.

"Yellow-haired. I don't know how banged up she is. He had a blanket over her . . . mostly."

"My Molly Mae!" Her name burst out like a sob.

"I'll get a wagon and go with you," the captain proposed. "If she's injured, we'll need a wagon, not a carriage."

"I'm going, too," the Marquesa insisted.

"I'll run tell Mama!" Quincy reported.

"You're not dressed," the captain protested.

"I'll hurry. I've done a lot of nursing. I can help! Mr. Merwin, you and Mr. Bray oversee the store until I return."

"If you're ready by the time the wagon's out front, you can go with us." The captain shoved his pocket watch back into his coat.

"I'll be ready."

She was.

Sort of.

She had on a dress.

Shoes.

And a shawl.

In her right hand was her bag.

In her left hand she clutched a hairbrush and a pair of earrings.

She crawled up into the wagon between Captain Mandara and Drake Quincy. With great patience and precision, she fastened the pierced earrings in the midst of bone-jarring bounces of the light wagon along the rocky road south of town.

Pressed in a human vise between two strong men, she found it almost impossible to brush her hair, which hung unrestrained down her back.

Captain Mandara whipped the matched pair of mules furiously as they reached the grade. Drake Quincy said nothing but kept pounding his clenched right fist into the palm of his left hand. The captain's clean-shaven face smelled of spicy tonic water. Quincy's smelled of bacon grease.

Isabel's folded hands rested on top of her canvas bag on her lap. She focused her eyes straight ahead at the laboring mules. *They'll kill him. He's just a kid. They're both kids. You do dumb things when you're fifteen. I did dumb things when I was fifteen.*

Of course, I didn't have a father to race after me.

Her head slumped, and she held her cheeks in her hands. *God, You don't know me. But You know July. I'm his friend. He's in trouble right now, God. Big trouble. I thought You ought to know that, because if You don't help him out, You better get his room ready in heaven.*

A slap of the line and a shout from the captain caused her to sit straight up.

You've got to gain control, Isabel. You're starting to slip. Praying? That's for people like Carolina. Or Ranahan. Or July. Or even Captain Mandara. I wonder if he's praying now? Probably praying to get his hands on July.

I wonder how God answers a prayer like that?

I've got to keep them from dismembering July. At least until he has a chance to explain himself.

Young man, I hope you have a mighty good explanation!

By the time they reached the top of the mesa on the south mountain, the mules were lathered with sweat and laboring for breath.

"Where are they?" Quincy growled, still pounding his fist in his hand. "Where's my girl?"

"Over there! By the rock pile! Isn't that her?" The captain turned the rig east and walked the mules toward the waving arms of a distant blonde-headed girl.

"I'll kill him," Quincy growled. "If he touched her, I'll kill him! Whip those mules!"

"I can't do it. They have to rest, or we'll have dead animals on our hands and no way to get her back to town," the captain reported.

Drake Quincy leaped from the rig, stumbled, fell, picked himself up, and trotted to the rocks.

Molly Mae ran toward him. "She doesn't look injured to me," Isabel observed.

"At least not on the outside," the captain mumbled.

"Where's July?" she asked.

"Maybe he's run off."

"He's not the type. He'd stay and face the music, no matter what."

"We'll find him," Mandara assured her.

They reached the embracing Quincys just as Molly Mae pushed her father back. "We've got to hurry. She's hurt."

Drake held her shoulders with his hands and stared into her eyes. "Who's hurt? Did he touch you?" he roared.

She raised light but anxious eyebrows. "July?"

"Honey, if he forced himself on you, I'll kill him!"

"Daddy! Just wait!" Molly Mae cried as she pulled away from her father.

"Where is he?" Mandara demanded as he swung down out of the wagon, pulling his gun from the holster.

"Over by those rocks," Molly Mae stammered, "but it's not what . . ."

"You stay here with the Marquesa!" Mr. Quincy barked. He pulled a shotgun from the wagon and ran after Mandara.

"Wait!" Molly Mae cried.

The explosion from Isabel's small handgun startled the mules. The men stopped running through the dry dirt and sage.

"Listen to her!" Isabel cried.

Both women jogged up to the men.

"Molly Mae, who is injured?" Isabel pressed.

The fifteen-year-old brushed her bangs out of her eyes. "It's Oliole."

"Who?" the captain demanded.

"Miss Fontenot!"

"What did he do to her?" Drake Quincy demanded.

Molly Mae shook her head. "July didn't do anything to anyone! Daddy, what are you talking about?"

"Are you saying he didn't touch you?" Mr. Quincy probed.

"He didn't do anything improper if that's what you mean. What's going on? Did you come up here thinking that July and me . . . but why?"

"You ran off without tellin' your mother," her father lectured.

Molly Mae looked down at the sage. "It was supposed to be a surprise."

"Who's this Miss Fontenot?" the captain asked.

"But you have on your Sunday dress." Mr. Quincy brushed the sleeve of his daughter's dress. "Why did you wear your best dress?"

"It was part of the surprise!"

"I'm going to give Mr. Johnson a surprise!"

"Daddy, please listen to me!"

"Will you two stop raving and let her explain!" Isabel Leon waved the small pistol in the air.

Molly Mae began to sob. "It was for your birthday."

Her father lifted her chin and stared into her eyes. "What do you mean, my birthday?"

"July and I wanted to surprise you on your birthday with a photograph."

"Is Miss Fontenot the new photographer in town?" Isabel asked.

"Yes, and she said a photograph with Cantrell in the background taken at sunrise would be extremely dramatic."

"As the captain well knows," Isabel interjected, "it *is* a dramatic view."

Mr. Quincy gazed toward the rim of the mesa. "You came up here this morning just to take a photograph?"

"It was supposed to be a surprise, Daddy!"

"I'm surprised, all right!"

"July and I posed on the rimrock, and Miss Fontenot was at her camera mounted on the back of the wagon. We were all waiting for the sun to get just right. And then a cougar screamed from somewhere in the rocks. Her horse bolted in the boulders and ran off, the wagon crashed, and Oliole was injured."

"Where are they?" Isabel shoved the little gun into her bag.

Molly Mae pointed to a barn-sized pile of boulders. "Behind those rocks!"

"Why didn't one of you hike back to town for help?" the captain quizzed.

"July refused to let me go by myself and wouldn't leave us alone up here. He said it wasn't safe."

All four trotted through the sage toward the wreck. July Johnson, wearing a soiled suit and tie, hovered over a woman with a long leather skirt and bloody white blouse. At one time the woman's bright yellow hair had been stacked on top of her head. It was now tossed and tangled in several directions at once. Isabel noticed the woman's pained bright blue eyes.

"Down here, Marquesa! Captain! Am I glad to see you! Thank You, Jesus!" July blurted out.

The Marquesa began to pick her way down through the rocks. *Yes, indeed. Thank You, Jesus.*

With a legion of would-be prospectors marching through town, there were no slack times at the Mercantile. There were busy times . . . and impossible times.

From the moment they returned to Cantrell, the Mercantile had been impossible. Around noon Isabel had slipped into her room, washed her face, and applied some makeup. She didn't bother pinning her hair up.

Then about 4:00 P.M. the store was suddenly empty of customers.

"What happened? Is there a fight?" she asked July, who was slicing a piece of cheese at the table near the woodstove.

"A big poker game," he announced.

She accepted a piece of the yellow cheese and nibbled on it. It tasted sharp. Very dry and sharp. "Poker game?"

"Your friend Mr. Phillips got a no-limit game rolling at the Diamond Queen," July reported.

"And everyone in town's over there?"

"Except us, I reckon. Think I'll let Tiny and Adam go have something to eat. We worked right through dinner."

"Maybe you should eat, too," she suggested.

"I reckon I better stay put. I don't think the Quincys are too happy with me."

"They were really scared," she cautioned. "Give them some time."

"Marquesa, did your daddy fret over you when you were a girl?"

My daddy never acknowledged my existence. "No, my father didn't act that way."

"See. Look at you. You turned out mighty fine."

She looked at his trusting blue eyes.

"Do you know why I became an actress, July?"

He pulled a huge green pickle out of a small wooden barrel. "No, ma'am, I don't. Why is that?"

"Because my real life was so pitiful and painful I couldn't stand to live it."

His mouth dropped open. "Really?"

"But you never mind about that." *Isabel, why on earth did you let down your guard with a fifteen-year-old?* She strolled across the store. "I do hope Miss Fontenot will be all right."

"It surely was superb of the captain to drive her to the doctor in Billings."

Yes, but I'm not sure what convinced him to do that. It might have been her injuries . . . or her long yellow hair . . . or the torn blouse. . . . I do hope he remembers Claire back in St. Louis.

But I don't know why I feel jealous.

He's not my husband.

Probably because if anyone flirts with Captain Mandara, you want it to be you, Isabel Leon.

May the Lord have mercy on my soul.

And my thoughts.

The man in the formal frock and top hat stepped to the center of the stage in the midst of the thundering applause. He smiled broadly at the enthusiastic audience, then held up his hands. "Please . . . please . . . let me speak!" he called out. "Your encouragement is tremendous. Please . . . be quiet! Thank you. Thank you.

"Now we do have an acknowledgment or two to make. First, let's thank once again Mr. Carlton Smyth-Leeds for traveling all the way from London, England, to play the part of Romeo."

Shouts and applause filled the theater.

Once again the man in the top hat quieted the audience. "And now we must thank our director, the woman who has done more to bring culture and elegance to Montana Territory than any other woman, the accomplished actress who demonstrated her talent so dramatically with her absolutely brilliant portrayal of Juliet—the exquisitely beautiful and world-famous Marquesa of the Yellowstone River Valley . . . Cantrell's very own, Miss Isabel Leon!"

In unison the crowd rose to their feet. Thunderous applause actually rattled the crystal chandelier above her head. A young boy handed her a huge armful of red roses. A handsome young man bowed before her and kissed her jeweled hand and then led her to the center of the stage.

It seemed like the applause would never stop.

More flowers were tossed onto the stage.

"Please," Isabel called out. "Please . . . you're so generous! If you let me speak, then we can go on with the evening! We have a wonderful buffet prepared, and then the orchestra will lead us into the ball. Remember, all the profit for this evening will go to build Cantrell's first hospital."

The applause of the audience completely drowned out her

words. Once again she waited on stage, roses in arm, for their ovation to subside.

"Now you behave yourselves!" she managed to shout. Her deep
blue silk dress seemed to rustle with every word. "That's better.
Governor, thank you for those kind words! Senator and Mrs. Parks,
Mayor Johnson, and all you wonderful people, please give no credit
to me. What little talent I possess is completely God-given. And
it has been my delight for ten years to live my life in the most wonderful area on the face of the earth. You have generously adopted
me into your hearts, and for that I will be eternally grateful.

"Romeo and Juliet is a love story that ends in tragedy. Before I
arrived in Cantrell, my life had been a tragedy, and you, dear people, have turned it into a love story."

She glanced over at the elegantly dressed Carolina Cantrell
Parks and noticed her wipe a tear from her eyes. "My pledge to you
is that I will always live here in Cantrell and continue to bring
quality performances to this theater.

"We live on the wild frontier, but we are not uncivilized!

"We have calluses on our hands, but I daresay there are none
more tenderhearted!

"We have labored in storm and battle for every penny we have,
and none are more generous.

"The air is clear. The stars are bright. And all that we do is
under heaven's gaze. God bless you all!"

For a moment Isabel was afraid the roof would collapse from
the deafening ovation. Then a crowd made up mostly of handsome,
well-dressed men packed around her. Most were calling out to her.

"Marquesa!"

One voice seemed more desperate than the others.

They are packed so tight I couldn't move if I wanted to.

"Marquesa, are you in there?"

Yes, yes . . . I'm here, of course. Dear boy, where are you?

"Excuse me, Marquesa, are you busy?"

Rough pine boards framed in the partially completed stage.
Sawdust and an occasional bent nail were scattered at her feet. Her
arms cradled not roses, but rolled-up hotel plans. And she sat not

on a velvet settee, but an empty nail keg. Her gown was homely brown and cotton. It constricted her neck and chest.

The ballroom was empty and only partially built.

But some young man was calling for her.

"Marquesa?"

She stood to her feet. "July?"

"Are you meditatin'?"

"Eh, I was going over the hotel plans."

"Is this the dancin' room?"

"It will be the ballroom and the dining room. Occasionally we'll use the stage for some theater productions."

"Won't that be fine! It surely looks different since they put up the siding on the outside."

"Yes, Captain Mandara said they will be hanging the doors tomorrow."

July stood a good two inches taller than Isabel. His white collarless boiled shirt showed some wear, especially at the cuffs. "Seems to me the captain's been happier ever since he took Miss Fontenot to the doctor in Billings."

"Oh? I hadn't noticed." *You lie, Marquesa! You have stewed all week over the very same thing yourself!*

"Well, he's sure a whistlin' today! He's going to town to pick her up, you know."

"Oh? I wasn't aware of that."

Isabel and July walked side by side back out to the front porch of the hotel.

"You know what I cain't figure?" July posed. "Why'd he up and sell his lumber?"

Isabel grabbed July's arm. "He did what?"

"You know that load of lumber he stacked up there on his lot to build his house? Well, he sold it."

"The lot?"

"Just the lumber, I think. I heard Moses Martin who owns the Black Elephant Saloon say that he was going to build a wood-frame building out of the lumber he bought from the captain."

"But that was his pay. That was for his house. That was the

arrangement I had with him—enough lumber to build a house and move his family here," she fumed.

July jabbed his hand inside his shirt and scratched his back. "Maybe he decided not to move them here."

"But . . . he'd talk to me before he up and decided not to . . ."

"Why? Why would he have to talk to you? Say, look at that pony!" He pointed across the street. "Did you ever see a horse with more sway than that sorrel? Anyway, the captain's your builder, but that don't mean you kin meddle in his life."

"I do not meddle in his life. I do not meddle in anyone's life, Mr. July Johnson," she barked. "I just thought we were close enough friends that he would discuss such things."

"Close friends do more than just talk over hotel construction, right?"

"We've done more than just business. Two weeks ago we rode up to the rimrock at sunset."

"And just what did you discuss up there?"

"Eh, hotel construction. But . . . the captain is a family man. I think it prudent that I keep away from personal discussions."

"I don't guess I know what prudent means, but I know he's a family man. Ever'one knows that. He even has a fifteen-year-old daughter with long brown hair and dimples when she smiles. I've seen the photograph."

"You seem to have an eye out for comely young girls."

"I've got a talent that way. Take Miss Fontenot. It's a good thing she's not ten years younger." He was speaking so rapidly his words ran together.

Isabel tilted her head. "Oh, what would happen?"

"I'd be goin' to town to give her a ride home instead of the captain." Johnson blushed.

"July, do I take it you came over here looking for me in order to let me know Captain Mandara is on his way to Billings to pick up Oliole Fontenot?"

"Oh, shoot, no! I almost forgot. I came over here because of who I seen go into the bank."

"Who's that?"

"Cigar DuBois."

The smile dropped off her face. "DuBois? Jacob Hardisty's bodyguard?"

"Yep. He was wearin' old clothes like a Texas drover, but it was DuBois, all right."

"But . . . Ranahan hauled him off to Billings last summer. We read he was convicted in Deadwood of murder."

"He either got a pardon or broke out. I didn't think it was my place to ask. I wanted to warn you 'cause he might be carryin' a grudge, and with Miss Carolina and Ranahan gone, you and me is the only two in town left who faced him down."

"That's a cheery thought," she sighed.

"I think you ought to carry a pistol just in case," July suggested.

"I have one. How about you?"

"I reckon I'll have to make do with my knife. If I start toting a pistol now, it would seem like I was lookin' for trouble. I don't aim to go up against a man like DuBois with a gun."

"What do you suppose he wants in Cantrell?"

"Ranahan, I reckon."

"You think he'll stay in town until the Parkses return?"

"Why not? We ain't got no marshal to chase him off."

"Perhaps we should notify the sheriff in Billings of DuBois's presence. If he's escaped from jail, maybe the sheriff would come out here and arrest him before Carolina and Ran bring their baby home."

"Are you sure you want the sheriff to come to Cantrell, Marquesa?"

"He just ran me out of Billings, that's all."

"But his jurisdiction's all of Yellowstone County. He might not be too happy to see you out here."

"If he comes to town, I'll hide in the back of the store."

"If the law comes after Cigar DuBois, I think I'll hide in the back of the store, too."

"You may be right, July. But let's notify the sheriff in Billings anyway. I'll take my chances. Has the captain left yet? We can have him let them know DuBois is in town."

"He left hours ago. He came into the store all clean-shaven and sweet-smellin', bought some stick candy, and drove off whistling

'Annie Laurie.' I've never knowed him to whistle much before, have you?"

She walked ahead of him as they crossed the street and headed toward the Mercantile. *This is not right. Yes, she is a strikingly handsome young lady. But she's too young for him. Besides, he's married. Maybe I should write to his wife.*

That would be a disaster.

"Dear Mrs. Mandara, I'm a lady friend of your husband, and I'm concerned that he is spending too much time with Miss Fontenot."

What I can't figure out is why I even worry about it.

I don't worry about who Logan Henry Phillips is visiting with. I don't worry who Jacob Hardisty is with. Personally, I hope she has a knife and knows how to use it!

Maybe I think too much.

I didn't used to think so much. I just did things. I was busy. I need a play to be in. That's what I should do. Direct a play. Why wait until the hotel is finished? We could have one right now. Set up some benches. Use local people. Molly Mae would love to be in a play! Let everyone come for a dime. Serve some refreshments. Sort of a preview of what's to come.

I suppose we'd need some costumes. We could hang a tarp for a curtain. Logan Henry Phillips would certainly be in it . . . just three or four more. I'll wire San Francisco for some scripts.

"Marquesa, are you coming to the store, or do you aim to hike to the river?" July hollered.

Isabel Leon glanced up and realized she had passed the Mercantile. "Oh, yes. I definitely want to go to the store. Somehow knowing that DuBois is in town doesn't exactly make me feel confident about going on a hike."

"You surmise he'll come calling on the store?"

"Would you if you were him?"

"Yes, ma'am, I reckon I would."

Isabel hiked up the stairs to the porch and into the sweet smells of leather and spices. She stopped just past the doorway and stared at the medium-sized, oak-framed photograph of Mr. and Mrs. Ranahan Parks taken on their wedding day.

I need someone to talk to.

I need a woman to talk to.

Carolina Parks, I never missed a virtuous woman so much in my life.

Isabel visited for a few minutes with Isaac Milton at the bank after making the daily deposits. She found out about another new Chinese laundry that had moved to town and a French bakery that was operating out of the back of a Second Street saloon.

"Mr. Milton, rumor has it that Cigar DuBois is in town."

"Yes, he stopped by here earlier today." Milton's complexion was as light as his cotton shirtsleeves held up by shirt garters.

"Was he putting money in or taking it out?"

"Neither. He wanted to know if Jacob Hardisty was in town. Says Mr. Hardisty owes him money."

"Is Jacob in town?"

"Of course not. Last time we heard, he was in South America. Something about a silver mine in Bolivia," Milton reported.

"You think DuBois is going to ride on out of town?"

"I certainly hope so. To tell you the truth, Marquesa, I never thought Mr. Hardisty's hiring DuBois was a good idea." He leaned across the polished oak counter and spoke in a very low voice. "I think the main reason DuBois came to town was to get even with Ranahan Parks. It just might be providential that they are gone."

She stood up straight. "I was thinking the same thing."

Isabel glanced at the huge eight-foot-tall safe that occupied the entire center area of the bank. "You know, Mr. Milton, DuBois is the kind that wouldn't be opposed to stealing the money out of that safe."

"Mr. Ostine and I discussed that very fact soon after DuBois's departure." He glanced around the room and then whispered, "Be assured your deposits are safe. We are taking extra measures of precaution."

She took the receipt of deposit, folded it, and slipped it into her bag next to the .32-caliber Lady Colt with mother-of-pearl grips.

Milton leaned across the counter, propping his small frame on his elbows. "Say, there is some talk among the businessmen that perhaps we should seek a charter and incorporate Cantrell. Some say it's about time to have a mayor and council, fix the streets, develop some sort of citywide water system, and, of course, hire a marshal."

"I presume that last idea has gained popularity since DuBois came to town." She noticed that the bank smelled as clean as a hospital room.

The gray-haired and balding Isaac Milton nodded. "Most definitely."

"Cigar didn't happen to say how he got out of that Dakota jail, did he?"

"No, he didn't, Marquesa. And to tell you the truth, I didn't have the nerve to ask."

"I can't blame you for that. I plan to stay put until he rides out of town."

She met Tiny Merwin and Adam Bray at the door of the Mercantile. They both seemed in a hurry.

"Things slowed down, so we're going to call it a day," Merwin announced. He was shorter than Bray, but his long face made him seem about the same height.

"That's fine with me. Did July tally your hours?"

"He's over at the cafe," Bray reported.

"So he finally had the nerve to see the Quincys again?"

"Miss Molly Mae summoned him." Tiny Merwin flashed a wide smile.

"How about Papa Quincy?"

"I reckon we'll find that out if he comes back in one piece." Bray's grin revealed a wide gap between his upper front teeth.

They all stepped across the porch. "I presume there are no customers inside?" she probed.

Tiny Merwin waved his arm at the front door. "There's one guy, but he don't seem to want to buy anything."

Isabel stepped through the doorway. Her eyes adjusted slowly to the shadows of late evening. She walked toward her room to leave her purse and then froze as she saw the man at the gun case.

DuBois!

No wonder they left!

Where's Ranahan when you need him?

Or even Carolina?

Or July?

They were all here when we captured DuBois last summer.

Where's Captain Mandara? Gone to visit some golden goddess!

Okay, Isabel. Time for a sterling performance.

I never owned a dress with a pocket before I started wearing Carolina's. Maybe she's smarter than I thought. Isabel slipped her revolver into the deep pocket on the brown dress and left her purse on the table next to the woodstove. She ambled over to DuBois.

She cleared her throat. "May I show you one of our fine Winchesters?"

DuBois spun around, his right hand resting on the grip of his holstered .45 Schofield Smith and Wesson revolver. He inspected her up and down intently. "You work here?"

I don't think he recognizes me. Either that or he's a better actor than I am. "Yes, sir, I do. I'm rather new here, but I think I know the merchandise. What do you want to buy?"

"I don't need to buy nothing! I'm just lookin' for some old . . . friends." His brown boots were almost worn through, his trousers covered with dust. A dirty gray bandanna was double wrapped around his neck. He hadn't shaved or trimmed his beard in weeks.

"Who might they be?"

"Ranahan and that fancy lady friend of his from back east. I hear they're out of town."

"Yes, they're back in the States."

The deep lines in his face defied age and emotion. "When will they return?"

"'I'm not sure. They never tell me anything. Not that I blame them. I never tell me anything either.'" *From* The Foolish Gypsy, *Act II, Scene 1.*

His piercing eyes surveyed her again.

Now he knows who I am.

Without moving her head, she tried to see if he was lifting his revolver. Her right hand was in her pocket clutching the mother-of-pearl handle of the Lady Colt. *The Gypsy girl Effie used a knife. I don't think I could actually stab a man. But I know I can pull a trigger.*

"It's important that I know when they return. I, eh . . . owe Ranahan something. I like to pay my debts."

"If you wish, I can collect the debt and give you a receipt."

DuBois shook his head. "Nope. Afraid I have to deliver it in person. Would you say they'll be back by next Sunday or next month?"

"'Time is merely a game with them. They use it to their advantage, always playing to win.'" *That was* Savannah's Mansion, *Act III, Scene 1.*

His mouth dropped open as he stared blankly.

"If I had to guess," she quickly added, "I'd say they'd be gone another month or so, but please don't hold me to it."

"How about Ranahan's partner?" DuBois pressed.

"Partner?"

"The one who sports the double-barreled shotgun and has kind of a high-pitched voice."

July was under the porch. He doesn't remember what July looks like!

"I'm sorry, sir, but Mr. Ranahan doesn't have a partner anymore. Other than his wife, Carolina." She stepped away and fussed with a stack of ready-made shirts. "I'm afraid I'm not much help to you. Would you like to try on a shirt?" *Or how about a nice hemp noose?*

"How about that dance-hall girl that hung around here and took a potshot at Hardisty? What was her name? The Duchess, I believe."

Dance-hall girl? Dance-hall girl! That's what you remember about me? "Was she the one with the long hair?" Isabel asked.

"Yeah, about the color of yours, but she let it hang down. She was a real firecracker. She wore brazen, indiscreet clothes." The memory seemed to send a flash through his dark, narrow eyes.

Brazen and indiscreet? This comes from a professional murderer?

"Oh, that Duchess! She went to San Francisco and starred in a lavish review and then married one of the Comstock Mine owners. 'He's old enough to be her father and foolish enough to be her son.'" *From* Mr. Taylor's Folly, *somewhere in the middle of Act II.* "The one that owns all the newspapers and half the trains. What's his name?"

"I don't know." DuBois's face was as wide as it was long. His hat looked slept in or run over—or both.

"My, you seem to have a lot of friends in Cantrell," she prattled.

He rubbed the grip of his holstered gun. "Yeah, I'm sorry to miss 'em."

Isabel fidgeted with the merchandise on the shelf but kept one hand in her pocket gripped on her pistol. "Will you be in town long?"

He surveyed her until she glanced away. "What's your name?"

"Miss Isabel Leon."

"Well, Miss Leon, ever'body I've met in this town keeps askin' when I'm leavin'. It's not exactly a friendly place."

"Oh, don't take it personal. Almost everyone in this town is leaving. Most people are passing through. They all assume there are still some good claims up in Devil's Canyon."

"They're all fools. Nobody makes money in gold strikes except lawyers and big companies."

"You know, I couldn't agree with you more. 'Gold is truly saint-seducing.'" *From* Romeo and Juliet, *Act I, Scene 1*.

He studied her again.

Relax, Isabel . . . relax . . . if he finds out who you are, he will probably kill you. Don't give anything away.

He started hiking toward the door, then spun around, his hand still on the grip of the pistol. "Say, I have an idea, Miss Leon. How about you letting me buy you some supper across the street?"

"Oh . . . my, Mr. DuBois . . . what a generous offer. But tonight is my night to work late at the store. I can't desert my responsibility."

He pushed his black hat back and rubbed his mouth with his hand. "You know my name?"

"Everyone in the Territory has heard of the legendary shootist, Cigar DuBois."

"Yeah, well, maybe we'll have supper together tomorrow night."

Isabel avoided his eyes. "'Would that my time were my own and all my days but blank slates.'" *I think that was* Darianna's Dare, *Prologue*.

"I'll check back by about this time tomorrow."

"That would be nice." She bowed her head slightly.

She watched Cigar DuBois exit the store, round The Hotel Marquesa, and head for Second Street. No sooner had he gone out of sight than July Johnson ran out of Quincys' Cafe and straight up to the porch of the Mercantile.

"Are you all right, Marquesa?" he puffed.

"Yes."

"What did DuBois want?"

"He wanted Carolina, Ran, you, and me."

"That's what I figured. Why'd he walk away?"

"Because he couldn't find any of them."

July's smooth face looked freshly scrubbed. "You didn't tell him where I was?"

"He was looking for someone older. He figured it was a man under the porch last summer."

"That's good news. Maybe he won't ever find out it was me. How about you? Didn't he recognize you?"

She and July strolled back into the empty store. "No, I presume not."

July broke into a huge smile. "Well, that's great!"

"I suppose. But I think I have to go out to supper with him tomorrow night."

"That's a joke, right?"

"DuBois doesn't know that yet." She opened the blue-enameled tin lid and gazed into an empty coffeepot. "How about you, July? Were you really summoned by Miss Quincy, or did you make that up to avoid Mr. Cigar DuBois?"

When July Johnson blushed, he looked twelve years old. "Both. I hope you don't think me too cowardly. I mean, if Ranahan were here, I'd stand right alongside of him. You know that. But I don't think I have the courage to face DuBois by myself. If he finds out I was one of them that done him in last time, he'll kill me. I got too much to live for, if you know what I mean."

"Speaking of too much to live for, how is Miss Molly Mae? Is her father still mad at you?"

"You know, Marquesa, she just might be the easiest woman to talk to on the face of the earth. Why, I can sit down with her on the porch and have nothin' much on my mind, and we visit for three, four hours. Ain't that somethin'? I only knowed three women who are that way with me, except for my mother, rest her soul."

"Which three women?"

"Why, you, Miss Carolina, and Molly Mae. But I think maybe you older women just know how to visit with men better. Do you suppose?"

July, how can you so innocently remind me of all the things I'd like to forget?

"I can't speak for all 'older women,' but I do think there are some who are better at holding a conversation with a man."

"Anyways, Mr. Quincy says I'm on probation. As long as I don't go off and do something dumb, he'll let me hang around his daughter. 'Course, he said if I tried to dishonor her, he'd shoot me right through the head."

"That could end a beautiful relationship."

"When he said dishonor her, do you suppose he meant sex?"

July didn't blush at all when he asked the question.

Isabel Leon did.

"Eh, yes, I do believe that's what he meant."

I am not the mother of a teenage son. I do not know how to raise children. I believe it's time for me to depart.

"Cain't figure out why he don't just come out and say what he means. Well, if you're all right over here, I think I'll go spend the evenin' at the Quincys'."

"That will be fine."

"Good night, Marquesa."

"Good night, son."

Isabel Leon placed Carolina's Bible on the nightstand and turned out her kerosene lamp at about 11:00 P.M. Then she lay awake, eyes open, staring at the ceiling.

The small room at the edge of the store smelled of stale perfume and flannel. It was too cold at night for fresh air. The one window on the right side of the bed had heavy crocheted lace curtains. The half-moon in the cloudless night sky reflected small rays of light into the room. After her eyes adjusted to the darkness, she could see the outlines of the room's furniture. A dresser. A mirror. Wardrobe. Chair. Dressing table. Coat racks. Paintings. Photographs.

It was a one-room home at the edge of the wilderness.

It wasn't her home. But she felt she was certainly on the edge of the wilderness.

I don't know why I have such a difficult time going to sleep anymore. I read until I doze. Then I turn off the light and lie awake for an hour. I didn't used to have this problem. I would just finish my performance, go out to supper with some man, dance with some man, visit for hours with some man. . . . I always went right to sleep.

So, Isabel Leon, you're living the good life. Fresh air. Clean clothes. Good friends. Building yourself a fine hotel. Finding respect in the community. Taking care of your body and your mind. Plotting cultural improvements for the town.

You're sitting in tall grass, Marquesa.

Why is it you don't go to sleep?

Why do you keep thinking you're missing something?

Someplace between thoughts of Captain Dawson Mandara riding in a wagon with a tall, slim, blonde photographer and compiling a list of excuses for not having supper with Cigar DuBois, Isabel Leon fell asleep.

It was not a deep sleep.

Not a restful sleep.

Still, she didn't hear the first shout.

But she sat straight up in bed at the second.

Someone was pounding on her door.

"Marquesa, wake up! It's an emergency! Hurry!"

She didn't bother reaching for a robe or even clutching her flannel gown. But she did reach into her bag and pull out the mother-of-pearl-handled .32 pistol.

She swung open the unlocked door to her room. Holding a lantern and wearing coveralls but no shirt or shoes was July Johnson. "Elias Prichard came to the door and said your friend Mr. Phillips has been shot over at the Black Aces Saloon and was calling for you!"

"Logan?"

"Yeah. I'll go with you, Marquesa."

"I . . . I need to get dressed."

"Yes, ma'am. I'll get some bandages and pull on my boots."

Oh, Logan! You've been living on the edge of disaster all your life. You don't know anything else. One of the things I shouted at you on the night we had our big fight was that I didn't want to be there when you got yourself killed! I can't believe you could wander out to this godforsaken land and get yourself shot in my town!

Hang on, Logan.

You can't go before I have a chance to say good-bye.

The Black Aces Saloon was a fifteen-by-thirty-foot room with wooden floor and white canvas walls. Running clear across the back wall was a custom-built mahogany bar complete with wood carvings and a well-endowed reclining damsel in a painting above the mirror. Scattered in front of the bar were several hastily built tables and a varied assortment of chairs and stools.

Half a dozen men stood at the bar drinking when Isabel and July entered the front door. At least two card games proceeded unhindered. Smoke curled around the lamps above the tables, and the air was dank with cheap whiskey and sweat.

One table was overturned, and a badly bleeding Logan Henry Phillips sat on the floor leaning against it. Two men knelt at his side.

"Logan!" She scooted to her knees beside him and kissed his sweating cheek.

"Thanks for coming, Marquesa."

She pulled his hand away from his right side just below the rib cage and shoved a wad of clean rags against the wound. "July, tear me some long linen strips so we can tie that bandage down."

"You're fightin' a losin' battle, Marquesa," Logan groaned.

"Logan, you promised me once you wouldn't go get yourself killed with me watching."

"I lied." He managed a momentary smile. "Ain't this something? I didn't even cheat him."

"Who?"

"I don't know."

One of the men standing next to her spoke up. "It was that new fella with the Smith and Wesson."

"Cigar DuBois?"

"That's him," a bystander confirmed.

"Where is he now?" she asked as she glanced around the room.

"He grabbed coins from the pot and plowed his way out the front door."

"I saw him ride south," one of the hangers-on spouted.

Phillips laid his bloodstained hand on her arm. "We hadn't been playing poker for even an hour. He was into the game about fifty dollars when he jumped straight up out of his seat, shouted that nobody was ever going to put one over on him in Cantrell again . . . and he shot me."

July handed her the linen strips.

"Can you get me a bowl of clean water?" she asked the man standing next to her.

"Cain't guarantee it's clean. But it ain't been used at least."

When the man returned, she washed Logan's face. "Maybe we should lay you down."

"I ain't dyin' stretched out on the floor of a two-bit saloon," Logan protested. "Sit me up at a poker table and shove me a royal straight. That's the way I want to go."

"I most certainly will not. We're going to take you to a doctor," she asserted.

"We don't have a doctor in town," July reminded her.

"Well, there are doctors in Billings. July, go and rent me a rig. I'm driving Logan to Billings."

"Tonight?"

"Immediately!"

"But, Marquesa, you go back there, and they'll throw you in jail," Johnson cautioned.

"Chances are, no one will even recognize me."

"There isn't any need for that," Logan choked. "He gut-shot me, and we both know I can't live 'til mornin'."

"Logan, it might not do you any good to get you to town. But it will do me some good. I've got to live the rest of my life thinking I did the best I could for you. Do you understand?"

He looked over at July and paused until he could suck in a deep breath. "Well, go get a rig, boy. Me and the Marquesa have a big finale ahead."

The half-moon in the sky made the dirt road a dim outline. It was impossible to distinguish rocks and ruts, but trees and boulders popped into view as they reached the river road. She had July tie Logan Phillips into the seat next to her and wrap him with blankets. There were no other people on the road, and she kept the drive horse at a trot.

Phillips's head rested on a blanket near her shoulder.

"There's been many a time in my life when a man had just cause to kill me. This isn't one of them. And I don't know why you're doin' this, Marquesa."

"Because you'd do the same thing for me in a minute. You and I both know that. Besides, if this is your time to die, I want you to be in a nice bed with clean sheets."

"And the sweet smell of perfume in the room."

"That, too."

"And a pretty woman . . ."

"Don't press it, cowboy."

He groaned. "Don't suppose you could miss some of them bumps?"

"This is the smooth part." She kept the horse at a trot. "But we'll have to slow down and walk the horse sooner or later."

"How long will it take us to get to Billings?" he asked.

"We won't get there before daylight."

"I'd like to see one more sunrise."

"You will, Logan." She reached over and stroked his matted blond hair.

"We're somethin', ain't we, Marquesa? Two of a kind."

"You mean, because we have nothing . . . no one . . . no home . . . never stay anyplace more than a season . . . have people in every town that want to kiss us . . . or kill us?"

"That about sums it up, doesn't it? You know, you're the finest-lookin' woman I ever met anywhere in the world."

"And you, Logan Henry Phillips, have the most irresistible smile God ever gave to any man."

"We lived life fast and hard," he panted. "But there were some good times, weren't there? You know when the audience jumps to its feet, and there's joy on ever' face. Ain't much that compares to that, is there?"

"Logan, never in my life did I ever have as much plain, uncontrollable fun as I did with you."

"Not even when you were a little girl?"

"Especially when I was a little girl."

"I surely hate to take away all your fun."

"Well, don't use up all your final lines. You just might live through this and have no more script."

"It wouldn't be the first time you and me operated without a script. We could make something up. Remember when Sally got sick, and you filled in for her in Cleveland?"

"It's not easy impersonating a 500-pound bear." Isabel chuckled.

"It was the funniest skit I ever saw. Eddy Foy was in the audience, and I thought he would roll in the aisle."

Phillips was quiet for several moments as Isabel continued to stroke his hair.

"Marquesa, I ain't feelin' too good."

"Be still and get some rest."

"Yes, Mama."

With a blanket pulled around her cloak, the cold night air struck only her face. It reminded Isabel of standing in the front of the ferry boat between New Jersey and New York. Other than the rhythmic clop-diddy-clop of horseshoes striking the roadway, it was a quiet night.

No other noise.

No movement.

No lights from ranch houses.

Nothing.

Just a worried woman.

And a dying man.

From time to time Logan would wake up and want to visit about some past adventure. But most of the time he was quiet, and

Isabel reviewed her career . . . town to town . . . theater to theater
. . . man to man.

*Sometimes it's so hard to find what is authentic in my life. Am I Miss
Penny Peters, the beautiful maiden held captive by the evil Cyrus
Charmayne? Or maybe Myra Anne Kelly, the songbird in "Col. Storm's
Musical Review"? Or the sickly but comely and heroic Cynthia Dollar
in Mother's Last Letter?*

*I should have worn one of my old theater dresses. That's the way
Logan remembers me.*

I don't want him to die.

Not in my arms.

I don't like dying scenes.

I never have.

Now, God . . . I know You don't have to listen to me . . .

Isabel glanced over at Logan, then felt tears roll down her face.

*I don't even know how to pray. Logan's dying, and I can't even pray
for him! Carolina . . . oh, sweet Carolina . . . how I miss you. That
soft Virginia voice praying so intimately to a God who has been your lifelong companion. Do you have any idea how wonderful that seems to me?*

With the Yellowstone River on the right side and the Northern
Pacific tracks on the left, she felt the ride smooth out as the roadway turned to river-bottom loam and packed sand.

*God . . . Logan and me, well, we've spent most of our lives com-
pletely ignoring You . . . so I know You don't have to pay us any mind.
But I read in Carolina's Bible that Jesus told this immoral lady that her
sins were forgiven her. Well, that's what I'm asking for Logan. I don't
know if he's strong enough to ask for himself.*

*And if You seem to be in a forgiving mood today, I definitely need
mine forgiven, too.*

— Four —

AT TWENTY-THREE YEARS OLD, Isabel Leon had been in a dramatic play about a crippled Civil War hero who returned home only to die in the arms of his childhood sweetheart. The finale included her cradling the man in her arms and singing "Amazing Grace."

It was still the only hymn she knew by heart.

So for the last six miles into Billings, she sang "Amazing Grace."

She was still singing it as she rolled into town.

Daylight had broken an hour before, and folks were just beginning to stir around. Compared to a city in the States, Billings was a tiny five-street village. Compared to Cantrell, it was a thriving railroad metropolis. Billings had hotels, newspapers, wholesalers, a courthouse, lawyers, doctors, and a jail.

She pulled the blanket up over her head as she drove past the jail.

Last time I was in this town I was trying to take a man's life.

This time I'm trying to save a man's life.

Lord, help me.

The black print on the white board sign read: "Dr. Abraham Hersmann, M.D., Room 21." Isabel pulled the carriage in front of the green two-story wood-sided hotel.

She gently brushed the blond hair out of Logan's eyes. "Logan?"

His eyes opened, but he seemed to be staring right past her at some sight known only to him.

"Logan, we're here. I'm going up to find the doctor. I'll be right back with some help." She cradled his slumping head in the palms of her hands.

His voice was surprisingly clear. "Where's the sun? I want to see the sun!"

"The son?"

"You know, that bright yellow ball that comes up every morning in the east?" His voice faded, hoarse and barely audible.

Isabel leaned away from the carriage and looked behind her. "It's coming up behind us."

"Turn the carriage around."

She put her hand on his shoulder. "I'll run get the doctor first."

"Please, turn the carriage around. I want to see the sunrise!" Logan pleaded. "It's the last thing I'll ever ask you to do for me. I promise you that. I've kept every . . . promise . . . I ever made you . . . you know that." Each phrase was now punctuated by a cough or a wheeze.

She slapped the lines on the horse's rump and drove the carriage in a U-turn, parking on the other side of the street. The sun was just starting to reflect under a light layer of clouds. "There's your sunrise. Right on schedule. When you recover from this, I promise you I'll dance all night with you, Mr. Logan Henry Phillips."

His pained eyes relaxed. "Will you wear that green dress?" he whispered.

Isabel leaned close, her ear just an inch from his mouth. "Which green dress?"

He placed a feeble kiss on her ear. "You know which one."

She sat straight up. "Oh, that dress! Logan, if you weren't critically wounded, I'd think you were lusting after me."

He tried to smile but closed his eyes and gritted his teeth instead. "I knew it would be this way." His voice now was just a whisper.

"What way?"

"I knew when it was my time to go that I'd regret not marrying you. We were good together, Marquesa."

"We fought like cats and dogs, Logan."

"Yeah . . . they were good fights, weren't they?"

She brushed her lips gently across his cheek. "They were the best fights I ever had in my life."

His strained eyes relaxed as she rubbed his face. Then he raised his head up. His voice cleared. "Who's in charge here?" he asked.

"Wh-what?" she stammered.

Then, with dulled eyes, he shook his head and laid it back on the carriage seat.

"I'm going to get the doctor. Now don't run off and get into a poker game while I'm gone!"

He didn't respond. Isabel leaned over and kissed him on the forehead beaded with cold sweat. Then she climbed out of the black leather carriage. Her legs were stiff from the long ride. She felt as if she'd slept all night in her clothes. Her hair cascaded down her back. She thought of tucking it under the cloak and pulling up the hood but didn't want to take the time.

Isabel jogged across the street and shoved open the ten-foot-tall etched-glass-and-oak hotel doors with crystal door handles. The small lobby was empty except for a thin, young man sweeping near the fireplace. His light brown hair was parted in the middle and greased down over his ears. He looked up.

"We're full up for the night . . . or morning," he told her.

"I need to see the doctor. Isn't his office in this building?"

"Yes, ma'am. Room 21 at the top of the stairs."

She hurried toward the stairway.

"But he ain't there. Doesn't open up 'til nine." With the reflection of the morning light, she could see he was trying to grow a mustache.

"This is a dire emergency. Does he have living quarters in this hotel?"

"Yes, ma'am. Room 22."

"Thank you." Isabel dashed up the stairs.

"But he ain't there!" he shouted and wandered over to the base of the stairs carrying the broom. "Done went to breakfast."

Isabel stalked down the stairs. "Did he happen to say where he was going for breakfast?"

"Nope. All he said to me was, 'Morning, Mr. O'Brian.' That's me. Doc always calls me Mr. O'Brian."

"Is there another doctor in town?"

"Nope. Doc Dennison is out at the Slash-Bar-Four until Saturday. They got a sick bull, you know."

"Well, I've got a critically wounded friend in my carriage, and

I must find the doctor. At which cafe would you suggest I start look-ing for the doctor?"

"He always eats breakfast at the England House."

"But you said he didn't—"

"No, ma'am, he didn't tell me he was eatin' there. That's what you asked."

Isabel bolted out the front door and gazed across the street at the black carriage with a man huddled under some blankets. The bright morning sunlight glared off Logan's pale face as she hurried down the covered wooden sidewalk.

Maybe I should check on Logan, but I need that doctor. Lord, please have the doctor be at the England House.

The England House! That's where I shot Jacob Hardisty. This is starting to feel strange.

Quite strange.

Only this time Carolina won't be there. Nor will those ranchers, Andrews and Odessa. Nor, for that matter, will Jacob March Hardisty.

I hope the sheriff won't be there either.

The dining room at the England House was about twenty feet by forty with white-painted tables, white linen tablecloths, a wall of windows along the street, and wood-paneled walls painted white, giving the entire room a light, cheerful look. The room was half-filled with patrons either chewing food or talking or both.

Isabel hurried over to a man in white shirt and black tie. "Excuse me, I need to talk to Dr. Hersmann? Which one is he?"

The man scanned the tables. "The man in the gray suit near the window."

"Next to the tall man with his back turned toward us?"

"Yes. That's Dr. Hersmann. He's just finishing his breakfast."

Isabel took one step, then turned back. "Is the sheriff here?"

The man shook his head. "No, the sheriff eats at the Bootstrap Cafe."

Thank You, Lord.

Her eyes focused only on Dr. Hersmann, she scooted across the hardwood floor. The heels of her borrowed black lace-up boots banged out a desperate rhythm, with the tinkling of glasses, silver, and china chiming the melody.

"Dr. Hersmann? You've got to hurry! I have a friend who's been shot, and he's in a desperate condition!"

"Isabel! You're supposed to be in jail!"

The tenor voice was sickly familiar. She had heard that same domineering voice in Baltimore, New York, and Cantrell, to name a few. She didn't have to turn to see who was sitting with the doctor.

But she did.

"Jacob!" she gasped. "You're supposed to be in South America!"

Hardisty turned toward the door and shouted, "Go get the sheriff! This is the woman who tried to kill me in this very room last summer!" He pulled a small sneak gun from his vest pocket and pointed it at her. "Get the sheriff," he hollered again.

Customers scampered out of their chairs and sprinted to the lobby.

"Jacob, I don't have time for this. Your wonderful associate, Cigar DuBois, gut-shot a friend of mine. Doctor, I need you to come with me!"

Hardisty spoke loudly enough so that any left in the room would hear. "My word, you shot another man?"

Isabel's voice was low as she spoke almost without moving her lips. "I didn't shoot anyone!"

"You once shot me!" he shouted. Hardisty waved the little gun close to her chest.

"Yes, I shot you. Regrettably, you lived!" She turned to the heavy-set, gray-haired man who hadn't moved a muscle since the ruckus began. "Doc, please! There really is a friend of mine out in the carriage."

Dr. Hersmann stood. "Yes, well, of course, let's go have a look at him."

"She's not going anywhere!" Hardisty shouted. "She's supposed to be in jail!"

Isabel grabbed the doctor's arm and tugged him toward the wide doorway into the lobby of the England House. Jacob Hardisty stood next to the table in a charcoal gray New York-tailored suit, waving the gun and shouting, "Come back here. I'll shoot you, Isabel! You leave this room, and I'll shoot you."

She glanced over her shoulder. "Jacob, most of the people watching us do not believe you're the type who would shoot an unarmed woman in the back. But I believe you would. Still, I'll take that chance!"

She trotted out of the hotel, the doctor at her side, while Jacob Hardisty shouted curses.

The sun had risen high enough to hide behind the clouds. A stiff wind blew down the street, swirling dust off the sidewalk and into Isabel's eyes. She continued to trot alongside Dr. Hersmann.

"My office is Room 21. Go get my bag!" he called to her as he stopped to catch his breath.

As Dr. Hersmann approached the carriage, Isabel held her skirt up to the top of her boots and darted into the street.

Room 21. He didn't give me a key. Is it unlocked? Room 21.

She didn't notice a stagecoach parked in front of the hotel. She didn't pay attention to two horseback riders in the street. And the strong callused hand that grabbed her wrist caught her totally by surprise.

"Miss Leon, I'll have to ask you to come with me!"

"Sheriff!"

"The judge told you clearly that the next time you came into town, you'd be thrown in jail."

She jerked her arm out of the man's hand. "This is an emergency!" She continued to run toward the hotel.

The sheriff caught her around the waist with one arm and lifted her off the ground, her feet kicking in protest. Isabel spun around in his arm and clawed at his face.

With parallel tracks of blood across his cheek, he dropped her to the street. His gun was out of the holster and only inches from her chest.

"Don't try that again, Marquesa!" he growled.

"Logan's dying!" she screamed. "A man's dying over there!"

The sheriff didn't take his eyes off her but yelled back across the street. The doctor was in the carriage with Logan while a group of men huddled around.

"You got a wounded man over there, Doc?"

"I've got a dead man over here, Sheriff!"

"No!" Isabel Leon cried. "No . . . no . . . no!" She dropped to her knees on the dirty, dusty street. "No . . . no . . . no. No, God, no! I tried to do it right this time!" she sobbed.

Isabel could feel the cold, hard dirt of the street on her legs, which were pulled up under her. She folded her arms across her rib cage and tried to stop crying.

I told you this would happen. I told you I didn't want you to die on me. Oh, Logan . . . it's not just you dying. It's me. We have nobody. Nothing. And no one but each other to mourn when we're gone. When you die, Marquesa, there will be no mourners at your grave.

"Come on, Marquesa, we don't need some dramatic act out in the middle of the street!" the sheriff prodded.

She found she could no more force herself to stop crying than she could make herself stop breathing. Each sob gave birth to the next.

The sheriff neither smiled nor frowned. "How do I know you didn't gut-shoot that fella?"

Finally she sucked a deep gulp of air. "I drove him all night all the way from Cantrell just to see a doctor!" She took the sheriff's hand as he yanked her to her feet.

"How do I know that? As far as I know, you shot him in the alley, took his poke, and are stagin' this for an excuse."

"What? I can't believe you'd be dumb enough to—"

"And I can't believe you'd be dumb enough to come back to Billings and think you could get away with a stunt like this!"

"Turn loose of my wrist. You're hurting me!" she wailed.

"It ain't nothin' compared to a hemp rope around your neck!"

She strained to look back at the carriage. "What about Logan?"

"I'll send his remains to the undertaker."

Isabel wiped her eyes on the sleeve of her brown dress. "Check with the people in Cantrell. They'll tell you what happened out there. It was a man named Cigar DuBois who shot Logan."

The sheriff's hand dropped off her wrist, and he stopped walking. "DuBois? He's in Cantrell? I thought he was in jail over in Dakota."

"So did we. Are you going out there and arrest him?" Isabel spotted a worried look on the sheriff's face.

"I'll, eh, send someone out to check on your story."

She stepped close to him. "When?"

He waved his left arm at the clouds. "Whenever this storm blows through."

"Storm?" she protested. "There's just a few clouds."

"Ain't sendin' a deputy out to Cantrell in a storm."

"Deputy?" Isabel sneered. "You mean you aren't going out there yourself?"

"Don't reckon I need to."

"Then how can you keep me in jail when you don't know what happened in Cantrell?"

"I'm keeping you in jail because you attempted to murder Jacob Hardisty." The sheriff pulled off his red bandanna and wiped his slightly bleeding cheek.

Isabel walked stride for stride alongside the man with a gun and a silver badge. "But the judge said there were extenuating circumstances."

"He also said for you to stay out of town."

She stopped, still in the street. "I haven't come to town in a year. This was an obvious emergency."

He prodded her with the gun barrel. "Call it what you want; you're going to jail. Only the judge or Hardisty himself can get you out of that."

"Hardisty?"

"If he dropped charges, and you could prove you didn't murder that man in the carriage, I reckon they'd let you go."

"Let me talk to Hardisty!"

"Won't do you no good. He's the one that looked me up and demanded I arrest you."

The Yellowstone County Jail had three cells. Each was six feet wide, twelve feet deep, and six feet high. All were made out of reinforced red brick and covered with a dirt-colored plaster. The floor was concrete. None had a window. Each had a wide iron-bar door on the front. The cot consisted of two-by-six planks stretched across a black iron frame about a foot off the floor covered with a worn and rancid-smelling one-inch straw mattress and two wool blankets. Next to the bed was an empty bucket.

There were no special facilities for women.

Isabel was shoved into cell number 3.

There were no other tenants in the cell or in the jail.

At least, no two-legged ones.

Isabel stood at the iron-bar door. "Sheriff, wait a minute! I've got to talk to somebody!"

"You got a lawyer?"

"No. Listen. Listen to me! I want to make arrangements for Logan. Can you send the undertaker by?"

"Has he got family?"

"No, I'm all he has. Please, can I tell the undertaker what to do?"

"I'll send word."

"Thank you. Wait! I must send a letter out to Cantrell to let them know what happened in town."

The sheriff flipped the ring of keys in his hand. "There's no mail delivery out there."

"I know, but, eh, Mr. McGuire will be delivering freight out to the Mercantile. Can he deliver my letter?"

"I reckon so."

"Could you get me a pencil and paper so I can write it? I'm helping out at the Mercantile for Ranahan and Carolina Parks. I've got to let July know what happened."

He dropped the keys into his vest pocket and shoved his hand toward the back of his head. "Seems like you're makin' a lot of demands."

"Sheriff, you know I haven't come to town for almost a whole year, just as the judge required. And you know that Logan was mortally wounded, and the only doctor was here."

"And how do I know you didn't kill him?"

Isabel dropped her head into her hands and sighed. "You aren't going to believe anything I tell you, are you?"

"I believe you're a mighty good actress!"

"Sheriff, I believe you have only slightly more intelligence than the back end of a mule. Could I please have a paper and pencil to write a note?"

The sheriff disappeared into the next room. She heard voices, but no one returned. The cell was cold, and she walked over to the cot. She tugged at the top blanket.

At least I can wear it like a shawl. What's on it? Are those crumbs?
She bent over to inspect the blanket more closely.

Lice!

She dropped the blanket and surveyed the dark shadows at the far end of the cell. *This is a bad dream. This is a very bad dream. I'm dreaming that I died and went to hell.*

She clutched her arms in front of her and felt a chill run down her back. She grabbed onto her arms as tightly as she could. Her entire body started to quiver.

"You want this paper or not?"

She spun around. The sheriff shoved a five-by-seven slip of white paper between the bars.

"Yes!" She ran over and grabbed the paper and pencil. "You've got to get me out of here. There are lice in the blankets!"

"Lice in the blankets? Shoot, Marquesa, there are roaches and rats, too. But you didn't expect it would be a hotel room, did ya? Throw them blankets down on the floor and stomp around on them some. You can get rid of most of the lice that way," he advised.

She held the paper to the grimy wall and began to scribble a few words. "Sheriff, wait until I finish. Then you can take it right over to Mr. McGuire before he leaves."

The sheriff leaned against a wall opposite the cell door under a high, iron-barred window. "Now what did you tell me you're doing in Cantrell?"

She stopped writing and glanced at the lawman. "Overseeing a store for a friend and building a hotel."

"A hotel?"

"Yes, I'm opening Cantrell's first hotel."

"You going to run girls in it?"

Isabel fought to keep from shouting. "No, I most certainly am not!"

"How do I know that's not just more crock?"

"Go to Cantrell and check it out for yourself!"

"I'll decide when I need to go to Cantrell."

She eyed the paper that read: "Dear July,"

Lord, help me know what to say.

"Captain Mandara!" she shouted so loudly the sheriff jumped.

"Who's he?"

"He's my builder. He's building my hotel, and he's here in Billings! He can vouch for my story."

"He saw that Logan fella get shot by DuBois?" the sheriff pressed.

"No, he had already left for town. But he can tell you about the hotel. He can vouch for my character!"

"Why should I believe him?"

"He's a man with an impeccable reputation!"

"Well, where am I going to find Mr. Impeccable?"

"Eh . . . he came to town to—to give a woman a ride back to Cantrell."

"Oh?"

"A lady photographer got hurt. Her name is Oliole. And he was supposed to pick her up and transport her back to Cantrell. They'll be leaving this morning. Hurry, tell him I'm in here and need to talk to him."

The sheriff lightly rubbed his scratched face. "I've never known a woman behind bars to make so many demands."

"But I must talk to him before he leaves town!"

"Where can I find him?"

"I don't know. . . . He's . . . well, ask Dr. Hersmann about a young blonde woman who busted her leg and wrist. He must know where she's staying. Please hurry!"

"Marquesa, I have other things to do besides run errands for you."

"But the captain is a very punctual man. He will want to leave early this morning."

"If I happen to run across this captain fella, I'll—"

"Please, Sheriff, I'm begging you . . . find Captain Mandara right now!"

"Well, they was right about you on one thing. You are a good actress." He turned and strolled out of the room.

"Sheriff, what about my letter?" she screamed. "You didn't take my letter!"

The door slammed shut, and she thought she heard a laugh. Then nothing.

Stifling. Constricting. Depressing. Silence.

She paced the tiny cell, staying away from the cot at the back.

Everything was going so good. I had a place to call home. A hotel to run. A town where I belong. No more packing a trunk. No more phony smiles. No more splitting headache and a guilty conscience in the morning. I've been trying to do it right. Is this what it gets me? I was better off doing everything wrong!

At least then I had a bed without lice.

Usually.

God, is this the way You answer prayers? Is this it? All I asked was to be able to get Logan to a doctor. I just needed a few more minutes. At least, I could have been with him when he died. Not all alone.

If I was a cold, hard, mean person like they seem to think, would I have loaded him up and drove overnight? I tried to do it right.

But Logan died.

And I'm thrown into this lice-infested cell.

Is that how You answer prayers?

Did I ask too much?

Well . . . I did ask that You'd forgive Logan's sins. Did You do that? Did he ask, too?

"'Amazing grace, how sweet the sound that saved a wretch like me.'"

Did Logan hear that and call out to You?

That's what I want to know!

Did You save him?

Isabel held on to the cold iron bars at the jail cell door. "Did You save him, Lord?"

Lord Jesus, save me!

Isabel had no idea how long she stood sobbing.

It wasn't an angry cry. Nor a sad one. It felt like a summer rain that cleans the dust out of the air, leaving a fresh feeling when it's gone.

Then she heard a sound, almost like hearing a voice from a distance. It started softly and began to build. "'Amazing grace, how sweet the sound . . .'" The song rolled off her lips over and over. Each verse built in volume and intensity.

"'. . . through many dangers, toils, and snares I have already come.'" It no longer sounded like a song, but a statement. A triumphant statement. "'Tis grace hath brought me safe thus far, and grace will lead me home. . . .'"

She was lost in the last verse and staring through the window across the hall at the clouds when she realized the song was now a duet.

Captain Dawson Mandara stood in the doorway in front of the sheriff. She stopped singing the moment she saw them.

"Oh, you surprised me!" She blushed.

"You surprised me," the captain replied.

"Because I'm in jail or because I know the words to 'Amazing Grace?'"

"Maybe a little of both."

"Did the sheriff tell you why I'm here?"

"Something to do with shooting a man."

"Cigar DuBois shot Logan last night, and I tried to get him to town to the doctor. They think I killed him."

"That's preposterous, Sheriff. The Marquesa is one of Cantrell's leading citizens. Logan was her good friend."

"But you weren't there when he got shot."

"No, but I know how close they were. Why, just the other night they had dinner together and spent three hours and eleven minutes eating, talking, and laughing together."

Isabel tried to look the captain in the eye, but his head was turned to the sheriff. *He was timing us?*

"Until you investigate the crime, you have absolutely no reason to suspect the Marquesa of shooting Logan. You can't arrest her because Phillips died!" the captain insisted.

She could see the sheriff start to puff up. "I'm getting sick and tired of people telling me how to run my office! She's going to stay in that cell because she shot Jacob Hardisty last summer and violated the judge's order about coming into town."

"There has to be some grace in that restriction when it comes to a life-and-death matter," the captain appealed.

"That's for the judge to decide."

"Where's the judge? I'd like to talk to him." Mandara wore his slightly worn suit without a tie. His collarless shirt was buttoned at the top.

"He's in session until noon."

Captain Mandara stepped over to the iron-bar door of her cell. "Marquesa, I'll go talk to the judge."

"Thank you, Captain Mandara. Your appearance was an answer to prayer." She dropped her chin to her chest. "I'm sorry to delay your return to Cantrell with Miss Fontenot."

"With Miss Fontenot?" the captain boomed. "Is she ready to return? You thought I came to town to bring her home?"

"Eh, July said that—"

"Yes, well, I'll be happy to give her a ride if she's ready. I understood when I brought her in it would two weeks before she would return. She mentioned something about going to stay with a sister in Deer Lodge for a couple of days."

"Oh." *But what about you and her? Whistling, smiling, laughing . . . a happy Captain Mandara. Don't tell me you only talked to her about house construction all the way to town? I'm not that naive!*

"I'll go talk to the judge, Marquesa." He put his hands on the iron bars just above hers. "Are you cold?"

"Wh-what?"

"You look cold," the captain said gently. "It's musty in here."

"It's a jail," the sheriff blurted out.

"Wrap yourself in those blankets," Mandara instructed. "I'll be back as soon as I can."

"The blankets are full of lice," she murmured.

"Lice?" He spun around to the sheriff. "Get this lady some clean blankets immediately."

"I don't put ladies in jail."

"Are you casting aspersions on the Marquesa's character?"

"All I'm sayin' is that a lady don't go around shootin' men! She's a dime-show actress, that's all."

Mandara stormed up only inches from the sheriff. "Mister, the only thing that's keeping you from getting your head split open is that silver-plated badge of yours."

"Are you threatenin' an officer of the law?"

"Captain!" she called out.

"I busted a general's jaw for insultin' a lady one time," the captain growled. "I surely won't hesitate to bust yours!"

"Captain Mandara!" she shouted.

"You don't come in here barkin' orders at me! One more word out of you, and you'll be in the cell next to her!" the sheriff screamed.

She saw Captain Mandara clench his huge callused fists.

"Dawson!" This time her voice was soft. Like a wife to a husband of many years. "Dawson, I need you!"

He spun around, eyes wide and mouth open.

"Dawson, I really need you to talk to the judge. My honor, if I have any left, cannot be damaged by the likes of this sheriff. Please go see the judge for me."

He took his hat off and ran his hand through his thick graying hair. "You're right. You're right, Claire . . . eh, Marquesa. I've got to go see the judge."

He called me Claire?

He pulled off his long coat and handed it to her. "Wear this. It's a little dusty, but there aren't any lice."

She was still holding the coat when the two men closed the door behind them.

The long black wool coat was sprinkled with red-clay dust, but the cotton lining was still warm from the captain's anger. She pulled it over her shoulders and cloak and then buttoned it under her chin.

It smells like a man.

It's a good, comfortable smell.

But no alcohol.

No tobacco.

And warm.

Thank You, God.

I'm still in jail.

There are lice in the blankets.

Rats are under the bed.

But the captain's working on my release.

Things are getting better.

She saw the door swing open. A man wearing a thick buffalo coat and a battered top hat walked in.

"Who are you?"

"The undertaker."

"I'm not dead, yet!" she protested.

"They told me to ask you about that Logan fella." His teeth wore years of tobacco stain.

She could feel her eyes puff, but no tears were left to fall. "Oh, Logan . . . yes . . . please fix him up handsome, and use a simple pine coffin. I'll, eh, I'll send you further instructions later."

"What about pay?"

"Use the pistol and the gold double eagle in his vest pocket for collateral. You did find the double eagle, didn't you?"

"Yes, ma'am, I did."

Somehow I knew that. "I'll settle up with you after I take care of this matter."

"Good luck, ma'am." He nodded and strolled back through the door. "I hear you're going to need it."

She paced the cold concrete floor for several minutes and still avoided the cot. Finally she leaned her back against the wall of the cell so she could see the door. Within moments she became so sleepy she began eyeing the bed.

I can't. Not lice. I didn't sleep last night. If I just had a clean floor to lie down on.

She propped her head in the corner where the bars met the wall and closed her eyes.

Captain, how long has it been since someone called you Dawson? Undoubtedly, only Claire calls you that. Thank you, Mrs. Mandara, for letting the captain come to my rescue.

With her arms warming up, she unfolded them and dropped them to her side, still inside the coat. Her left hand slipped inside a deep inner pocket and rested against several folded papers.

Whatever it is, it is private. Just leave the papers where they are.

She pulled the tightly folded papers out and held them in front of her.

A letter and a brochure? Isabel Leon, you do not need to read these things.

She shoved the letter addressed to Capt. D. Mandara, Billings, M.T., back into the pocket.

It's probably from Claire and certainly none of my business.

She opened the illustrated brochure and began to read:

Lyman Bridges Building Materials and Ready-Made Houses, Corner of Carroll and Sangamon Streets, Chicago, Illinois.

Ready-made houses? They can just ship the walls and lumber pre-cut and ready to assemble?

Number 27? That's the one he circled. Lumber? That's why he sold the lumber at Cantrell! He's buying a ready-made house! Two stories . . . three chambers upstairs; a parlor, dining room, kitchen and bedroom downstairs; dormer windows . . . little balcony. It looks charming!

They ship them by rail?

But how will he get it to Cantrell? I wonder if they have wagons strong enough to haul a whole house. Is that why he came to town? To pick up his ready-made house. But we talk every day. Why didn't he mention it?

Or did he?

Maybe I was so busy thinking about the hotel I really didn't listen.

I have plenty of time to listen now.

It will be, Captain Mandara, the nicest house in town.

She shoved the brochure back into the pocket and felt the letter with her fingers.

I have no intention of reading the letter.

He gave me this coat out of kindness. He undoubtedly forgot what was in the pocket.

She pulled her hands out of the pockets and shoved them into the outside coat pockets. Her right hand came up with a bent nail, a broken pencil, and a tiny, still-sealed bottle of quinine water.

Quinine? Has he been ill? Was he expecting to get ill?

The other pocket held only a small single-blade folding knife. Isabel glanced over the ivory handle and carefully opened the blade. She held it so she could read the inscription by the light of the high small window across the hallway from the cell.

"For Capt. Mandara, from the men of the C Company."

He said he busted a general's jaw for insulting a lady. What general was it? It couldn't have been Custer. He was a colonel, wasn't he? "Oh, Colonel Custer, how can we escape from this box canyon?" Custer on the Plains, Act I, Scene something. He must have slugged some other officer. No wonder he got dismissed from the army. I wonder if someone insulted Claire.

Probably not or else the captain would have been executed.

For murder.

If he's that protective of me.

Woe unto any that say disparaging words about his wife.

She dropped the small knife back into the pocket and began to pace back and forth.

It's not my letter.

It's a private matter.

I will not read it.

She circled back and forth several more times. *Well, it wouldn't hurt just to see who wrote the letter. I'm certainly not going to read a letter from his wife.*

That would be wrong.

Very wrong.

She pulled out the letter and glanced toward the doorway.

What if he came through the doorway and saw me reading his letter? I'd die.

She pulled the rest of her long hair out from under the collar of the captain's coat and let it flow freely down her back.

I could turn and face the wall. Maybe he wouldn't see me read it.

She pulled the small brown envelope out of the pocket and then turned with her back to the door. The envelope was slightly crunched, but the letter inside was folded. The words were gracefully formed with sweeping strokes in black India ink.

She looked quickly at the back side of the letter, then folded it, slipped it back in the envelope, and shoved it deep inside the pocket.

"I love you." Signed, "Georgia Claire Mandara."

It's from her.

It would be a horrible sin to read his personal mail.

Lord, I will not read a letter from his wife.

Georgia Claire?

Nellie is fifteen.

The boys are the youngest.

A daughter named Georgia? About twelve or thirteen—is that what he said?

Maybe it's from his daughter. They could have named their daughter Georgia Claire . . . after Mama.

But then his wife could be Georgia Claire, and everyone calls her Claire.

The penmanship was flawless. It was not from a child.

But she's not a tiny child. She could be quite good at writing. She's an officer's child. He probably drilled all his children in their studies.

The salutation would tell me. Then I'll put it back.

She pulled out the envelope once more and opened it up.

"Dearest Daddy,"

His wife wouldn't address him, "Dearest Daddy."

Would she?

May the Lord have mercy on my soul.

Again!

Dearest Daddy,

It is my turn to write to you, and Nellie is in a tiff. Just because she's older, she thinks she's the only one of us kids who can write a decent letter. I think my penmanship is quite sufficient, don't you?

Nellie has a boyfriend. His name is Gerald, and he is really dull. He looks like that Edwards boy that used to live next to us and drive you and Mama to torments. He hangs around the house with a silly grin. You should see him!

Philip and Grant go fishing almost every evening with Grandpa now that the weather's better. I'm sick of eating fish myself. What does buffalo meat taste like? I hear they eat the brains. Did you ever eat buffalo brains?

Nellie told us about the house from Chicago you ordered. It sounds wonderful. Do I really have to share a room with her? I could have the little room off the kitchen just for myself. Then I could get up and make you coffee every morning. Grandma taught me how to make coffee. Actually I can cook pretty well, but my sewing is ugly! I'll never, ever be able to sew as good as Mama.

I miss, miss, miss, miss, miss, miss you!!!!!

(I miss you a whole lot more than Nellie does!)

I can't believe it will only be a few more weeks until we can all move out to M.T.

Say hello to the nice lady with the dark hair for me.

From your adoring daughter (the pretty one).

Love,
Georgia Claire Mandara

Isabel folded the letter and jammed it back into the inside pocket of the captain's coat. She turned around and faced the door. She could feel her face burn.

Nice lady with the dark hair. Is that me? I mean, of course it's me. Isn't it?

I shouldn't have read that.

I'm glad it wasn't from Mrs. Mandara.

Captain Mandara, you have a precocious thirteen-year-old. And a fifteen-year-old with a dull boyfriend. You and Claire will need wisdom, grace, and patience over the next several years.

I think I like Georgia. She sounds a bit like a thirteen-year-old Isabel Leon.

If I had a daughter like . . .

She reached up with the heavy wool coat and wiped the corners of her eyes on the dusty sleeve.

You will never have a daughter, Isabel.

Nor a son.

Jacob Hardisty saw to that.

I wish I had killed him! No . . . maybe it's best this way. Lord, perhaps You have something stored up for him worse than death.

Isabel dozed off while standing and leaning against the jail cell wall. The sound of the door handle turning caused her eyes to open. The creak of the door stood her straight on her feet. With his thick gray hair shooting out from under his hat, Captain Mandara marched into the hallway leading two women. Both wore long dark dresses and straw hats. Their hair was pulled back so tight that it seemed to stretch the wrinkles out of otherwise middle-aged faces.

Isabel felt tense neck muscles relax. "Captain!"

"Are you all right, Marquesa?"

"I am tired. The cot is too filthy to lie upon." She gawked at the two ladies as she spoke.

"Judge Westfield is busy in court for another hour. However, this is Mrs. Westfield, and this is Mrs. Duvall, the mayor's wife. Ladies, this is the Marquesa, Isabel Leon."

"Hello, Marquesa. Captain Mandara told us all about your plight!" Mrs. Westfield boomed.

"This jail is simply wretched," Mrs. Duvall added. "I cannot believe anyone, let alone a lady of your obvious status, would have to endure one minute in such a place as this!"

"Lice, roaches, and rats? This looks like something from the Dark Ages! I will tolerate none of this!" Mrs. Westfield stepped back to the doorway and commanded, "Sheriff, you come here right now!"

A slump-shouldered Yellowstone County Sheriff appeared at the doorway. His badge tilted to the right on his stained leather vest.

"Release this woman at once! She needs better quarters. This is quite unacceptable."

"I cain't do that, Mrs. Westfield. You know that. She stays right there until your husband tells me differently," he protested.

"Nonsense," Mrs. Duvall blurted. "You will release her immediately into our custody." From her skin tone, Isabel couldn't tell if she was tan or had some Mediterranean heritage.

"But I have no authorization!"

"Sheriff, do you expect to run for reelection next fall with Mrs. Westfield and me endorsing your opposition?"

"Look, ladies, she has to be confined until the judge says."

"But she doesn't have to be confined in squalor. Release her into our custody, Sheriff," Mrs. Westfield insisted, swinging her dress that had tiny pearl buttons from her neck to the floor-dragging hem.

"I cain't do that!"

Mrs. Duvall's face grew beet-red. "Are you insinuating that we are not to be trusted for the guardianship of the Marquesa!"

"I believe he has just impugned your honor, ladies," the captain added. Isabel thought she caught a slight smile on his face. It quickly vanished.

"Stay out of this, Mandara!" the sheriff bellowed. "I will have no part of this!"

"Then would you please leave us your keys?" Mrs. Westfield asked in a high, almost-sweet tone.

In obvious disgust, the sheriff shoved the keys straight at the judge's wife.

She took them and nodded. "Thank you!"

The sheriff charged out through the office. Mrs. Westfield handed the ring of keys to Dawson Mandara. "Captain, could you release the Marquesa for us?"

"Certainly, ladies." He fumbled with several keys before he found the one that opened the cell. The door squeaked open, and Isabel Leon stepped forward. She followed the others out through the empty sheriff's office and down the hall and out to the boardwalk in front of the building.

"I can't even begin to thank you enough!" The Marquesa's voice quivered.

"Well, it was the captain's idea," Mrs. Duvall explained. Her flower-crested straw hat raised up and down with each word. "Did you know he's building a ready-made home? It sounds quite intriguing, doesn't it? It's precut and shipped in from Chicago."

"Oh . . . I, eh . . . did see a brochure," Isabel stammered.

The captain's eyes lit up. "The brochure in my pocket? Isn't it a winsome model?"

"It will be quite dramatic on that lot you've chosen." Isabel pulled off his coat and handed it back to him.

He slipped on the coat and shoved his hands into the pockets. "Did you read my Georgia's letter?"

"No . . . no, I didn't think it right to . . ."

Lord, forgive me, please forgive me. I just can't tell all of them I read his letter!

He pulled out both the illustrated brochure of house designs and the letter. "Here, show the ladies the house design. They were interested in the ready-made schoolhouse. And please read the letter from Georgia. She's my little firecracker!"

Isabel took the letter and the brochure. "Where will you be going?"

The captain tugged the front of his hat down. "Would you like for me to talk to the undertaker about Logan?"

"No, I've already done that. At least for now. But I don't know about the carriage."

"I'll put the horse in the livery."

She held the edge of her cloak and curtsied. "Thank you, Captain."

"After that I'll sit outside the judge's chambers waiting to talk to Judge Westfield," he offered.

"Tell Horace I have a custard baked," Mrs. Westfield added. "I expect him home early for dinner. And tell him that I want to discuss this matter about the Marquesa with him before he makes a ruling."

"Yes, ma'am, I will," the captain concurred. "Now where will you ladies be holding the Marquesa in custody?"

"We'll go over to my house first," Mrs. Duvall replied. "We all want to wash up after that horrible ordeal in the jail."

"Then we'll stop by the Imperial Hotel for tea and biscuits," Mrs. Westfield explained. "And if she doesn't mind, we'd like to take the Marquesa to the opera house. We're redecorating for the summer season and would really appreciate her professional advice."

"Ladies, I'll be delighted to give you my opinion provided I don't fall asleep. I was awake most of the night driving to town. And, of course, that cell was no place to sleep."

"Well, come to my house, dear. By all means, you need your rest," Mrs. Duvall insisted. "Mrs. Westfield, how would you like to help me on a campaign to build a new jail?"

"With a women's ward?"

"Of course."

"I'd be delighted!"

The two ladies strutted down the sidewalk.

Captain Mandara leaned close and whispered into the Marquesa's ear, "Remember, to these women you are the Marquesa. Enjoy it."

Isabel stood on her toes and kissed his suntanned cheek. "I prayed to the Lord, and He rescued me."

The captain stepped back quickly. But he didn't blush.

"I do believe you are right, Marquesa. I believe you are right."

The Hutchins Boarding House Cafe was not England House, the Imperial Hotel, nor even the Bootstrap Cafe. But it was clean and served plenty of hot food. Isabel Leon sat at a small rough wood table with her back to the wall and her eye on the front door. She sipped coffee from a chipped porcelain cup. She looked up every time a customer came through the doorway. Especially the men.

Finally, with posture perfect and worn suit obviously brushed clean, Dawson Mandara marched into the room. She glanced at his dark eyes and then at the empty chair across from her at the table.

Doesn't he ever relax? It's like he's on review all the time. Everything so somber. Clean shaven. Tonic water. Straight tie. I've never known anyone who took day-to-day living so seriously.

The captain hung his hat on a peg on the wall next to their table and sat down. "Marquesa, did you finally get some sleep?" He glanced around the room and signaled with his hand toward a girl in a long white apron.

Isabel set the cup down on the saucer. The stiff collar of her dress felt tight at her neck. "About twelve hours' worth, thank you."

The girl in the white apron filled the captain's cup with steaming coal black coffee.

"Yesterday was quite a day for you."

She licked her lips with the tip of her tongue, then spoke softly. "I was just thinking about that when you arrived. It was like I visited heaven and hell all in the same day."

He gazed over the top of his coffee cup. "Maybe you did."

She nodded and sipped her coffee.

Mandara seemed to be examining the patrons at each table. "Well, I hope this boardinghouse was all right. It was the one place in town I figured you wouldn't run across Hardisty or the sheriff."

She tried to see what he was looking for and then returned her gaze at his square jaw and narrow eyes. "After I talked to Judge Westfield, I came right here. I've seen no one at all," she admitted.

As if signaling that the coast was clear, the worry lines melted from his face, and he turned his penetrating stare to her. "I think I have all the arrangements made. I even have a headstone for Logan Henry Phillips."

Her brown eyes widened. "They carved it already?"

"They were quite accommodating," he reported. "Especially since the mayor's wife was with me."

Isabel tilted her head to the right and instantly a strand of hair popped out of her comb and over her ear. "Do those ladies run this town?"

"Yes, but don't tell their husbands." The captain tapped his finger on the table while gazing around the room.

Isabel held her arms straight out from her sides. "They bought me this dress."

He glanced at it for only a second and then resumed his room search. "It looks very nice."

Isabel scrutinized the dark blue cotton material. "Sure, if I want to look like a middle-aged ranch wife."

This time his eyes pointedly locked onto hers. "I said, it looks very nice."

You made your point, Captain.

She glanced across the room at three men who entered. Each wore holstered revolvers strapped low. "When will we be leaving for Cantrell?"

For the first time the captain leaned against the back of the chair and relaxed his shoulders. "In about an hour. McGuire is still loading his wagons."

A young girl about twelve scooted to their table carrying two steaming plates piled with thick chunks of ham, eggs, and biscuits. She returned with a pitcher of gravy.

Isabel broke off a piece of biscuit and ate it with her coffee. "What kind of arrangements did you make for your ready-made house?"

She watched Mandara flood his plate with white gravy. "I loaded my wagon and two of McGuire's. He held up yesterday's shipment to the Mercantile and is sending it today. There will be five wagons. And your carriage. Are you sure you don't mind?"

"Driving a carriage?"

"With a coffin on the back," he reminded her.

"I drove Logan to town. I can drive him home."

"He really doesn't have any folks back east?" The captain loaded his fork and crammed the half-biscuit bite into his mouth.

"He's from New Mexico."

Mandara swallowed hard, then took a swig of coffee. "He is? I thought he was a friend of yours from the East."

"That's true, but he was born near Fort Bliss, Texas. His parents were shot in a border raid. He might as well be buried in Cantrell. At least there will be one person there who will remember him." She ran her fork through her scrambled eggs but didn't take a bite.

"I'm sorry about Logan. I know it's difficult to lose someone . . . close." His voice was soft.

"The thing is, Logan and I were just friends. We only saw each other a few times over the past years, but neither of us had anyone else. So we kind of adopted each other, without really talking about it. It's difficult to explain."

The captain scooped up a forkful of biscuit and gravy and then baptized it with a spoonful of honey before he chomped down. After a swig of coffee, he said, "Marquesa, tell me all the judge told you again. You were tired last night, and I didn't want to press you much."

"He said the sheriff would come out to investigate Logan's death, but that they were waiting to find out if Cigar DuBois had a pardon or had escaped."

"What difference does that make? Why wait?"

Isabel's eggs were cold, but the gravy tasted spicy. "Obviously the sheriff has no intention of facing down DuBois. I think they're hoping to get word that he's left the county. The judge said it would be judicious for me not to be in Billings at the same time as Hardisty in the future."

The captain took the still-white napkin and wiped his mustache. "So the banishment from Billings is officially over?"

"It would seem so. Although I have so many less-than-pleasant memories here. I don't plan on coming back very often."

"Sounded like the ladies want you to return."

"Oh, yes. I agreed to sing at a benefit in September to raise money for the new jail."

"You fitted right in with them, did you?"

She could not tell if he was teasing. "They were kind, but I could never be like they are. You're sort of born with that, I think."

"You might be surprised." He piled his fork with gravy and eggs.

"What do you mean, Captain?"

"Take Mrs. Westfield." He waved his inverted empty fork at her. "She's half-French and half-Cheyenne. I first met her when she was living with an old trapper down on the Washita during a military campaign."

Isabel sat back in her chair.

"You didn't think that was all suntan, did you?"

"Does the judge know that?"

"Yep. It's no secret from anyone. It just doesn't matter to these folks."

"And Mrs. Duvall?"

"She was a servant girl for some rich folks who moved to Fort Benton. She ran off and chummed with the Wolfe Creek gang of bank robbers until she met Duvall, who was a petty horse thief himself."

She glared at him. "Captain Mandara, are you making all of this up?"

His eyes seemed to burn into hers. "Why would I do that?"

"Well, I like them. Even before I found out all of that. Before I forget it, Captain, here is your letter from Georgia. Mrs. Duvall kept the Ready-Made House brochure. They were talking of sending for both the schoolhouse and the church."

She smiled as he looked over the letter. "Your daughter has excellent penmanship, you know."

"Claire taught her that. They all have learned much more from their mother than they ever will from their father."

He sighed and tucked the letter into his coat pocket.

"It won't be too long until you have them with you," Isabel encouraged him.

He pushed his chair back and drained his coffee cup. "Yes, and we had better get going. There's a hotel to finish."

"And a house to build," she added.

He combed his fingers through his newly washed hair. In the

dim light of the cafe, it didn't look nearly as gray as on previous occasions.

The rain the night before had made the road muddy and slick. But the air tasted cool and fresh as Isabel drove the carriage east along the south side of the Yellowstone River. The valley was green, and the box elders, willows, and cottonwoods along the river were at full leaf. Up on the rim of the plateau to the south, the scattered short grass was about the same color as the sage.

Rain-heavy clouds still hung in the sky. Isabel couldn't tell if they were going to stack up or blow away. Captain Mandara insisted on leading the caravan with his wagon loaded down with precut lumber, windows, and doors.

"Marquesa, I don't want you to be first in the line of fire," he had said. *Line of fire for what? It is just a muddy road out to Cantrell. I had no problem driving in the other night.*

It's the officer in him, I suppose. Line up, move out . . . hup-two-three. Women and children in the rear. I can't believe they let you out of the army.

Even if you did punch a general in the nose.

I'm sure the man deserved it.

God, this is Isabel. How are You this morning? I'm doing well, thank You. Look, I'm not sure what You did for Logan yesterday. I'll just have to trust him into Your hands. I know You'll do what is fair.

But You really did something in my life.

I don't mean just getting me out of that jail.

I mean, whatever that thing was You did in my heart.

I like it.

I just wish Carolina would hurry up and get back so she can tell me what happened to me. You know, God, I know a lot of things—things about acting, singing . . . surviving . . . men . . . surviving men! But there are some things I'm pretty dumb about.

But I can learn.

She drove along at a walk as she kept the slow pace of heavily loaded wagons on a muddy road. She gazed ahead at the back of Captain Mandara's wide-brimmed hat.

God, I'll tell You one thing I don't understand. I mean, I feel like

You've given me a new chance. And I don't have that horrible burden of guilt anymore for all the things I've done wrong in the past.

But I'm still worried about what I might do wrong in the future. Like when the captain was talking with me this morning, there was that little leap in my heart and a tickle in my throat. And sometimes my thoughts about him and me are . . . you know . . . rather shameful.

Weren't You supposed to take away those feelings yesterday?

In a few weeks his wife and family will be here.

And I'm scared to death I'll do something wrong before then.

Something very, very wrong.

— Five —

ISABEL LEON EXPECTED to return to a Cantrell in confusion. All during the plodding day-long trip back down the Yellowstone River, she imagined a town terrorized by the likes of Cigar DuBois. She worried greatly for July's safety, fearing that he could have been killed and the Mercantile burned to the ground.

She didn't feel fear but more a sad resignation.

As they finally turned south for the short climb up the riverbank to Cantrell, she checked to see that her small handgun was loaded. The road dust lay like thick gloom on the sleeves of her dress. She didn't bother to brush it off.

What she found when she pulled into town was a surprise.

July was so busy with customers that he hardly had time for a greeting. Molly Mae was helping out at the store since she had finished her chores at the cafe. Word around town was that DuBois had lit out for the Devil's Canyon diggings. No one had seen him since the night he shot Logan.

Isabel had been away for less than forty-eight hours, and yet she immediately found out that a drugstore was being built just east of the Mercantile. Several men had met and formed a volunteer fire company, and two Englishmen on Third Street were talking about constructing a tennis court.

The captain went to work on the hotel and his house. July and Molly were now inseparable. And Isabel took the lead in forming the Cantrell Cemetery Association. She collected enough money from city businesses to hire a couple of men to build a fence around a bluff of scrub cedars above the town. The

first resident was Logan Henry Phillips, whose stone was at the base
of the largest cedar. The headstone faced the morning sun.

The Hotel Marquesa's windows and outside doors were
installed, and Isabel spent as much time wandering from room to
room as she could. The upstairs veranda was usable, although the
railing was not completed. She spent several evenings toward the
end of the week sitting on a stack of boards on the veranda watching the sun set in the west.

It was a week after Logan's death that July Johnson banged on
Isabel's door at 7:00 A.M.

"Marquesa, you've got to come see this!"

With pastel green cotton stockings in her hand, she scooted to
the door. "July, I'm still getting dressed. What is it?"

"A sack of mail." His voice was as excited as it could be dis-
cussing a subject other than Molly Mae.

She tried to stand on one foot and pull the stocking on but only
succeeded in hopping around on one foot. "Someone brought the
mail out from Billings?"

"No, ma'am. This came right off the train to the stagecoach
and then to us!"

She caught hold of the bedpost. "We don't have a post office."

"We do now! It says it's sent to the United States Post Office,
Cantrell, Montana Territory. That's us!"

She scurried to the door and peeked out. "Is anyone else in the
store?"

July looked around. "No, ma'am. You want me to bolt the front
door?"

"No, I'm dressed. I just haven't put on my shoes." She waltzed
over to the woodstove. July trailed behind and poured her a cup of
coffee.

"Now what's all of this about a post office?" *No makeup, jewelry, shoes? There was a time, Marquesa, when you would have let no
man see you like this—even a fifteen-year-old boy.*

"Right there." July waved his arms with the enthusiasm of a
child with a Christmas present. "Look at it. That's what it says."

A brown canvas bag about one by two feet with leather trim
lay on the floor next to the table.

"Did you open it?"

"No, ma'am. It says that it can only be opened by the post-master or the assistant postmaster of Cantrell, M.T."

"But we don't have any postmaster. We don't have a post office!"

July shook his head. "Ain't that something?"

"Then we'll have to peek in and try to figure this out."

July flashed a wide, dimpled grin. "I was hopin' that's what you'd say. There's a dispatch attached to the top of the bag. Maybe you ought to open it," he suggested.

Isabel raised her eyebrows. "Why me?"

"It might be against the law," July offered.

"You mean, since I've had more experience at being arrested and thrown into jail, I ought to be the one who opens it?" she jibed.

With wide eyes, July nodded. "Thanks, Marquesa!"

Did he think I was serious?

Isabel unfastened the string on the large dispatch envelope, unwound it, and then opened it up. Inside were two smaller envelopes. One brown. One white. Written on the brown one were the words, "Open First."

She slipped the paper out of the brown envelope and unfolded it. July hunched behind her and peered over her shoulder. "Who's it from?"

"It's from the Postmaster General in Washington, D.C.!"

"Read it to me, Marquesa!"

"Dear citizens,

"It is my pleasure to inform you that your town, Cantrell, M.T., has been awarded a United States Post Office. I do hereby appoint Mrs. Carolina Parks as postmaster and Mr. July Johnson as assistant postmaster."

Isabel stopped reading and looked at July.

"Me? I'm the assistant postmaster?" His expression was some-where between "your dog died" and "Molly Mae is waiting for you in the barn."

"That's what it says!"

"I can't believe it! I ain't even old enough to vote!"

"Let me finish the letter," the Marquesa insisted.

> "*The United States Post Office in Cantrell, M.T., will be housed in the
> building known as Cantrell's Mercantile. Mail will be delivered by stage on
> Mondays, Wednesdays, and Fridays until such time as daily delivery is war-
> ranted. The contents of this sack cannot be legally sorted and delivered by any-
> one other than the above mentioned.*"

The Marquesa looked up at a beaming July Johnson. "Then the
letter's signed by the Postmaster General himself."

"I just can't believe it."

"Well, let's read letter number two. Maybe it will explain.
Would you like to open it?"

"Nope. You read it, Marquesa. It wasn't in the bag, so I reckon
you can look at it, too."

"Thank you, Mr. Assistant Postmaster."

July threw his shoulders back and raised his square chin.
"You're welcome. Who's that one from?"

The Marquesa glanced down at the bottom of the letter. "It's
from Ranahan, Carolina, and David Parks!"

"Who's David?" July interrupted. "I mean, her brother's name
was David, but he got killed and . . . he was a Cantrell anyway.
Who's—"

"He's their baby, July!"

"They had a baby? I mean, they already had the baby, and they
didn't tell us?"

"They just told us!"

"Yeah! Oh, I have to go tell Molly Mae!" July raced toward the
door.

"It's too early to go visiting," she cautioned.

"She's cookin' breakfast today," he explained.

The Marquesa waved the envelope in her hand. "Don't you
want to hear the letter first?"

"Oh, yeah, the letter!" He scampered over to the table and
threw himself into the chair.

> "*Dear Isabel and July,*
>   "*We miss you and the store and Cantrell so dearly. It was good that we*

came east. Mother has been ill, and I've needed to take care of her and some business matters. Ran absolutely hates the East. (I told you he would!) I fear I'll never get him to come back here again.

"David Joshua Parks came into the world on May 15. He is a perfect little one, with his mother's face and his father's strong will. I can't wait to bring him home!

"While in Washington I spoke with a former friend of my father's. He's the Postmaster General. So, as you can see, we now have a post office. It was obviously the Lord's leading that we came back here. Now I want Him to lead us home. We hope to be there by the week of the 3rd.

"July, make sure you record all your hours spent in sorting the mail. You are on the government payroll now. You should be receiving a shipment of oak mail boxes, a cancellation stamp, and other items in the next two weeks. We'll put the boxes alongside the counter at the back of the store. Until then you'll have to hand out the mail.

"Please give our regards to all.

"Yours truly,
"Ranahan, Carolina, and David Parks"

"I've got to go tell Molly Mae about the baby! Little baby David." He sprinted toward the door, then spun around. "I wonder if they'll call him Davy?"

"She always called her brother David. I'd guess she likes David best."

"Yeah!" He yanked open the door. "Are you going to be all right? With the store?"

"I'll pull on my shoes. Go on."

"Thanks!"

"Don't forget to tell the Quincys about the post office and your new position."

"Oh, yeah, I forgot! I didn't really forget. It's just . . ." July's face lost its grin, and he stood still. "Marquesa, do you reckon it's possible to have too many good things happen to you all at once?"

Isabel pondered July's anxious blue eyes.

"No," she proclaimed.

"I didn't think so!" He ran across the porch, leaving the door wide open. She waited a moment and saw him spin around in the middle of the street. "Don't touch that mail, Marquesa! I'll take care of it when I get back."

By 7:30 A.M. there was a line of residents waiting for mail out in front of the Mercantile. Even though the store was open, July had posted a handwritten sign: "U.S. Post Office, Cantrell, M.T., 8:00 A.M. to 6:00 P.M., Closed Sundays."

At 8:00 Mr. July Johnson personally handed out fifty-six pieces of mail. That was all but two of the items in the mail bag.

Those two were in Isabel's hands.

"I'm sure it will be all right if I carry these over to the captain," she explained.

"But I'm supposed to deliver them right to the person on the envelope," July protested.

"When the Quincys drove to town for supplies, didn't they always bring mail out for everyone?"

"Yep."

"Well, just think of me as doing the same thing."

"I reckon you're right." He ran his fingers through his neatly trimmed brown hair. "This is a responsible position, isn't it?"

The Marquesa put her arm around his shoulder. "July, do you realize at this moment you are the only government official, whether federal, territorial, county, or city, in the entire town?"

His face turned solemn. "It humbles a man, don't it?"

To say nothing of what it does to a boy of fifteen.

Captain Mandara was hanging a door on an upstairs room when Isabel found him.

"Did you hear the news?" she asked.

"About the Parkses' baby boy, David? About Cantrell having a post office? Or that July is our assistant postmaster? Or the news about the *Courier?*"

"The what?"

"The *Cantrell Courier*—the town's first newspaper."

"We have a newspaper?" she gasped.

"A fella from Virginia City pulled a big wagon in last night. Said he brought a printing press. Asked me if he could rent a room in the hotel to establish a newspaper."

"A room in my hotel?"

"Yeah, I told him he was a few weeks too early but that he could talk to the Marquesa."

"What did he say?"

Mandara kept hammering. "He asked, 'Which one's the Marquesa?'"

"What did you tell him?"

He stopped hammering and pulled a nail out of his nail apron. "Told him he'd know you when he saw you. You're the only one in town who looks like a Marquesa."

"I don't look much like one this morning. I haven't even put on my jewelry."

"You look nice."

"Thank you, Captain. But I really feel quite plain without a little more makeup."

He took two nails out of his mouth and leaned closer to her. "I said, you look nice!"

Yes, sir!

She walked into the empty hotel room and gazed out the window at the nearly finished veranda. "Even if the hotel was finished, I don't want to have a newspaper office for a tenant."

"His name is Garrard. I told him he'd be better off building his own office. He said he'd stretch a tarp between some trees down in the cottonwoods and print a few papers."

"Right away?"

"Nope. Said he couldn't possibly get a paper out before . . . Saturday."

She glanced over to see if the captain was smiling. He wasn't. "This Saturday?"

"He was a persistent fellow." The captain pointed toward a piece of wood on the floor. "Could you hand me that shim?"

She walked over with a small scrap of shingle. "But what will he report on? Nothing newsworthy happens around here."

"I hear there was a murder last week." He swung the door closed between them, then opened it up quickly.

She folded her arms in front of her. "He'll put that in the paper?"

"I surmise he'll put in everything he hears. You could give him the news about the Parkses' baby, as if folks haven't heard it by now." He stepped back out into the hall. "These doors turned out quite nobby, didn't they?"

"Yes, they did."

"What color are you going to paint them?"

"The wall will be a light gray. The doors will be white."

"I think I'll have the painter get started by Monday. Maybe we can put a Hotel Marquesa construction report in the paper."

"If he really is going to print a paper, I'll post an advertisement for hotel staff."

He walked across the hallway to work on another door. "We can have an article about our new post office."

"That's why I'm here. There were two letters for you. Shall I put them in your coat pocket?" In the background she could hear some of the other workers hammering.

"Why don't you just read them to me? I don't want to turn loose of this door 'til I get it hung right."

"I don't feel comfortable reading someone's mail before they get a chance to see it first."

"You officially have my permission." The captain continued to screw a brass hinge into the doorjamb. "Marquesa, I do not get embarrassing mail."

"That's not what I meant. It's just, well, it's like reading some-one's diary."

He stopped to glance her way. "You've never done that?"

"Yes, I have. But I've felt burdened with guilt every time."

"Well, the only emotion you'll experience reading my mail is boredom. But I'll tell you what." He handed her the screwdriver. "You hang the door, and I'll read."

"All right, you win." She handed the screwdriver back. "The captain gives the orders. Here's the first letter. It looks like it's from your daughter Georgia."

"Hold it up. Let me see."

She turned the outside of the letter toward him. "Nope. That's my Nellie."

"How can you tell?"

"'Capt. D. Mandara.' She abbreviates captain. Georgia never abbreviates anything."

The Marquesa held it up at eye level. "Okay, here's the letter:

"Dear Father,

"We are all very healthy. In fact, I believe the boys have added ten pounds since you saw them. Georgia still fusses with her food, but Grandma told her to sit up and act mature like me!

"Georgia's such a pill every time Gerald comes over to visit. Remember, Gerald is that really cute boy I told you about in my last letter? Well, every time he comes over, Georgia tries something really dumb. Last night she spilt lemonade all over his shirt on purpose.

"Father, you must write to her. No one here can get her to do anything.

"All of us, except for you know who, are doing quite well with our studies. Did you know school will be out only two days before we move?

"All we seem to talk about around here is moving to Montana and being with you. The house sounds wonderful! I was thinking perhaps it wouldn't be such a good idea to put me and Georgia in the same room. You know how provoking she can be! So why don't you put her down in the bedroom off the kitchen, and I'll keep the upstairs room all to myself.

"Did I tell you Gerald really wants to move to Montana, too?

"Maybe he could work for your Marquesa. Everyone is dying to meet her. But each one has a different idea of what she looks like. You know you aren't very descriptive in your letters.

"Philip and Grant say 'hi!'

> *"Your firstborn,*
> *"Nellie Elizabeth Mandara."*

"There you have it, Marquesa." It was a relaxed, proud smile. "Now you know why my hair is nearly gray at forty-two."

Forty-two? Why did I think you were fifty-two? "Actually I think your daughters sound delightful."

"They are nothing alike. They don't even look alike. Nellie is just exactly like her mother, and Georgia . . ."

"Like her father?"

He held a couple of nails between his lips and balanced a two-foot level on top of the door. "It's uncanny," he mumbled. "Now Nellie, she's got Daddy wrapped around her fingers. She knows how to get anything she wants out of me. But Georgia—that little princess knows the words I'm going to speak before I ever say them."

"And what are the boys like? Are they like their mother or their father?"

"Philip is officer material from boots to hat. He'll go to the academy. If he wants to. But Grant—he'll either end up owning a gold mine or swinging from a rope."

"Oh, my!"

"When he was five, I sent him to the store to buy one pound of sugar. He came home with eight pounds of sugar and all the money I sent him with."

"What happened?"

"He bet the clerk double or nothing and won three times in a row."

"At five years old? What did you do?"

"Took him back to the store and made him return the sugar, of course. That's Grant!"

And how about Claire? Tell me about Claire. Tell me that she's a horrible wife, a lousy mom. But she's wonderful, isn't she? I'm sure she is. On second thought, don't tell me about Claire. I don't think I can handle the comparison . . . just yet.

He motioned at her with the level. "Read that other letter before I get to missing those kids too much."

"All right. Here goes. This one is from the War Department.

"Dear Captain Dawson Mandara,

"I regret to inform you that your request to be reinstated into the United States Army has been denied. The circumstances surrounding your discharge prevent us from taking action at this time.

"As you are well aware, you are allowed by law to reapply twelve months from the date of this letter.

"Yours truly,
"General Nelson Miles"

"And there's a hand-scribbled note that says, 'Give my regards to your Nellie.' Gen. Miles knows Nellie?"

"She was named after him."

"Captain, I'm sorry about the rejection letter."

"I get one every year. They have to do it. It's the army way." He shrugged.

"You apply for reinstatement every year?"

"Yep. Till the day I die, I suppose."

"Captain, this is none of my business."

"You're right—don't ask."

"About your discharge."

"Yes. I have nothing to say about it."

She looked at him, expecting to be glared at.

She wasn't.

Instead, he just moved down the hall and began to work on another door.

"Captain, when was the last time you had a really happy day?" she blurted out as she followed along behind him.

"Marquesa, what makes you think we are supposed to have happy days in this life?"

"You didn't answer my question."

"Nor you, mine."

"You know the answer to my question," she insisted. "I am not wise enough to know the answer to yours."

He stopped and dropped his head.

"You're right. And I deserve your disdain. I just can't talk about it yet. I'm trying desperately not to let the past distort the future. I know that all sounds cryptic. Forgive me."

"You are certainly forgiven. I have spent most of my life blurting out personal things that should have been kept to myself," she declared.

"Perhaps we can learn from each other."

"I think we are, Captain. . . . I must get back. The assistant postmaster is expecting me."

"If you don't have other plans, could we have supper together tonight? I want to finalize these upstairs plans with you before I get the painter in here."

"At 8:00, Captain?"

"I'll see you then."

Isabel Leon walked slowly back toward the Mercantile.

It's 8:30 in the morning. It's a two-, well, three-street town, and I won't see you until 8:00 P.M. tonight? Are you going to hide out in the hotel all day?

With business still booming, Isabel Leon spent most of the time scurrying around the store. The clerks, Tiny Merwin and Adam Bray, went home around five, and fortunately so did most of the customers. July and Isabel sat at the little table by the woodstove.

She pulled off her heavy lace-up shoes, tugged off her stockings, and wiggled her toes.

July did the same.

"The tally looks good again, but I don't reckon we can keep this up all summer, do you?" he asked as he bent his fingers back one at a time, cracking his knuckles.

"I've heard some say that by the first of June everyone who's spending the summer in the Big Horns will be outfitted. If so, we'll have a slow time then." She held her hands up in front of her and examined her long manicured fingernails. "It will slow down about the time I open the hotel. The men partnered me in the hotel building, but the business is up to me. I'll need to turn a profit quickly. I'm a little nervous about that."

"You've got a number of permanent residents lined up. Then when the snow drives them out of the mountains, you'll have everyone wantin' a room . . . just like last winter when we had 'em sleepin' on the Mercantile floor."

"What's the weather like in Devil's Canyon, July?"

"I ain't been up there in almost a year. Don't aim to go back neither. The upper end is over 9,000 feet elevation. You can't live there in the winter. But there weren't more than a couple dozen men in the canyon last year. They was scattered up and down the crick. In the springtime it was sort of like a picnic. But then the Crow came and kilt some. They run the rest off, at least for a while."

"Well, it is their land."

"Not for long. Everyone's saying the government will open it up. It makes you wonder if they'll just build a big city up there and bypass Cantrell."

She began to massage the back of her neck. "I suppose there's always that chance."

"Kind of makes you just want to get in and enjoy what you got right now, don't it?" He sported a familiar smile.

"I presume you have Miss Molly Mae on your mind?"

"Yes, ma'am, I do!"

"Well, go on. I'll take these daily receipts to the bank."

"Be sure and lock the door. Don't want Cigar DuBois standin' in here again when you get back."

"I hear he's up in Devil's Canyon," she put in.

"I doubt it. They haven't been bringin' any dead bodies down with them," July noted as he hung his apron on a peg near the door. "Ever'where DuBois goes, there seems to be dead bodies."

With the store closed, July gone, and supper still over an hour and a half away, Isabel Leon carried the pail of boiling water into her room and dumped it into the enameled iron tub that sat behind the screen in her room.

The routine she learned from Carolina Parks: Boil the pail of water and the large teapot full of water three times, and by the time she dumped the third round into the tub, the first two would be cooled enough to allow her to slip into the bath oils without scalding herself.

Isabel had once thought that anything less than a bath a day was uncivilized. That was until she had to pump her own water from the well and wait for it to boil. She had learned how to survive with cold sponge baths and two hot dips in the tub a week. They were just about the highlight of the week.

They were especially leisurely with Ranahan and Carolina gone. Her suite at the hotel had a separate bathing room, with a hand-operated dumbwaiter to draw up hot water from the kitchen.

One of the maids will pour my bath each day.

With her long black hair stacked high on her head, Isabel slipped out of her robe and into the steaming bathwater.

For a sweet fifteen minutes I'm in New York . . . or San Francisco . . . or even Paris . . . not that I've ever been there.

With her green silk robe draped around a very clean and sweet-smelling body, Isabel studied the dresses laid out on the bed.

I can brush and press the one the ladies bought me. He said he liked

*it. He emphatically said he liked it. But it is rather plain. To be honest,
it's horribly dull!*

*Then there's Carolina's blue dress. Very fancy if the right accessories
are used. But even then very modest.*

*Or, of course, I could wear my green silk dress, which is really not
that outrageous . . . in San Francisco after the theater! Maybe I could
tone it down a bit. I could wear a coat over the top and keep it buttoned!*

Why does that black lace have to dip so low?

*Be honest, Marquesa. You love that dress, low-cut lace and all. "A
woman in plain clothes is a misuse of cloth . . . and womanhood." The*
French Dancer, *opening line.*

Isabel stomped back across the room and peered out the window toward the partially constructed drugstore. She ran her hands
through her hair, which now flowed down her back.

I will wash my hair tomorrow.

She sat on the edge of the bed and again examined the three
dresses.

*This is ridiculous, Isabel. Totally ridiculous. You are going to supper with your builder to discuss hotel construction. You have had meals
with this man on numerous other occasions. He is a married man. In
three weeks his family will be here living with him.*

*In three weeks he will live in his own house, in bed with his own wife,
surrounded by his children, and occupied with building a town.*

*Me—I will be in my hotel suite, scurrying around trying to make
things run smoothly. Once or twice a month we will pass each other in
the street, and he'll tip his hat and say, "Evenin', Marquesa." I'll nod
and say, "Good evening, Captain . . . Mrs. Mandara." Then Claire
will say, "We really must be going, Dawson." And they'll stroll down
the street arm in arm, and I'll crawl in bed that night alone and read.*

*So what difference does it make in the whole world what wretched
dress I wear tonight?*

She felt tears come to her eyes. She tried to brush them back
with her fingers. "Stop whimpering, you big baby! You've got more
things going right for you right now than you ever had in your
whole life! So straighten up. You chose the kind of life you wanted
to live. Now you pay!"

If only . . .

I wonder, if I had met a single Captain Mandara when I was younger would I have had enough sense to latch onto him? Probably not. When I was younger, I had no sense at all!

Isabel picked up the dress Mrs. Westfield and Mrs. Duvall had purchased for her. She held it under her neck and looked in the mirror.

"'I said, it looks very nice, Marquesa!'" she mimicked in a deep voice. Then she hung the dress up in the crowded wardrobe closet near the bed.

Now, Lord, You know that I don't know much. I know I turned everything over to Jesus when I was in that jail cell singing "Amazing Grace." And You know I am never, ever, going to go back on that deal.

But I don't understand. If You're in control, why do I keep thinking about Captain Mandara more and more? I thought with You in control, I'd never feel this way about a man again . . . especially a married man.

"Lord Clarington, I will not be a part of this immoral scene. This is demented, outrageous, imprudent, mad, absurd, and bizarre. And I wash my hands of the matter entirely!" *The King's Mistress*, Act II, Scene 1.

She snatched up Carolina's dress and held it up to herself in front of the mirror. *I wonder if she'll be able to wear this dress after having a baby? She won't be able to wear it right away. Of course, if anyone could, she could.*

"Carolina Cantrell Parks, you are the most disgustingly organized and self-disciplined woman who ever sauntered across the face of this earth! And I wish you'd hurry up and come home. I really miss you."

Isabel hung Carolina's dress in the wardrobe and began tugging on the shiny green silk one.

This is me. This is who I am. I'm the Marquesa. I'm comfortable in this dress. There aren't five women in America who could say that. But I can.

I'm a good me.

But I'm me.

I'm not Mrs. Duvall or Mrs. Westfield.

I'm not sweet Carolina.

And I'm not Claire Mandara.

Isabel Leon . . . the Marquesa of the theater. Lord, You don't mind me just being me.

Do You?

Carolina's crocheted black shawl had an extremely wide design, and wrapped around Isabel's shoulders and pinned with a gold brooch, it made the lace bodice of the dress somewhat less risqué.

Although the stones in the dangling diamond and emerald-like earrings were fake, they captured every ounce of available light and reflected it around the room. It was the only legacy Isabel had left from a short-lived music review called "Cleopatra's Follies."

Eye shadow.

Rouge.

Lipstick.

And a discreet amount of Dr. Sylvan's Miracle Wrinkle Cream and Skin Tonic.

Then just a little Rose of the Evening perfume.

Isabel brushed out her wavy black hair and gazed in the mirror. "Well, Miss Isabel Leon, you shore do look purdy tonight!" she drawled. *I keep expecting someone to rap on the door and shout, "Curtain's going up in five minutes, Marquesa!"*

I probably won't hear that again ever.

Perhaps the stage at the hotel will be large enough for a condensed version of Pirates of Penzance. *I'd have to bring in someone to be the Pirate King . . . and I could play—*

"Marquesa!" It was a muffled shout outside the front of the store. "Marquesa!"

Somehow I don't think it's a curtain going up.

She adjusted the shawl on her shoulders and strolled across the empty store. She opened the door a few inches to see an extremely dusty man wearing worn chaps and vest over his suspendered duckings and grimy gray shirt. His wide-brimmed hat looked like it hadn't been off his head for months. Dirty brown curls of hair shot out wildly over his ears.

"Marquesa?" He leered at her up and down.

It was not a feeling she enjoyed, but she had experienced it before.

"Yes?"

"Mr. Milton at the bank asked me to see if you had a couple of minutes. He had some mix-up on your deposit, and he wanted to check it out with you."

"Mix-up?"

"Don't ask me, ma'am. I ain't much on bankin'. I jist stopped by to deposit my poke. It's been a good week at the diggin's up at Devil's Canyon."

"Tell him I'll be there in a minute."

"Yes, ma'am! Reckon I'll see you later at the dance hall."

"Cantrell does not have a dance hall, and if they did, I can guarantee that you would not see me there!" She shut the door and threw the lock.

He gives me the shivers. At least the bummers in the East are fairly clean and mostly polite.

When she reached her room, she raised a foot to the padded stool and began to lace up her shoes. Then she grabbed up her flower-print cloth purse, opened it, and glanced at her pistol.

That man has been on the trail a long time.

He might have been pushing cows.

But he wasn't wading in a stream panning for gold.

She snapped the purse closed.

But then everyone in this town wants to pretend they struck it rich in the goldfields. Especially if they're looking for a dance-hall girl to spend money on.

The door to the Assay Office and Bank opened as she approached. The cowboy who had summoned her held the door handle in one hand and his hat in the other.

"Welcome, Marquesa," he greeted her and jammed his hat back on his head.

She was convinced his hair had not been combed nor washed in a year.

"What's this all about?" she asked.

A large man with a full black beard and dusty black derby stood behind the front counter. A fresh black tie was neatly attached over a once-blue-but-now-dusty-gray shirt.

"Marquesa, I'm one of the new owners in this bank. I purchased it from Jacob Hardisty. And I'm in the process of reviewing accounts."

"Where are Mr. Milton and Mr. Ostine?"

"They're tied up with business in the back. All I want to know is the exact amount of your deposit today. The records seem to be unclear."

"I need to talk to Mr. Milton," she insisted.

"It will be awhile before he is free."

"I'll wait."

"I don't want to spoil your party. It looks like you're dressed to celebrate." He managed a yellow-toothed smile.

"And it looks like you borrowed Mr. Milton's tie," she observed.

"You're right about that! Very perceptive. My trunk hasn't caught up with me. We've been on the road awhile, as you can see. My associate and I have ridden all the way from Deadwood. Now what was that deposit amount today?" he pressured.

She looked back at the dirty cowboy. He was blocking the doorway, a hand resting on his gun handle.

"Well, now, let me see. I'll check the receipt." She opened her purse and slipped her hand on the mother-of-pearl-handled Lady Colt. "The deposit was for one dollar," she divulged.

"What?" the man behind the counter bellowed, his face reflecting red through the black beard.

"That's right. It was a slow day," she declared.

"You don't expect me to believe that!"

"And you don't expect me to believe you. Mr. Grime back here said he made a bundle prospecting at Devil's Canyon. You said you two rode in from Deadwood. Get your story straight, boys," she seethed. "I want to talk to Mr. Milton!"

Out of the corner of her eye, she could see the man behind her hold his gun in his hand now, pointed at her. She released her own gun and left it concealed in her purse.

"Go on back there, and we'll all talk to Mr. Milton." He

motioned to the backroom. The barrel of a gun at her back prodded her along.

The first thing she spotted in the office at the back of the bank was Isaac Milton and Ted Ostine tied to their chairs.

"This is what you meant by being tied up? What's the meaning of this?" she demanded.

"You! It's you!"

Isabel looked to the right. Cigar DuBois crouched against the wall.

"You know her?" the one with Milton's tie asked.

"She's one of that bunch that jumped me, Rosto! Fired a shotgun right through the ceiling at me!"

"What's going on here!" she demanded again.

"First, we're going to rob the bank, and then . . . I'm going to take care of you!" DuBois snarled. "You thought I didn't recognize you the other day. I don't ever forget someone who takes a potshot at me."

He didn't recognize me. That's obvious. He would have killed me then if he had.

"Marquesa, whatever beef Cigar has with you is none of my business. My name is Rosto Rollins. Maybe you've heard of me," the man with Milton's tie introduced himself.

"No, but other than Cigar DuBois, I know very few horse's rear ends by name!"

"You ain't heppin' matters none!" the man behind her boomed, prodding her in the back again with his gun.

"What do you want from me?" she pressed.

"We want to know how much your deposit was," Rollins shouted.

"The safe's empty. You've got the money. What difference does my deposit make?"

"We think Mr. Milton might be holding out on us."

"How much was in the safe?" she asked.

"Just tell us the deposit amount!" Rollins stalked back and forth in front of the bound bankers.

Isaac has the main deposits stashed away somewhere. That's what he meant by putting it in a safe place!

"I told you our deposit was only $1.00," she repeated.

"That's absurd!" Rollins boomed. "The store was full of customers when we rode by."

"We do a lot of business on credit," she explained.

Rollins stopped pacing and waved his finger at her. "Show us the receipt."

"What?"

"You said you had the receipt in your purse. Show us the receipt!"

"She can show me a whole lot more than a receipt!" the man behind her snarled as he ran the barrel of the gun slowly down her back and across her derriere. She spun around, holding her purse in front of her, forcing him to step back. His gun now was aimed at her chest.

A single-action Colt, and the hammer's not back. Mister, you're molesting the wrong woman.

Isabel opened her purse slightly and slipped her hand over the grip of the pistol. "You want proof? I'll give you proof."

"What have you got in there?" he snarled. He dropped his head to peek into her purse.

The moment his head lowered, the barrel of the Colt cracked like a hatchet splitting wood into the man's chin. His hat tumbled off his head, and his gun crashed to the floor. Blood streamed down his chin. By then she had a secure grip on his dirty hair and the barrel of the Colt shoved into his ear.

Both Rollins and DuBois had revolvers pointed at her.

Hammers cocked.

"Drop it, Marquesa!" DuBois shouted.

"You aren't going to fire that," Rollins scoffed. "It's probably not even loaded."

The explosion from her gun caused both men to dive for cover. She had pointed the gun to the ceiling, and the bullet tore its way through roof and shingles.

The man in her grip dropped to his knees and cried, "I'm deaf! Did she blow off my ear? I cain't hear nothin'! I cain't feel nothin'!"

The acrid smell of gun smoke filled the room.

"Drop the gun, Marquesa!" DuBois shouted.

"I'll kill your partner!" she snapped. "You know I'll kill him!"

"What'd she say? Get her off me! She's crazy!" the bleeding man screamed.

Someone beat on the front door and yelled, "What's going on in there? Is everything okay?"

"They're gatherin' out front, Cigar. Grab the money and let's get out the back way," Rollins ordered.

DuBois's face was almost bright red under the dirty beard. "I want all the money!"

"We'll just have to come back and pick it up another day!"

"I ain't going to leave her alive," DuBois growled.

Isabel could feel her hand starting to quiver. *Which one of these guys is in charge?*

"Kill her this way, and 100 men will ride after us. We pull out now, and not one will try it," Rosto Rollins exhorted.

With guns still pointed at her, Rollins and DuBois started backing toward the side door.

"Wait! Git me out of this!" the man on the floor shouted. "Git her off me!"

"You're on your own, Odin!" Rollins called out.

"What did he say? I cain't hear!"

"We goin' to leave him?" Cigar pressed.

"He got himself caught by a woman and has a gun at his head. He ain't much use to me," Rollins growled as he stuffed a money sack into his shirt.

"Hey! This ain't funny! Git her off me!" Odin shouted.

"What's going on in there?" a deep, resonant, and very familiar voice shouted. "Milton, are you all right?"

"I ain't through with you, Marquesa!" DuBois blazed. "I'll come back for all of you. You can count on that!"

"I cain't believe they'd go off and leave me!" Odin moaned.

The Marquesa didn't loosen her grip. "You'd better believe it."

"What?" he cried. "A proper woman wouldn't do this to a man."

She yanked his hair even tighter. "I haven't been proper very long. I'm just learning."

"What?"

Captain Dawson Mandara led a company of men into the bank. "Marquesa! Are you all right?"

"I got my dress soiled, and my hands are dirty. Other than that, I'll survive."

"Git her off me. She's a crazy woman! She deafened me and split my chin open," Odin cried out.

"Who are you?" Mandara asked.

"What? Cain't you see I'm bleedin' to death?"

Two of the men who burst in with Mandara shoved Odin to the floor and kept him down with their boots and their revolvers.

The captain hurried over to release Isaac Milton. "Is he the only one?"

"There are two others, but don't follow them, Captain," Milton cautioned. "It's DuBois and Rollins, and they'll shoot you down any way they can. They only got $200. I don't want anyone to lose their life over $200."

"I'm bleeding bad. You've got to help me," Odin whined. "I think she shot my ear off!"

"We'll be happy to haul him out to the cottonwood on the bluff and take care of him," one of the men offered.

"What did you mean by that?" Odin yelled.

"So you can hear," Isabel challenged.

"I'm gettin' better."

"Bandage up his chin and tie him up, boys. We'll have to figure out what to do with him," Milton ordered.

Captain Mandara addressed Isabel Leon, still holding her bloody-barreled gun. "Excuse me, Marquesa, but if you're all through with your bankin', maybe we could go have our supper."

"I've just been in the middle of a bank robbery," she stormed. "My hands are shaking, and my throat is so dry I could choke from just breathing, and you say . . ."

It was the widest smile she had ever seen from Captain Mandara.

She steadied herself. "But then, of course, I do need to eat supper sometime."

"I thought maybe a quiet meal would help you relax," he suggested.

"I need to clean up a little."

"And you'll need to change your dress," he commanded.

I knew he wouldn't like it! Change my dress? Are you telling me you won't eat with me unless I wear what you want me to wear? Well, I've got some news for you, Captain Dawson Mandara. You're not in the army anymore, and I'm not a . . .

"Change my dress?" she managed to choke out.

He took her arm and escorted her toward the front door. Leaning close, he spoke softly so that the others couldn't hear. "Frankly, your dress is stunning. But there is blood splattered on the back. If you soak it in cold water, I think it will wash out."

"Oh?"

"I don't know much about washing clothes, but I know quite a bit about trying to get blood off them."

The army man. "It will take me a few minutes."

"I reckon a good half an hour. I've waited for a woman to change cloth⟨es⟩ ⟨b⟩efore."

Yes . . . ⟨th⟩e married man. "I'll meet you at Quincys' then in half an hour."

"No. I said you needed a quiet supper. There's nothing quiet at Quincys' in the evenin'," he declared.

Her mind quickly inventoried the other eating establishments, a couple of lean-to chophouses and a few saloons. "What did you have in mind?"

"How would you like a private table in the dining room/ballroom of The Hotel Marquesa?"

"Wh-where?" she stammered.

"Miss Quincy and young Mr. Johnson have spread us a table in the ballroom. Would you join me?"

"You aren't kidding me, are you?"

"Why would I do that?"

Remember, Marquesa, he doesn't kid. "Captain, that is the most delightful surprise I've had in a long time! I will see you at the hotel!"

She ambled up the boardwalk to the Mercantile next door to the bank. She locked the door behind her.

The dress is stunning!

I knew it!

Well, I didn't really know it.

An intimate dinner!

Oh, Captain . . . oh, Captain, everything is so perfect . . . except for this little matter of your marriage!

Isabel retrieved a new galvanized bucket from the store and filled it with cold water. Then she soaked the hem of her blood-splattered dress. She scrubbed her hands over and over but could still feel the grease and grime of Odin's hair.

I'm glad I carry that little Colt.

I think I'm glad.

Maybe it's wrong.

But what would I have done without it? I could have fainted. I do a pretty good faint.

"Miss Lampierre? It is with a sorrowful heart that I must inform you that Lt. Geoffrey McCowell was slain at the battle of Vicksburg."

Isabel staggered backward, her hand on her forehead, her face grimaced in feigned grief, and then collapsed on the bed.

A Lily for the Lieutenant, Act III, finale.

She lay on the bed in her petticoats and scrutinized the ceiling. *It impressed them in New Haven.*

Finally she sat up.

Well, Carolina, I'm wearing your dress after all. It won't be stunning, of course. But with the right accessories, it could be alluring.

I could leave the top four buttons unfastened.

Lord, forgive me for that.

I do not need to be alluring. It's not that kind of supper. But I do like to be alluring sometimes.

Maybe that's wrong. Is that wrong, too, Lord?

She stood in front of the mirror. "Carolina Cantrell Parks, you get home, and you get home right now! I have a thousand questions to ask you! I'm going to do some things wrong, and then I'll regret it and ruin everything and spend the rest of my life as a spinster in a little hotel room looking out through lace curtains, wishing for what never will be!"

Bravo! Bravo! The audience can hardly contain themselves.

I ought to write a play sometime.

It could be based on my life story.

But I don't know whether to call it a comedy or a tragedy.

She tugged on Carolina's blue dress and began to fasten it.

All the way to her neck.

Well, Captain Mandara, you completely surprised me. Never in my dreams would I imagine you're the type to plan a little dinner like this! The first meal in The Hotel Marquesa!

Living in Cantrell has been different from anything I've ever done in my life . . . terrifying and tremendously exhilarating all at the same time.

Sort of like you, Captain.

She inspected herself in the mirror.

Are you ready for outfit number two, Captain?

I wonder what he looked like in his dress uniform? Tall, straight, a slight smile on his closed lips. The square chin. The absolutely disarming glance.

Oh, my.

Be careful, Isabel Leon. This isn't a scene from a play. This is real. It's just a relaxing, enjoyable supper with a friend.

A good friend.

If you don't think it's right for me to eat with a married man, Lord, then I won't.

That's all there is to it.

Oh, please . . . please . . . please let me do it!

A solitary kerosene lantern hung from a small chain that drooped down from the ceiling where the chandelier would one day sway. Under the lantern were two sawhorses with a door lying across them. On top of the door was stretched a white linen tablecloth. There were two candles glimmering from brass candlesticks, two china plates, silverware, and crystal goblets.

Next to the impromptu table stood Captain Dawson Mandara.

Suit, tie, hat in hand, polished black boots, neatly trimmed graying mustache, penetrating brown eyes, and that tiny smile that some regarded as a smirk.

"Welcome to the ballroom at The Hotel Marquesa," he trumpeted.

"Captain, this is enchanting! I'm almost in tears."

"Well, there might be tears of pain after having to sit on a nail barrel all evening. But I needed to do something. Someone told me I should have more fun."

"This is just about the most thoughtful thing anyone has ever done for me. To have a nice private dinner in a boomtown like this is a rare pleasure. But to have one in my hotel, it's . . ." Isabel picked up a linen napkin from the table and dabbed her eyes. "I'm sorry . . . I'm not a crying woman, Captain. Not usually."

"Tears are the overflow of the soul, Marquesa, whether tears of joy or sorrow. I am happy your soul is so full of joy. I would slide out your chair for you, but there's really no way of sliding a barrel."

She sat down, brushing her skirt as flat as she could. "We have a waiter, do we?"

"Two of them, I believe. Miss Quincy was watching for your departure from the store. She and July will be bringing our supper."

"Where did they get the china, crystal, and silver?"

"I supplied them. Some of our personal items from home arrived in Billings. I had them shipped out already."

"Is your house far enough along to need furnishings?"

"No, but it's far enough along to store them."

She lifted the napkin and spread it across her lap. "I don't believe I've ever seen a house go up that fast."

"Nor have I. It's surprising what can be done when all the boards are precut and the walls arrive framed and sided."

"It's chow time!" July blurted out as he and Molly Mae entered, both carrying large trays.

"July, that's not what you should say. You should say, 'Captain, Marquesa, dinner is served.'"

"It ain't dinner. It's supper," he corrected.

"He has a lot to learn," Molly Mae said as she set bowls and platters of steaming food in front of them. "But I'm a very good teacher."

I'll bet you are, honey. I'll bet you are.

"The Captain said to bring all the food at once 'cause you two didn't want to be interrupted," Molly Mae informed her.

"Nah," July corrected, "what he said was he didn't want us to have to make more than one trip over here."

"The way I said it was much more . . . intriguing," Molly Mae insisted.

"Intriguing?" July shrugged. "What's intriguing about eatin' supper?"

Molly Mae raised her eyebrows and shook her head at the Marquesa. "You can see I have much work left to do."

"Thank you very much!" Isabel replied.

July stacked the large wooden trays on the floor a few feet from the table. "You can thank the captain for most of the food. He had that pheasant and lobster shipped in on the stage."

"Pheasant and lobster? In Cantrell?"

"He even had to show us how to cook the lobster!" Molly Mae exclaimed.

The two fifteen-year-olds giggled their way out the door, leaving Isabel sitting staring at the feast in front of her.

"Captain, you continue to surprise me. This kind of thing only happens in plays and melodramas."

"Marquesa, in a couple of weeks, my work on your hotel will be through. My family will join me. You will have a hotel to get operational. Life is going to be hectic for a while for both of us. So I thought we could have our completion celebration a little early."

"I think it's a splendid idea. Where shall we begin?"

"I think a prayer of thanks would be appropriate in light of the construction of the hotel, my home . . . and your being kept from harm at the bank this afternoon."

He means, he'll pray, I trust.

The captain prayed.

They both ate.

And they talked.

And talked.

The night noise from town was only a slight hum in the background as they discussed all the details of the hotel, the ready-made house, and the future of Cantrell.

The coffee was cold by the time Isabel picked at her rice pudding. She didn't care.

"I'm a little apprehensive about hiring staff," she announced. "Right now I'm wondering if I can run the place with six to eight employees."

"It will be difficult to keep any of them very long," the captain advised.

"That does bother me. I'm afraid I'll just get some trained, and they'll leave." She glanced at the shadows of the ballroom.

"Unless they have roots here for some other reason. Family, friends, or something."

"Yes, well, not many have very deep roots in Cantrell." *Captain, I wonder if you dance.*

"I have a suggestion, but I want you to understand there is no compulsion on your part," he offered.

"What is that?" *Of course, you dance. All army officers dance, don't they?*

"My Nellie would make a good worker. She still has schoolwork in the fall, but that would only be about half a day. I think she would do well at housekeeping the rooms."

"Really? Do you think she'd be willing to work for me?" *If he has an orchestra hidden on the stage, I'll lose any self-control I have left.*

"She has begged me to ask you in several letters."

"Well, she's hired!" *Who am I kidding? Self-control?*

The captain loosened his tie and unfastened the top button. "I think you should interview her first."

"Oh, I know I want her." *And I want her father!*

"She needs to look you in the eye and ask you herself for a job. I won't tell her it's for certain until she interviews."

"That's wonderful." She sipped water from a crystal glass. *I should pour this on my head!* "How about Georgia? Would she like to work some, too? I know she's only thirteen, but if she'd like to work in the kitchen or with Nellie, I'm sure I could . . ."

"She would be thrilled to earn some money, but please don't put her with Nellie."

"How old are the boys?"

"Too young." The captain turned to the side and stretched his legs out in front of him. "Not too young to learn a little responsibility, but too young to get any decent work from them."

"Well, as soon as you think they're ready, I'll use them, too. Oh, but you'll probably want to teach them how to build."

"That thought did cross my mind. Of course, if I . . ."

"If you what?"

"Well, it's not a real possibility, but if I ever got reinstated in the army, we'd all have to pack up and move, of course."

The Marquesa sipped her cold coffee and gazed at the captain through the flickering shadows of the almost empty room.

"Captain, I have a personal question to ask you."

"And I have a dozen to ask you."

"You do?"

"Yes, but I promised myself I wouldn't," he disclosed.

"Why?"

"They might seem to you inappropriate. Go ahead. Ask your question." As always, he stared right into her eyes.

Isabel had a sudden urge to put on more lipstick and perfume. *Think of something, quick, Marquesa.* "I'm curious about the origin of the name Mandara. Is it perhaps Spanish or Basque?"

"No, but that's a good guess. My father was a delta barge oper-ator in New Orleans. Cajun to the core."

"Cajun?"

"Mama was from northern Ireland. She died when I was twelve, and Daddy sent us kids to live with my aunt. She and her husband made the run into Kansas. That's where I lost any south-ern accent I had. All I carry nowadays from that heritage is a nice permanent tan and a fiery heart."

"Do you have brothers and sisters?" Isabel quizzed.

"At last count one brother, Antoine, was still alive. But I wouldn't have any idea where he is. My sisters moved back to Louisiana after the war. Both of them died there. Claudine died of malaria. Erin had scarlet fever."

The captain stared off into the darkness.

"It sounds extremely sad."

"We don't get to choose who lives and dies. We just accept what we've been assigned and do our best not to disappoint the Lord. Growing up with my aunt and uncle in Kansas brought sev-eral good things into my life."

"Oh?"

"My uncle's best friend ended up being a congressman. That got me an appointment to West Point. And it was in Kansas where I met the Lord . . . and Claire." He looked back at Isabel with quiet eyes. "You see, God was in control all along. Now how about you, Marquesa? It's your turn for a life story."

"You don't want to hear it all," she began. "I was born in Puerto Rico. My mother was French. My father was Spanish. Well, that's not completely true. Anyway, we moved to New York when I was three. When I was five, dear Daddy went back to Puerto Rico, but not without sitting me down and explaining that I was not his daughter, which can be rather devastating when you're five."

"Or at any age," the captain suggested.

"Yes, I'm sure you're right."

"Did your mother ever explain the situation?"

"No, she said I knew all I needed to know."

"Is she still living?"

"Yes, she is," Isabel replied. "I usually see her when I'm performing in New York. She always comes to the theater."

"To watch her daughter?"

"No, to ask for money. As far as I know, she never watched any of my plays or musicals."

"Well, that sounds more sad than my story."

"We are protected when we're young. I didn't know it was sad. I enjoyed my childhood. Well, most of the time I enjoyed it. Mother drinks a lot." She set down her cup, still half-filled with cold coffee. "Now, Captain, just what were those personal things you wanted to ask me?"

"Marquesa, I don't want to be out of place. If this conversation gets too personal, just tell me to be quiet."

Dawson Mandara . . . get to the point!

"Captain!"

Molly Mae's panicked cry brought both of them to their feet. "Captain, July went after them! He got a shotgun and horse and went after them, and nothing I could do would stop him!"

"July went after who?" Isabel asked.

"DuBois and Rollins!" Molly Mae cried.

"Why on earth did he do that?" the captain asked.

"He didn't know it was Rollins with DuBois until Mr. Ostine mentioned it over supper. It was Rosto Rollins's gang that killed his mama and daddy in Custer City!"

The captain turned to Isabel. "Rollins killed his parents?"

"I didn't know who was involved. But July told me once that his parents were caught in the crossfire at a bank robbery."

"July said he was going to kill Rollins! Captain . . . Marquesa . . . you have to do something!"

— Six —

THE SHEETS FELT ROUGH. The flannel gown stiff and dirty. The comforter seemed to weigh 200 pounds. The down mattress was lumpy. The pillow feathers scrunched and crackled every time Isabel Leon tossed and turned.

The air in the bedroom was stuffy and lifeless. The aroma from a vanilla candle she had burned earlier in the day now smelled like a rotting bouquet. Her back throbbed with a stiffening pain. The headache she got when Captain Mandara rode off into the Montana darkness seemed to play a throbbing, neverending chorus in her skull. At 2:30 A.M. she quit staring at the blackness of her ceiling and got up.

Wearing her green silk robe over the flannel gown with tiny pink flowers and a pair of Carolina Cantrell's slippers, Isabel carried a lit kerosene lantern out into the storeroom and built a fire in the woodstove. Within ten minutes there was a pot of coffee boiling. Then came a soft knock at the door.

It's them! No, July has a key. Maybe it's the captain. Perhaps he couldn't find July. What if he did? What if DuBois and Rollins killed both of them and now are coming after me? I need my gun. No, Lord, I've got to trust You, don't I?

The knocking persisted, this time a little louder. Isabel scooted over to the door, still unarmed. Her ear on the door, she listened for a man's voice.

What she heard was a girl's soft whimper.

"Marquesa? It's me, Molly Mae. I see your light on. May I come in?"

Isabel unlocked the door quickly and swung it open.

Wearing her father's thick heavy wool coat over her flannel gown and moccasins, Molly Mae Quincy scooted into the store and edged through the shadows over to the woodstove. Her blonde hair caught the glimmering reflection of the one lantern, as did her anxious blue eyes.

"I couldn't sleep," she admitted.

Isabel poured herself a cup of coffee and then one for Molly Mae. Without saying anything else, both women dragged the straight-backed wooden chairs up to the woodstove and sat down facing each other. The aroma from the cups smelled of morning, even though the sky would remain black for several more hours.

"I've been sitting in the cafe staring out the front window ever since the captain left," Molly Mae admitted.

Both their voices were hushed, even though there was no one around to eavesdrop.

"I went to bed and lay there wide awake," Isabel admitted.

Molly Mae sniffed the steam from her coffee cup. "They'll be back pretty soon, don't you imagine?"

Isabel glanced across at the soft, smooth complexion of a fifteen-year-old and the worried eyes that defied age.

A woman worried about her man looks the same at any age. Molly Mae's got a legitimate concern. July is wholeheartedly hers. And the captain? He's my . . . builder . . . and friend. That's all. But my heart keeps trying to send my brain a different message.

"I was thinking," Isabel suggested, "even if the captain caught up with July, they might build a fire and wait until day breaks before they head back. It kind of feels like a storm blowing in. It would make sense to wait until morning, wouldn't it?"

"Yes," Molly Mae admitted, "but nothing else makes sense. I don't understand how July can run off and get himself killed. He doesn't know anything about shooting men. Rollins is a notorious killer."

"Miss Molly Mae Quincy, I've been around twice as many years as you have. And, being in the theater, I've certainly had to deal with a considerable number of men. I'm convinced that we will never totally understand why men behave the way they do."

"Why would he want to ride off into the dark and get himself killed when he could have stayed with me?" the young lady sniffled.

The Marquesa stared across the darkened store and thought of darkened years. "Don't take it personal. Actually this is one case where I do understand July's behavior. It must be a lifelong terror to watch both your mother and father get shot down. July told you about that scene in Custer City, didn't he?"

"Yes, but that happened years ago." Molly Mae's small, dainty mouth was lifted in a pout.

"He was a young boy, totally helpless to assist his mother or father." Isabel suddenly felt like a schoolteacher. "It eats on a person. Especially a boy. July spent all those years alone. Bumming a meal. Working for someone . . . anyone. No family or close friends."

"Yes, but he has a home now. He has Mr. and Mrs. Parks, and you, Marquesa . . . and me! Why doesn't he let the sheriff or the U.S. Marshal handle this? It's their problem, not his."

Isabel gazed down at her dull beige slippers and wiggled her toes. "Until this land settles down, there is no law in remote places like Cantrell. Even though Rollins was convicted once, he obviously found a way to get out. The chances are pretty good that no one is going to track him down now. The land is too big. Too unsettled. Too wild. So July sees this as a way to help out after being so helpless before. He's doing this partly for his parents, and he's—"

"But this won't help his parents one twit," Molly Mae intoned somewhere between a plead and a whine.

"And," the Marquesa continued, "I think he's doing it for the sake of justice. If this land is ever to be settled and established for families in the future, there has to be a commitment to law and order. Bringing one killer to justice helps the whole land become more fit for settlement. Some men, and boys, think that way."

"Yes," Molly Mae whimpered, "but what if he fails and gets himself killed? It will just make this land more barbarian."

"That might be. But at the time he left town, I'm sure July had no intention of failing."

"I begged him not to go. With tears . . . and everything!"

Everything? Just what did you do, young lady?

"Well, Miss Molly Mae Quincy, over the years I learned that there are some requests we should never ask of a man. A good man cannot violate his conscience without completely breaking his spirit. Such a man, no matter what he does after that, is not much better off than a drunk or a dolt."

Molly Mae leaned so far forward that her shoulders were even with her knees. "But how do we know what demands not to make on a man?"

Isabel Leon shook her long black hair from shoulder to shoulder. "That, dear girl, is what women have been trying to figure out for centuries. Each man is different. You've got to know him and learn from experience."

"Like tonight?"

"Yes."

"Are you saying that when he rides back to town, I should forgive him and not be angry and pout?"

Isabel sipped her coffee and then nodded her head. "Molly Mae, if I were you, when July comes riding into town, I'd hug that boy, kiss him, and say, 'I just about died from worry with you gone.'"

A wide, wonderfully innocent grin broke across Molly Mae's face. "You would?"

"Yes." The Marquesa sipped the lukewarm coffee.

"That sounds a lot better than being furious at him and not speaking to him for days."

"And a lot more fun." The Marquesa raised her dark sweeping eyebrows.

"Is that the way you're going to greet the captain?"

"If he were my man, that's what I'd do. But he's just a friend, of course."

"Marquesa, may I ask you something very, very personal?"

Oh my, this could be embarrassing. "Yes, you may. But that doesn't necessarily mean I'll answer."

"How come a woman your age isn't married?"

My age? How old do you think I am? "It's pretty easy for a woman to say she just hasn't met the right man. The truth is, I probably met him and was too busy being an actress to notice. For fifteen years I've been living in one town for a season . . . or a week . . . or a night . . . and moving on. You get to visit with a lot of men but not know very many well."

"But don't you ever get tired of traveling?" Miss Quincy stood and pulled off her father's coat, tossed it across a barrel of carriage bolts, and sat back down. "Didn't you ever say to yourself, 'I've had it. . . . That's it. I'm going stay right here'?"

"That happened once," Isabel admitted.

"What did you do?"

"I built a hotel."

"Oh, you mean here in Cantrell!" Molly Mae stood and spun toward the door. "Is that them?"

The Marquesa set down her coffee cup and cocked her head sideways. "Sounds like a wagon out in the street."

Molly Mae padded over to the door, opened it a crack, and peered out. She shut the door and turned back around. "It's just a wagon." She walked slowly through the store coming back to the table. "Marquesa, do you pray very much?"

"A lot more than I used to." Isabel folded her hands on her lap. Her fingers felt thin, weak, and cold.

"Why more now?"

Leon studied Quincy's slender face and inquiring eyes. *Was I ever young, beautiful, and innocent?* "Molly Mae, did your parents ever tell you about Jesus when you grew up?"

"Yes, they always read the Bible aloud. And anytime we're near a church on Sunday, we go. Is that what you mean?" She pulled her one long braid of blonde hair in front of her and rubbed it with her fingers.

"Yes, well, when I grew up, I didn't have anyone around to tell me about things in the Bible." The Marquesa opened the iron door of the woodstove and shoved in a fat piece of red fir. "Once in a while I'd learn some things from a friend, a person like Logan, for instance. He knew a lot about the Bible actually. So during all those years in the theater, I didn't pray much. I didn't know if God was real, and if He was, I figured He didn't want to listen to me."

Molly Mae dipped her finger in her lukewarm coffee and then stuck her finger in her mouth. "I guess I've always known that God hears me when I pray."

"I know that now."

"What made you change your mind, Marquesa?"

"About a year ago, when I finally started making some right

STEPHEN BLY

choices. It was people like Carolina and Ran. Did July tell you how much Carolina and I disliked each other when we first met?"

Molly Mae rolled her eyes. "He just said it was like tossing two bobcats in a gunny sack."

"When I came back from San Francisco, I started reading Carolina's Bible. Then all this trouble in Billings last week, and . . . well, I finally made up my mind. Where did all this conversation begin?"

Molly Mae ran the end of her braid across her lips like a brush. "I was going to ask you to pray for July and Captain Mandara."

"Oh, I have."

"No, I meant right now."

"Aloud?" the Marquesa gulped.

"Yes."

Isabel Leon gazed into the expectant eyes of Molly Mae Quincy. *I can't pray in front of someone else. I don't know how to do it. Lord, this is too new. It's just between You and me. My new faith is a private thing. I can't . . .*

The Marquesa bowed her head. "Eh, Lord? Now Molly Mae and I are really worried about July and the captain—"

Suddenly Molly Mae blurted out, "Yeah, we're afraid those men are going to shoot them dead! Please, don't let it happen, Lord."

Miss Quincy's silence caused Isabel to feel uncomfortable. She coughed, then continued, "We would like You to bring them back to us safely because—"

"Because I love July, and the Marquesa loves . . ."

I love whom?

"Amen!" Molly Mae blurted out.

Isabel Leon was staring at Molly Mae Quincy in the shadows of the Cantrell Mercantile when the fifteen-year-old raised her head and opened her eyes.

"I'm sorry, Marquesa. I didn't mean to say that. I've never . . . I just don't know how to pray out loud good like you."

Isabel could feel cold sweat on her forehead; her hands were clammy, and her knees still quivered. *Good like me? I haven't had this much stage fright in fifteen years.*

"Marquesa, can I wait the rest of the night over here with you? Please!"

"Do your parents know you are over here?"

"I left them a note."

"Yes, well, by all means, stay with me. I'd enjoy the company."

The two women downed the rest of their coffee and then sat in silence until Isabel's eyelids grew heavy, and she started to nod off.

"Marquesa!"

Isabel Leon sat up straight. "Yes?"

"I'm getting sleepy. Let's talk."

"What would you like to talk about?"

Molly Mae shrugged. "I don't know. I just don't want to go to sleep."

"Let's don't talk about July and the captain," the Marquesa insisted. "We'll just get more worried."

Molly Mae stood up and looked at the door. "Did you hear that?"

"No."

Miss Quincy's flannel gown was almost identical to Isabel's. "Okay, what do you want to talk about?"

"How about you picking a subject, and then I'll pick a subject," the Marquesa suggested.

"Okay." Molly Mae beamed. "I want to know what it feels like to be in a play and have hundreds and hundreds of people watching you. I want to know what it's like being an actress. Now what's your subject?"

"I want to know what it feels like to be fifteen and in love."

"You were fifteen once; you know how it feels."

"I can't remember," the Marquesa sighed. "I want you to remind me."

Sometime before sunup they stumbled weary-eyed into the Marquesa's room and collapsed on the bed. As exhausted as they were, the banging on the front door brought both of them to their feet and scurrying across the store.

"Who is it?" Isabel called out.

"Drake Quincy. Is my daughter still there?"

Molly Mae opened the door several inches. "Hi, Papa."

"Marquesa, this girl isn't bothering you, is she?"

"Mr. Quincy, it has been a delight and comfort to have your daughter sit with me. She is quite a mature young woman."

Quincy stuck his head into the store and looked his daughter up and down. "Is the Marquesa talking about you?"

"Papa!" she pouted.

"Did they come back yet?" he queried.

"No." Molly Mae's slumped shoulders emphasized the answer.

"I reckon they wouldn't have started back until daylight," Mr. Quincy suggested.

"My thoughts exactly," Isabel concurred.

"Mama needs some help with serving breakfast," he advised.

"I'll be right there, Papa."

Mr. Quincy disappeared back out into the Montana morning.

Molly Mae padded across the store and retrieved her father's heavy wool coat. "I guess I need to go."

"Go on. We both better get to work."

Molly Mae lingered at the open door. "Thanks, Marquesa, for talking with me and praying and everything. I don't think I could ever be an actress, but in a lot of ways, I hope I can grow up to be just like you."

"What on earth for?"

"Oh, because you're so—so beautiful and self-confident, and because of the way you light up a room when you walk into it. You're such a good example for me."

"Molly Mae, Carolina Parks is a good example of how to live a meaningful life. I'm a good example of the grace of God."

"Well, I hope you never ever, ever move away from Cantrell because I really like having you for a friend."

"Molly Mae, those are about the nicest words I ever heard from a woman of any age."

"I meant them."

"I know you did. Now go to work." *Before I begin to cry.*

Using the skill of a seasoned performer with only a few minutes between costume changes, Isabel Leon got ready for the day. By the time Tiny Merwin and Adam Bray showed up to work in the Mercantile, she had clothes, jewelry, and makeup in place, as well as a fresh pot of coffee brewing on the woodstove.

It took her a few minutes to explain the situation of the night before at the bank . . . and the fact that July wouldn't be in for a while. She left the two clerks in charge and hiked over to the hotel.

All three carpenters were huddled around a little scrap-wood fire behind the building. "The captain's going to be late today. You men know what he needs done?"

"I reckon," nodded a gray-headed cabinetmaker she knew only as the "old man."

"Well, go ahead and get started."

"If we run out of somethin' to do, we could finish roofin' the captain's house," the old man replied. "It looks like a storm blowin' in."

"Yes, by all means, do that. Forget the hotel and go roof his house. We need to get that done before the rain."

Isabel hiked up the staircase at the back of the lobby. The upstairs at The Hotel Marquesa stood like a bride fresh out of the tub. Clean, perfect, ready . . . but needing hair combed, clothing, jewelry, and a touch of makeup.

As she had before, Isabel went room by room to stare at big empty boxlike rooms with windows. When she reached the upstairs sitting room, she opened the tall leaded-glass double doors and strolled out to the still unpainted veranda. She sauntered along the now-completed railing, the cool Montana air rushing past her face. She dragged an empty crate to the northwest corner where she could view both the road south to the mesa and the road north to the river.

"*Like a seaman's wife watching the seas for her man to return, the lonely queen gazed across the heath for a sign of the return of . . .*" The Prince's Last Ride, *Act II, Scene 1.*

The return of her what?

Her prince?

Her lover?

Her friend?

Lord, Molly Mae was right.

I think I love him.

She dropped her head into her hands and began to cry.

Lord, that's the way I am. Surely Jesus didn't die for me. How can You forgive my sins? At the very moment I believe and trust in You most, I fall in love with a married man. And I don't know if I can change!

Maybe You have some understudy parts in Your plan. I don't need to be a star. I don't have to be on the center stage. Just a stagehand or an understudy. That's all right with me. Maybe that's what I am—Claire Mandara's understudy.

If he would have said something or asked me to do something last night . . . anything, I would have let him!

I'm ashamed.

He's a good man. A loving family man. And I was willing to ruin it all.

Just for me.

I'm horrible.

But You knew that.

Maybe it's good that he's gone.

Isabel pulled a small lace and linen handkerchief out of her sleeve and wiped her eyes. Then she stood and adjusted her shawl, stepped up to the railing, and looked up and down the street.

Lord, for the last twelve hours I've been asking You to bring the captain safely back to me.

That's not right. Lord, bring him home safely for Nellie, Georgia, Phillip, Grant . . . and Claire. The pain of losing him to a murderer, or a Marquesa, is something none of them should have to bear.

After walking through the rooms that would be her suite, Isabel descended the stairs and paused for a moment in the ballroom. She stood and gazed at the door stretched across the sawhorses and the nail barrels squatting beside them.

Captain Mandara, you were about to ask me some potentially personal questions. It seems like days ago. Someday I would like to know, at least, what those questions were going to be.

Perhaps it is best I don't.

I don't know when I'll see the captain again, and I'm quite certain we'll never have a chat that private and personal again.

On the way back to the Mercantile, Isabel stuck her head into the Assay Office. Ted Ostine greeted her.

"How is everything in here this morning?" she asked.

"Fairly quiet once we assured everyone their money is safe," Ostine reported.

She strolled on into the room. There were no other customers. Ostine's white shirt looked freshly starched and pressed. His long brown mustache was heavily waxed. "Did you have some folks wanting to withdraw their deposits?" she asked.

"Only a couple. Most figured if DuBois and Rollins couldn't get anything out of us, it's a pretty safe place to put their money. Of course, we didn't tell them they threatened to come back and get the rest."

"Yes, well, do you have contingency plans for that?" Isabel tugged at the tight collar of Carolina's dress.

"Yes, we do."

"Good, but I don't want to know what they are."

"I wouldn't tell you if you asked." Ostine glanced at the locked safe. "Besides, I don't think we have to worry about those two. I heard that a vigilante posse was formed and went after them."

"Posse? Hardly. It was just July Johnson and Captain Mandara."

"They're both brave men."

"Yes, and it's my hope that they're smart men and that they'll return home quickly."

"Don't worry about them, Marquesa. We got some mighty good men in this town—men like Ranahan and Captain Mandara . . . and even young Mr. Johnson."

"Yes, I know that. Unfortunately, those 'good men' are all out of town at the moment. I'm glad to have you and Mr. Milton for neighbors."

"Isaac went to Billings last night. He took that man, Odin, to the sheriff."

Clutching her canvas purse in front of her, she rubbed the bridge of her nose with her right hand. "Good. I'm glad to get him out of town."

Ostine closed a ledger and slipped it into a drawer under the counter. "Lots more talk this morning about needing a town marshal."

"I'm all for it," Isabel concurred, "but how do we pay his salary?"

"I don't know. But most folks already know who they want."

"Ranahan?"

"Yep."

"I think they're right about that. Do you think we can elect someone marshal who isn't here?"

"I don't know." Mr. Ostine pushed his round gold-framed glasses up higher on the bridge of his long, narrow nose. "I suppose we'll need a mayor and council first."

"Would you or Mr. Milton be willing to serve?"

"I reckon we'd take our turns. Providing we had the right man for mayor."

Isabel could feel her thick black hair start to sag at the back of her head. "Who would that be?"

"Captain Mandara, of course. He's a natural-born leader," Ostine declared.

"The Parkses are going to be coming home in about two weeks. If we last until then, we should have some sort of community meeting and discuss all of this, I suppose." *I'm either going to cut my hair or wear it down. This is getting to be a bother. I am not Carolina!*

Two clean-shaven prospectors wearing new clothes entered the bank. "Marquesa, you're looking at a couple of rich hombres!"

She turned and smiled. "Struck some color, did you?"

"I ain't braggin', mind you, but we made more money in a week of diggin' than we did in a year in those dreary Black Hills."

"Well, boys, I'm really happy for you."

"Don't suppose you're going to have the hotel open this week?" The speaker was one of those men who looked somewhere between twenty-five and sixty-five years old.

"I'm afraid not," she replied.

"You takin' reservations?"

"I hadn't thought of it, but I suppose I could."

"Well, put us down for your two best rooms for the Fourth of July week. We'll come to town to celebrate!"

"And we'll pay for them right now," the other one bragged. "How much you want?"

"Deluxe rooms, right?"

"Not just deluxe but the best you got."

"I believe I'll charge $2.50 a night," she advised.

The one prospector pulled out two twenty-dollar gold pieces and dropped them into her hand. "That ought to do us for a week apiece."

She rolled the coins over in her hand. "I'll save the rooms for you."

"Thank you, Marquesa." The sleeves of his new shirt were several inches too long and made his fingers look like tiny stubs. "If we ain't here by July 1, you keep the money and rent the rooms to someone else."

"Oh, I'll save your money for whenever you do arrive in town."

"Marquesa, if we ain't here by July 1, we're either filthy rich or dead. Either way, the money's yours."

"All right, boys. That's the way we'll do it." The Marquesa turned back to Mr. Ostine. "Someone should order in some fireworks for the Fourth. We ought to have a celebration."

He rocked back on his heels. "I'll bring it up with Mayor Mandara."

Isabel returned to the Mercantile and busied herself helping Merwin and Bray. Business was fair but definitely slower. It gave her time to glance out the window about every time a rig or a rider pulled into view.

Twice during the morning, Molly Mae ran across the street to confer with the Marquesa. At straight up noon, Isabel Leon headed out of the Mercantile to have lunch at Quincys' Cafe. The clouds were stacking up and hanging heavy. She stepped back inside the store and retrieved her black shawl. Just as she tromped again across the porch, a lieutenant led twelve cavalrymen down Main Street. Most folks ceased what they were doing and stared at the troops as if they were a parade. The entire patrol stopped in formation in front of the store.

The lieutenant tipped his hat. "Ma'am, I'm Lieutenant Sarret." He was so clean-shaven that Isabel wondered if he was old enough to shave. He was tall, thin, and obviously intense.

"I'm Isabel Leon. Lieutenant Sarret, what are you doing in Cantrell?"

"I heard that a retired cavalry captain by the name of Dawson Mandara lives here."

"Yes, he does. However, he's out of town this morning. I'm a friend of his. Can I help in any way?"

The lieutenant dismounted and hiked toward her, leading the black horse by the reins. He stopped and turned back. "Master Sergeant, check in that cafe to see if they can accommodate thirteen of us for dinner."

"Yes, sir!" the man shouted and scampered down off his buckskin horse.

"Ma'am," the lieutenant began, "we've been following an escaped bank robber and murderer by the name of Cigar DuBois. Do you know if he's been in this area?"

She folded her arms in front of her. "Yes. He and a man by the name of Rosto Rollins tried to rob the bank next door yesterday."

"Rollins? He's a harder case than DuBois. Rollins killed two sheriff's deputies when he escaped from the Sweetwater County Jail," the lieutenant informed her. "What do you mean, they tried to rob the bank?"

"The bank manager and some local citizen prevented them from stealing very much."

"How many got killed?"

"None," she reported.

"None? That's unusual for those two. We've trailed DuBois all the way from fifty miles north of Fort Laramie. Tracked him clear across the Crow Reservation."

"We think they might have headed north toward Devil's Canyon," she added. "Captain Mandara and another person, our assistant postmaster, rode south to try to find their trail."

"We scoured the Big Horns for two weeks and rode up the southern trail this morning. There was no sign of DuBois or Rollins."

"So you didn't see Captain Mandara or a young man?"

"No, ma'am." The lieutenant rubbed his slick chin. "So DuBois and Rollins pulled a holdup, and no one got hurt. That is amazing."

The cool drift of air up from the river caused her to hold the shawl tight under her chin. "They had an accomplice by the name of Odin who was injured and was apprehended by local townspeople."

Lieutenant Sarret's blue eyes lit up. "Perhaps I could interrogate him."

"Mr. Milton at the bank drove him to Billings late last night. He should be in the county jail by now."

Lieutenant Sarret led his horse a little closer to the porch in order for a freight wagon to creak its way between him and his mounted troops. "If we can't pick up their trail along the river, we might have to go to Billings and pay a 'visit' to this man Odin. How badly was he injured?"

The Marquesa felt her toes begin to chill. "He bled a lot, but I don't think it was all that bad. I just shattered his chin with the barrel of my revolver."

The lieutenant stared at her from head to foot. "You? You're the citizen that apprehended the man?"

What do my looks have to do with this? Why do men use anything unusual as an excuse to study a woman's appearance? Keep your eyes focused a little higher, Lieutenant.

"Look around!" She adjusted his focus with the wave of her arm. "As you can see, Cantrell is a boomtown. We don't have a marshal. The county sheriff is too busy to come this far. So we do what we can."

"Yes, ma'am, I didn't mean to imply anything less than respect for your courage."

Lieutenant, your heart might be in the right place, but your eyes seem to be wandering. I know what a man's implying when he looks at me like that.

"Lieutenant!" the master sergeant called out as he trotted across the street. "They got room for us now."

"Good, have the men dismount and tie off at the cafe or the . . . Is that going to be a hotel?"

"Yes, it is. Actually it's my hotel," Isabel proclaimed.

"My word, do you own the entire town?"

"Hardly."

The sergeant took off his hat and nodded to her. "It's a handsome building, ma'am."

"Thank you. Captain Mandara is building it."

"You know Dawson, I mean, Captain Mandara?" the battle-tough sergeant asked.

"Yes, I do," she admitted. "I take it you know him as well."

"Served with him for ten years! Yep. I know him pretty good."

"Sergeant, tie up my horse," the lieutenant commanded.

"Yes, sir."

Sarret turned to Isabel. "Miss Leon, would you join me for dinner? I'd like to hear about this bank robbery attempt."

"Actually I was hoping to eat with the master sergeant," her voice sirened.

The sergeant, who looked about forty, with neatly clipped gray hair and mustache, turned back and beamed. "It would be my pleasure, ma'am."

"We have a mutual friend," she tried to explain to Sarret.

The lieutenant mumbled something and followed the enlisted men into the cafe.

Isabel ate very little, but the master sergeant forked down food like a man unsure of his next meal. She allowed him to gorge awhile before the questions began.

"Sergeant, were you with Captain Mandara when he was discharged?"

"Call me Tommy, ma'am." He tipped his hat and smiled, revealing tobacco-stained teeth. "The captain was illegally drummed out—that's what he was. He probably just said he was discharged. That's the way he is. He won't put down the army. If he hadn't done it, one of us would have. 'Course, they would have tossed us enlisted men in the brig and left us to rot."

"Tommy, I'd be very interested in your version of the story. You know how close-lipped the captain can be." She thought the meat on her fork was veal, but she couldn't remember what she had ordered. She pushed it across the plate.

"I figured you wanted to talk about him. It ain't my devilishly good looks that caused you to eat with me, is it?" He winked like a man who has done a good deal of winking.

"Actually," she ran her finger around the top of her coffee cup, "I was just looking for an excuse to get away from your lieutenant."

The master sergeant slapped his hand on the table, then leaned forward and spoke in hushed tones. "I know what you mean, miss, but he'll be all right once West Point wears off, and I've schooled him a little more. So you want to know about the captain? He graduated from West Point in '64. Served with Phillip Sheridan near the tail end of the war, where he made captain. I first met him in '70 right after he married Miss Claire Nell McCarty."

She fought to make sure there was no emotion in her voice. "Where were they married?"

"Fort Dodge, Kansas. Anyways, you don't want to hear all of that about the two of them. What a handsome couple! The kids look just like 'em. Have you met the children?"

"Not yet."

"Both the captain and me were under Gen. Jack Clarkston."

"*The* General Clarkston?"

"Yes, ma'am." The master sergeant leaned forward again and whispered, "In the presence of a lady and almighty God, I can't tell you what I think of him. It is my opinion that the world would be a better place if he were taken out and shot."

"Oh my!" Isabel's hand went to her mouth. "That's not what you read in the papers. Especially in the East."

"Do you want to know why the captain never made major? He's a military man that should be a general. But Gen. Clarkston saw to it he never even made major."

"Why?" Isabel stabbed a piece of cooked carrot with her fork.

"One time out in Dakota, we were moving some of Red Cloud's bunch back up to the reservation from the Indian Territory. A couple braves up and fled camp one morning. As it turned out, they met up with some buddies of theirs just north of the Platte. So General Clarkston had Captain Mandara send half a dozen men out to round them two up and bring them back." The sergeant crammed a forkful of meat and gravy into his mouth, swallowed hard, smacked his lips, and then began again.

"Well, they didn't come back by nightfall, and the captain wanted to send out a scouting party to see what happened. But the general refused."

"Why?" This time she popped the carrot bite into her mouth.

"We had some reporters from New York City in camp, and the

general figured they would write a story about how he let some of the Indians escape. So he refused to send out a relief column."

"He hid the fact that two men escaped?"

"Correct. By morning the men still hadn't returned, and Captain Mandara was beside himself, but the general again refused to send a scouting party."

"What happened then?"

"The captain stormed out of the general's tent, ordered up a patrol of twelve men, and rode out with them."

"Against the orders of a general?" she gasped.

"Yep. I rode with him that day."

"What happened?"

"We found the men surrounded by about fifty warriors. We managed to drive them off and rescue the men. Three of the six men were dead; the other three were wounded. One of 'em died back at camp."

"I presume there were repercussions?"

"Not for the general. But the captain paid sorely. The general locked every one of us up and started court-martial proceedings. But the captain told them that all of us were merely obeying his orders. They let us out after one day."

The Marquesa abandoned any idea of eating. "What happened to the captain?"

"General Sheridan intervened and got the matter dropped. But, as you might reckon, General Clarkston hated Captain Mandara after that. 'Course, us men would ride into Hades with him if he asked us. Captain Mandara is a man who understands the men under him."

"He didn't transfer to a different outfit?" she quizzed.

"General Clarkston wouldn't allow it. Not only that, but every time he sought to be promoted, Clarkston turned him down. We had majors and colonels that would come to Captain Mandara for advice. Everyone knew it was just spite." The sergeant scraped the lumpy white gravy off his plate with half a biscuit.

"You still haven't told me why he was discharged," she reminded him.

"I know. I know. I'm gettin' there." The sergeant rubbed his

wide, crooked nose. "Now one night later on, when we were sta-
tioned at Fort Gambel, it was cold, and the captain let us build fires
for those on guard duty. About midnight Captain Mandara came
out to check on the men just to make sure they weren't getting
frostbit or nothin'. That's the kind of man he is. So there were four
or five men, me, and the captain outside, mostly huddled around a
fire trying to keep warm, when Mrs. Clarkston came running out
of the general's house. She was barefoot, and her flannel gown was
half torn off her. She was bleedin' all over the face, screaming, and
crying that the general was drunk and trying to kill her."

"That's incredible!" Isabel gasped.

"We had seen the general's wife with bruises before, but she
always had some explanation for them. Well, the captain yanked
off his coat and wrapped her up. We gave her our blankets and got
her near the fire. General Clarkston came storming out of the
house, screaming and cussing and waving his .45 revolver, saying
that he was going to kill her.

"By now most of the camp was awake and out watchin' all of
this. We had two colonels and four majors with us, but they just
stood there on their porches watching, afraid to do what, by regu-
lation, they should. The general stomped over to us and demanded
we give his wife back to him."

"What happened then?" she quizzed.

"The captain refused. So the general threatened court-martial
and ended up pointin' the gun at the captain's head and cocking
the hammer back, saying he'd kill him."

Isabel could envision the stoic look on the captain's face.
"Didn't anyone try to stop him?"

"We just stood there with our mouths open. No one knew what
to do. That was when the general's wife called out that she wanted
to go back with the general. We tried to talk her out of it, but she
insisted. If she wanted to go back, what could we do?"

"She obviously said that only to keep Captain Mandara from
getting killed," Isabel surmised.

"I reckon that's what the captain thought, too." The sergeant
picked his teeth with his fingernail and paused a moment. Then he
leaned over the table and continued in hushed tones. "So she was

barefoot, and there was a dustin' of snow on the ground. She was still wrapped in the captain's coat, hiking back alongside the general. Well, he got to screaming that she was not about to wear another man's coat, and he pulled it off her, exposin' some of her privates to the whole camp. She started cryin' and grovelin' in the snow to retrieve the coat when the general just up and slugged her right in the nose."

"No!" Isabel covered her mouth with her hand to keep her voice down.

"That was when Captain Mandara lost control. He tackled the general and battered him to the ground with his fists. I've never seen a man get whipped so quick and so thorough. At that moment most of us were hopin' the captain would just kill him. And I think he would have, but the two colonels ran across the grounds and pulled him off.

"When the general recovered, he had the captain arrested and immediately proceeded with court-martial. Some of the officers intervened with testimony, supporting the captain. But this time Sheridan said the best he could do was give the captain a discharge. It was either that or court-martial."

"And the captain chose discharge?"

"It was a sight to see, the day the captain left the fort." The sergeant wiped the corner of his eyes with a cloth napkin. "Trail dust," he explained.

"What happened?"

"I suppose the officers said their good-byes inside. But when Captain Mandara came out wearin' civilian clothes, every enlisted man at the fort stood at attention right where they was. Scattered all over them grounds was about 400 men at attention. He stood right there on the steps and saluted them. We stayed at attention until he left the fort."

"Whatever happened to Mrs. Clarkston?"

"They're still married, so I hear."

"No!" *There are worse things than not being married.*

"Yep. I don't think they live together too much, but they are still married. I guess she likes them Washington, D.C., balls and all that." The sergeant gazed at a huge piece of apple pie with white melted cheese over it as intently as the lieutenant had gazed at the Marquesa. "I got myself out of that outfit as soon as I could. Most all of us did. There are lots of really good men in the army. Clarkston ain't one of them. On the other hand, ain't none much better than Captain Mandara. But I reckon you know that." He stuffed his mouth with apple pie.

"I haven't known the captain long, but I've certainly found him to be a man of integrity." She stared across the crowded cafe. Everyone seemed busy eating and talking at the same time. "It's difficult to imagine that the general's wife went back to such a deplorable situation."

"Life is hard to figure, isn't it?" He swallowed hard, then dove in for another huge bite of pie. When that bite had been chewed and swallowed, he wiped his mouth with the back of his hand. "Life ain't always fair. Here's a lady in a horrible marriage, and she stays with it. The captain moves his family down to east Texas, and in six months Claire gets sick and dies. That don't hardly seem right, does it?"

Every muscle in Isabel Leon's body felt frozen. She didn't move her arms, her fingers, her lips, her tongue. Nor did she blink her eyes. Her heart rose; she felt dizzy.

"Ma'am, are you all right? Looks like you had a spell."

"Claire's dead?" she choked out the words.

"For nearly five years. Got that flu the year the epidemic swept through Galveston. You didn't know that?"

It was not a glamorous scene. She could almost see it from a distance. She had excused herself and then numbly strolled out of the cafe, ran across the dusty street, tears streaming. She almost got run over by a freight wagon. She burst into the Mercantile, startling both clerks and customers. She slammed the door to her room behind her and threw herself on the bed and cried.

Tiny Merwin knocked at the door. "Marquesa, is everything okay?"

"Yes!" she sobbed and rolled over on her back.

I'm in tears, near hysteria, and he asks is everything all right. Why do men do that? Do they think we like being in this condition? How in the world do I know if I'm all right?

That's the absolute best news and the most horribly depressing news

I ever got in my life. I feel like dancing and singing on the roof of the hotel and then jumping off.

She pulled the pillow out from under the comforter and wiped her eyes on the pillowcase. Then she put the pillow under her head and sighed.

I've known him for six weeks, and most of the time I wished he wasn't married. But I didn't wish that Claire was dead. I just wanted some romantic world where we both were perfect and pure and unattached.

Claire died.

Nellie and Georgia . . . Oh my, that explains Georgia . . . and Phillip and Grant don't have a mother. I've been whining around because he's married, and I never once thought about those children being without their mother.

She sat straight up on the bed. "He lied to me!" she blurted out.

He led me to believe his wife was alive. He even told me she was alive, didn't he? Didn't he talk about picnics and child-raising and how she cooked . . . or did he? Did he say now, or did he say then? Did I just assume he was talking about her in the present, but he meant it in the past?

Captain Dawson Mandara, you never once, not once, said in a clear statement that you were a widower! You made me believe you still love her!

She flopped back down on the bed.

Of course, he probably still does love her.

Obviously, he didn't want me to know she was gone. Why would he do that? Because he didn't want me to get serious. He wasn't interested in me and figured being married would keep me away! He didn't want me to pursue this relationship, did he?

But . . . but why all the long talks? Why the private little dinner in the ballroom? Captain, you were leading me on! If you didn't . . .

I can't believe I fell for it.

I can't believe this.

It's just like New York. Nothing changes!

"Oh, Marquesa, let's have a little tete-a-tete . . . but it can't be permanent. After all, I'm a married man!"

Love them and leave them.

*But you knew I'd find out when your family moved to Cantrell and
there was no Claire. What did you think would happen then?*

Are you toying with me, Captain Dawson Mandara?

*But he's not that way. True blue. Defender of women. Even if it
costs him a career.*

She began to sob uncontrollably.

This time it was Adam Bray who knocked on the door and
called out, "Marquesa, are you sure you're all right?"

"Yes!" she sobbed. "Everything's perfect! Now leave me alone!"

"Yes, ma'am . . ." came a faint reply.

Isabel Leon pulled herself up from the bed and stumbled across
the room. She dipped the flour sack towel in the bowl of tepid
water and began to wipe her face.

I don't know if I love him or hate him.

It's one of the two.

Or both.

The United States Cavalry left under a curtain of thick, drooping black clouds around 2:00 P.M. The three carpenters reported
that the captain's house was roofed around 4:00 P.M. And just
before dark, it began to rain. The street turned muddy and slick.
The customers left, and the Marquesa was left alone in an empty
store, with lamps burning and front door open.

Her eyes were red.

And tired.

But dry.

She pulled off her shoes and her stockings and wiggled her toes.
The coffee in her cup was lukewarm, but she was too tired to go and
warm it up from the pot on the stove.

*At this rate, I'll be lucky to last two more days. In the past twenty-
four hours, I've had my life threatened by bank robbers, had an intimate
supper with the captain, seen him ride off in the dark, spent most of the
night awake, worked all day . . . and had an emotional rocket explode
in my heart.*

I need a break.

"Hi, Marquesa!"

She didn't bother to stand. At the door, with a basket in one hand and umbrella in the other, stood Molly Mae Quincy.

"I brought some supper over for you and me. Are you hungry?"

"I don't know. I suppose."

Molly Mae, wearing her father's rubber boots, tromped across the store to the stove.

Isabel sorted through the basket of food. "You have enough in here for six people."

"I was hoping for four. They have to be back soon, right?"

"I don't know anymore, Molly Mae. I don't know which way they went. The lieutenant said they weren't on the south road to the Big Horns. I don't even know if the captain caught up with July. So maybe they're together, maybe they aren't . . . maybe they went south . . . or east . . . or west. Maybe they're in trouble, or perhaps they're safe."

"Wherever they are, they're wet," Molly Mae added. "Marquesa, if they don't come in before bedtime, can I spend the night with you again?"

"Of course, if your parents agree."

"They said it was all right, but if I become a bother, you should kick me out."

"You have to promise me a couple of things."

"What?"

"That we'll get more sleep than last night and that we won't sit around talking about all the bad things that might have happened to them."

"I promise."

They listened to the rain pelt the roof of the Mercantile. The steady rhythm of the downpour filtered out any other sounds. The only additional noise they heard were the words of their lips and the wistful sighing of their hearts.

After standing out on the covered front porch until it got dark, they scooted their chairs over by the woodstove.

"Marquesa, would you show me how to use makeup?"

"What on earth for?"

"So I can look beautiful like you."

"Do you know why I wear makeup?" the Marquesa asked.

"No, why?"

"So I can look as beautiful as you."

"Me?"

"Molly Mae, a fifteen-year-old girl's complexion is just about perfect. You don't need to worry much."

"That's what my mother says. But I'd still like to learn. That way I'll be prepared when . . ." Her voice softened, and she glanced down.

"When you're old like me?"

"I didn't say that."

"Well, I'll show you a few things I've learned from the theater. But I do believe you've got ten to twelve years before you need any of them."

"Could we have the first lesson now?"

"Let's wait until we both have a little something to eat."

They picked at the basket supper. Finally the Marquesa looked over at the cookie-eating fifteen-year-old. "Molly Mae, I have a question for you."

"Yes?"

"Did you know that Captain Mandara is a widower?"

"Oh, yes. Too bad about his wife dying of the flu down in Texas, isn't it?"

"How long have you known that?"

"For at least a month. July told me all about it."

"July? July knew he is a widower?" Isabel gasped.

"Everyone in town knows that." Molly Mae threw her hand over her mouth. "Oh, my word . . . you mean . . . you didn't know?" She began to giggle.

"I don't see one thing funny," the Marquesa snapped.

"You don't?"

"Certainly not!"

"It's just . . . I mean, you've been all over . . . and on the stage and everything. I figured you knew everything . . . about, well . . ."

"About what, young lady?" Isabel demanded.

"Well, gosh, Marquesa, everyone in town knows how smitten he is with you."

"Smitten? Is that what it is?"

"That's what he calls it."

"The captain has told you he's smitten with me?" Isabel questioned.

"Oh, yes. But he told me more than that. Why did you think he wanted that private little dinner last night?"

"To talk over the hotel plans."

"Didn't he tell you about how he feels and what his children said when he wrote and mentioned they might be getting a new mama and—"

"He did what!" The words exploded from her lips and brought her to her feet.

Molly Mae's eyes widened. "He didn't say any of that last night?"

"No, he didn't. He did say there were some personal things he wanted to talk about, but before we got to them, you came running in about July."

"You were in there talking for over three hours! He never said any of that?"

"No, he didn't."

"Oh." Molly Mae dropped her blonde head to her chest. Her voice was almost inaudible. "Oh, heavens, I busted in on you and ruined everything, didn't I?" She started to weep.

Isabel brushed her eyes, but there were no tears.

"Molly Mae, relax. Don't cry now. You haven't messed up everything."

"Yes, I have!" she whimpered.

"No, you haven't."

"Yes, I did!"

"Well, maybe just a tad."

Molly Mae stopped crying and looked straight at the Marquesa. "Really?"

"Look, we'll get this all straightened out once the captain returns."

"You really think so?"

"Certainly." *Actually it's getting so complicated I can't even guess what will happen from here.*

"But . . . but what if, you know . . . he never comes back, and you never get to hear those things he wanted to talk to you about?"

"Then I shall hate you forever."

Molly Mae gasped.

"I'm teasing you. Remember, we weren't going to talk about them not coming back?"

"Oh, yeah."

"So, Miss Quincy, what exactly did the captain want to talk to me about last night? Since you are the one that interrupted us, I think you might fill me in on what I missed."

"He told me he had to find some way of telling you how smitten he is with you. What do you think he meant by that?"

"I hope to find out."

"Anyway, July said the reason the captain took so long to get around to talk to you was because he was afraid you would find him presumptuous and impertinent."

"Just why would I think that?"

Molly Mae took a deep breath and let it out slowly. "Well . . he told me and July one time that he thought you were young, vibrant, intelligent, and without doubt the most handsome woman he ever met. He said it was ludicrous to think you'd be interested in an older man with four active children and a background that included being kicked out of the army."

"He told you two that?"

"Yeah. What's ludicrous?" Molly Mae gritted her straight white teeth.

"Outlandish, laughable . . . preposterous."

"Do you think that you two getting married would be ludicrous?"

"Married? I hardly think . . ."

"The captain said he wasn't good enough for you. Said you deserved someone younger and richer, someone who hadn't burned all his bridges and stuff like that. He even told July he was praying that some rich, young mine owner would come along and court you."

The Marquesa paced the room with her arms folded in front of her. "I can't believe this."

"What? That the captain feels this way?"

"Yes. And that you and July knew this and I knew nothing!"

"See, if he doesn't come back, you'll go to your grave hating me," Molly Mae sniffled.

"That's not true. I'll forgive you."

"You will?"

"Certainly. In twenty, thirty years maybe."

Molly Mae held her breath until Isabel relaxed and smiled.

"Do you love the captain, Marquesa?"

"Why is it I keep thinking he ought to be here asking me these things instead of you?"

"You're right. I shouldn't be prying into other people's business."

"Young lady, you know more about my affairs than I do! Which means, you know the answer to your question."

"Yeah. I know you love him. But I don't know if you want to marry him."

"Molly Mae, I don't know if I want to marry him either. I'm going to need a whole lot more than just some second-hand talk, that's for sure."

"Oh? What are you going to need?" Molly Mae raised her blonde eyebrows.

"That was just a figure of speech. I didn't mean I would need . . . of course, if we got married, I'd need . . . what I mean is . . ."

"Yes?"

"I just think I should . . . well, I need to hear all of this from the captain's lips." *That's not all I need from his lips!* "What I'm trying to say is that I need to know his heart in this matter."

"Oh, that. Well, I told you what is in his heart."

"Molly Mae, would you rather have me tell you how July feels about you, or would you like to have him tell it to you himself?"

"I see what you mean. But, you know, you could tell me what July thinks, too. I mean, that wouldn't be as good as him saying it, but it would do for the time being. What does he think about me?" Molly Mae urged.

"He thinks you are, without question, the most wonderful girl God ever created."

"Really? Those were his words?"

"Close enough." *At least, that's what his eyes keep telling me.*

"Oh," she swooned. "That's the way I feel about him, too! Marquesa, it sure is tough being a woman in love, isn't it?"

Isabel nodded. *You can't even imagine how difficult it is, young lady.* Suddenly the Marquesa's forehead relaxed for the first time in hours. *Perhaps my longings for the captain haven't been all that sinful. At least, not all my longings.*

After the two ladies picked at their food, they adjourned to the Marquesa's room, where Molly Mae Quincy received her first lesson in makeup, jewelry, and hair design.

They laughed and cried and giggled for an hour.

Molly Mae begged to try on the Marquesa's green silk and black lace dress. Isabel had to pin it in several places to keep it from sliding off Miss Quincy's shoulders. She let her wear the dramatic matching jewelry as well. Finally they pinned her hair up on top of her head in a dramatic swoop and then plopped one of Carolina's fanciest hats on her head.

With a slight amount of rouge and a touch of lipstick, Molly Mae Quincy posed in front of a mirror. "Wow! I look so . . so mature! Makeup really makes me look pretty, doesn't it?"

"Honey, there isn't any makeup in the world that can give you that beauty. It's all you. We just accented it a little differently than you've been accustomed to."

"I look nice enough to be your . . . your . . ."

"Don't you say daughter!"

"I could be your little sister!"

"Yes, if it weren't for our totally opposite hair color, skin tone, and general body shape."

"I don't have much . . . eh, shape, do I? Mama says I still have time to grow."

"You're a beautiful young lady. You don't need anything to show that."

"Thanks anyway. It was fun. Kind of like a costume party."

The noise of the continuing rain almost kept them from hearing the knock at the door. They scurried out of the Marquesa's room to see a soaking-wet July Johnson and Captain Dawson Mandara shivering in the doorway of the store.

The women shouted in unison.

"Molly Mae . . . is that y-you?" July stammered.

"Of course, it's me!"

"Why in the world are you wearing all of that stuff?" he complained.

"We've been walking the floor for two days worried sick that you might be shot dead by murderers, and the first thing you do when you come home is complain about what I'm wearing?" Molly started to cry. She spun around and retreated to the Marquesa's room.

"I don't suppose we could find a warm meal, could we?" the captain asked.

"A meal? That's all you have to say?" the Marquesa barked. "What I want to know is, why didn't you tell me you were a widower and were smitten with me? Don't you think that's something I'd need to know?"

She left July and the captain, mouths open, and rushed to her room a few steps behind Miss Molly Mae Quincy.

— *Seven* —

ISABEL LEON ABSOLUTELY hated Captain Dawson Mandara for almost two hours.

After that she sat next to the woodstove and talked to him until daylight.

There were some laughs.

There were some tears.

Mostly laughs.

That conversation ended with a soft hug and a kiss.

On the cheek.

It wasn't the last long conversation she had with the captain. For the next six days they took all meals together at Quincys' Cafe. In addition, the lamps at the Mercantile stayed lit late into the night. And most folks on Main Street could see the Marquesa's frequent trips to the hotel to check on construction and painting.

And the builder.

In her free moments she hired a staff of six and supervised the hanging of a huge The Hotel Marquesa sign on the railing of the upstairs veranda facing Main Street. She also wrote long personal letters to each of the Mandara children.

On the day the hotel furniture arrived, Isabel Leon was dressed and ready before July had the coffee boiling.

She held out her sleeve. "July, can you button these for me? They are almost impossible to fasten after the dress is on."

He fumbled with the tiny mother-of-pearl buttons gathered about her wrists.

"I don't know how Carolina ever buttoned these," she fussed.

"You've got a busy day, don't you, Marquesa?"

"You know, July, one time I was in this musical review called 'Bavarian Festival' with sixty-two people and an elephant on the stage at the same time."

July dropped his hands. "An elephant?"

"It was a huge circus number—total chaos trying to get it coordinated." She held her hand back out for him to finish the job.

He took a button in his hand. "Wow! An elephant right on the stage!"

"It was a little elephant. To get things ready, there was yelling, confusion, people running everywhere. Then someone screamed, 'Five minutes until curtain!' It was like a riot or something." She held out her other arm.

"I cain't believe it!" July began fastening the new sleeve.

"Yes, you can't imagine what it's like when you've got sixty-two selfish actors and—"

"A real, live elephant right on the stage! Don't that beat all? Don't that beat all." Again he dropped his hands to his side.

She waved her arms back in front of him. "Yes, but my point is, all that confusion and turmoil was nothing compared to—"

"I ain't never seen an elephant." He picked up her sleeve again. "In person, that is. Miss Fontenot has some stereoscopic photographs of an elephant. Those are really something!" He finished the job and stepped back.

The Marquesa brushed down her sleeves with her hand. "Today is going to be even more hectic than the opening scene of that musical."

July's face flashed a look of excitement. "Did you ever see Miss Fontenot's stereoscopic photographs?"

Isabel plucked a miniature peppermint from a jar and popped it under her tongue. "After all, I've got to try and get the furniture unloaded without getting mud tracked in on the floors, not to mention—"

"Sure am glad Miss Fontenot's recovering from her injuries. She's a nice lady, but her hair ain't as pretty as Molly Mae's, no matter what other folks say! Miss Fontenot said we'd go back up on the mesa next week and give it another try," July announced.

"And the captain is going to . . ."

"Think we'll try for a sunset picture this time, instead of a sunrise one."

". . . finish the cupola if it's not raining. It's not raining again, is it?" the Marquesa quizzed.

"Won't it be fine to have me and Molly Mae in our very own stereoscopic photo?"

"I hope things will be fairly manageable here at the store because I won't be able to help out much today," she informed him.

"Did you ever notice how many handsome women live in this town? There's you, Carolina, Miss Fontenot . . . and Molly Mae. Just to name a few."

"You know, if I'm still standing at the end of the day, it will be a miracle," Isabel proclaimed.

"I think I'll run over and see Molly Mae. It's her shift for cooking breakfast. I've got to tell her about that elephant. Now that was really something!"

The Marquesa swished toward the counter at the back of the store. *I'm talking to a wall. He doesn't have anything on his mind except elephants and Molly Mae. Mostly Miss Quincy, I suppose.*

She slid the money box behind the counter and then looked up to see one of the most handsome, nearly gray-haired forty-two-year-old men she had ever met come through the door wearing his old canvas work coat and slightly drooping wide-brimmed hat.

"Good mornin', Miss Leon."

"Good mornin', Captain!" She waltzed out to where he stood.

"I'm glad to see you!" July exclaimed to the captain. "Now you can visit with the Marquesa while I go to the cafe."

Mandara and Leon watched the white-aproned July Johnson burst out the doorway into the street.

"Sorry, Captain." The Marquesa grinned. "You got stuck with me."

"Well, I suppose I should make the most of it!" he laughed.

"And just what do mean by that, Captain Mandara? Are your intentions honorable?"

"Not completely."

"Good!" She scooted over and slipped her arms around his waist. She laid her head on his chest.

It felt good.

Real good.

The captain kissed her hair; then she stepped back. "You know, Marquesa, if you keep that up, I'm going to fall helplessly in love with you."

"I certainly hope so. I would hate to think I did all this work for nothing," she purred.

He poured himself a little coffee but stopped when he noticed it hadn't boiled long enough yet. "Just exactly what 'work' did you do today?"

She swirled around as if modeling the dress. "You don't think I wake up in the morning looking like this, do you?"

"No, I don't know how you look first thing in the morning. But I've been thinking about that a lot lately," he conceded.

"Good! That way I won't be the only one with such thoughts."

"Did you ever get to thinking that we are acting about as mature as July and Miss Quincy?" the captain asked.

"That thought did occur to me."

The captain stared back at the open doorway. "What was his hurry this morning?"

"He was using a story I told him about an elephant as an excuse to go visiting."

"An elephant?"

"I'll tell you about it sometime. Maybe I'll wait and save it for the children. I've been trying to think of things to talk to them about. I've told you over and over, I have never spent much time around children."

"You'll do fine," the captain assured her.

"It won't be long, will it?"

"They'll be here in ten days."

"Did you write to them about us?" she asked.

"Oh, yes."

"What did you tell them?"

"I told them there would never be another woman in the world who could take the place of their mother in their hearts or in mine.

But I told them that God had opened up a whole new beautiful room in my heart for the Marquesa, and my prayer was that He would open up a new room in their hearts as well."

She slipped her arm into his. "Captain Mandara, you're a jewel!"

"A rough old stone. You're the diamond. Every time I see that heart-stopping smile of yours, I feel like a prospector staring at the mother lode."

She shook her head and laughed. "I don't think I've ever been compared to the mother lode before. I hope your children will be at least half as enthusiastic as you, Captain Mandara."

"I laid awake half the night thinking that we should get married in Billings when we go in to pick up the children next week."

"And what did you think about the other half of the night?" She grinned.

With his naturally tanned skin it was sometimes difficult to tell when he blushed.

Not this time.

"If it were just me and you, Captain, I wouldn't wait until noon today! But I won't do that to your children. A month ago I would never have felt this way. But now, well, if it's the right thing to do, the Lord will see that it happens."

"I reckon you're right, but I don't think there's anything immoral or unchristian about getting married right away."

"Your children need some time to get used to me. Especially Nellie."

"She's the most enthusiastic about the matter."

"Yes, but maybe that's what she thinks you want her to say. She's the oldest. She'll do anything and say anything on earth that pleases her daddy. But I want to win her heart first. She hasn't seen you hold my hand or kiss my lips. That will be a real test."

"Maybe we ought to practice up a little before the children get here," he teased.

"Oh, sure, make some amorous suggestion on the busiest day of the year."

"What time are your wagons due in?"

"They were supposed to camp at the river last night. McGuire said they would roll in by eight this morning."

Through the open doorway of the store they heard the echoing peel of a bell ringing.

"You have the bell installed!" she exclaimed.

"Yep. Got it up there this morning at daylight."

"The hotel will seem like a school with the bell in the cupola."

"It's the town alarm," he reminded her. "Just seems like it ought to be there. I told Philip he could be the official bell ringer."

"I thought perhaps you would give that job to Grant."

"Oh, no!" the captain insisted. "Grant would go around town selling the right to ring the bell to other kids for a penny." He stepped to the doorway. "It has a nice tone, doesn't it?"

"Yes, but I have a suggestion." She hung close to him. "Let's not ring it at 7:00 A.M. again. My hotel guests might complain."

"You think we should go to 8:00 A.M.?"

"I was thinking noon."

"You're joking, right?"

She looked straight into his brown eyes. "Why on earth would I do that?"

"Do I hear echoes of my own words?"

"Perhaps. Maybe you should slip on over to the cafe and get some breakfast while you can," she suggested.

"I'll wait for July to return. Then we can go together."

"Well, I think the coffee's boiled. Shall we just sit here and talk?"

"Do you really want to talk?" he asked.

"Captain, what I want to do is hug you and hold you close for the next 100 years without letting go. But I'm afraid the furniture would never get unloaded, to say nothing of how bored your children would be waiting all that time at the train depot in Billings."

"Did you ever consider that perhaps it was the Lord's design that the next ten days are extremely busy ones?" he proposed.

"Yes, I've rejoiced and whined about that very matter quite often."

One time Isabel Leon had done two shows a day for thirty-six days straight during the World's Fair in Philadelphia. When the run ended, she thought she would never be able to move a muscle for the rest of her life.

Sitting in a wooden chair on the balcony of The Hotel Marquesa, Isabel was sure that the run in Philadelphia was a simple walk in the park compared to how she now felt.

Seated in a chair next to her was a slightly crumpled-looking Captain Mandara. Strolling hand in hand along the railing of the veranda were July Johnson and Molly Mae Quincy.

"Did you know you can see the front of the captain's house from here?" July called out.

Isabel lifted her head off the back of the chair and opened her eyes. "Yes, I planned it that way on purpose. I can just step out here and keep an eye on him."

"You're going to live over here and the captain over there?" Molly Mae asked. "Even after you're married?"

"How do you know we'll be getting married?" Isabel quizzed.

"Everybody in town knows that!" July added.

"Well, everybody's just going to have to wait awhile. We've got to get to know each other better and—"

"Why?" Molly Mae pressed.

"And I need to visit with the captain's children and make sure they like me and—"

"Everybody likes you, Marquesa," Molly Mae insisted.

"Oh? I can think of a few who don't."

"Who?" Molly Mae quizzed.

"Well, there's a man named DuBois and another named Rollins, not to mention Jacob Hardisty."

July let Molly Mae's hand drop and gazed off at the rimrock behind town. "If that storm hadn't come up, me and the captain would have shot them two by now. We couldn't follow their trail after that rain."

"They circled around and came back to the river, didn't they?" the Marquesa asked.

Captain Mandara continued to keep his head on the back of the reclining wooden chair and his hands folded in his lap. His hat was pulled over his eyes. "I figure DuBois knew the troops were south, and there's no place to go east or west, so he circled back to cross the river."

"You think they rode up to the Slash-Bar-Four?" July quizzed.

"Not if they knew anything about Andrews, Odessa, and that bunch of cowboys," Mandara replied. "I reckon they rode up or down the railroad until they found a place to spend their money."

"You think they'll be back?" Molly Mae asked.

"I hope they wait until Ranahan Parks returns, and we can make him town marshal," the Marquesa replied.

July looked down at the white clapboard siding of the Mercantile. "Are Ran and Miss Carolina and little David coming in this week or next?"

"We don't know. Their last letter was vague. It has something to do with the furniture Carolina's bringing out from Maryland."

"It will be nice to have them home," July added. "They're about the closest thing I have to a mama and a daddy."

Molly Mae leaned over the railing and peered at Main Street crowded with dirty men and tired horses. "Cantrell has changed a lot since they've been gone. I surely like your hotel sign, Marquesa."

"It makes it seem like we are open for business, doesn't it?" Isabel started to roll the sleeves of her dress down past her elbows and then abandoned the project.

"Are you going to open Monday for sure?" Molly Mae pumped.

"If I can get all the staff trained." A pain shot through the Marquesa from the base of her back up through her shoulder blades. "I still think I ought to hire a night clerk. If not, I'll be the one who has to get up in the middle of the night for emergencies."

The captain sat up and jammed his hat down on his head. "I wish the weather had cooperated so we could paint the outside."

July watched the traffic on the still muddy street. "I reckon the cafe's gettin' full. We'd better head down for supper."

"I think I'll just sit here a spell. How about you, Marquesa?" the captain probed.

"I might not move for days," she groaned.

"Ain't you goin' to eat?" July challenged. "You two got to come eat. Besides, it's getting too dark up here to just sit."

Molly Mae tugged at his sleeve. "Come on, Mama will be lookin' for me to help serve. Besides, maybe they like sitting in the dark."

"Sounds boring to me," July responded and headed for the door back into the upstairs sitting room.

Molly Mae turned to the Marquesa and the captain. "It will take me years to train him."

"You bragging or complaining?" the captain teased.

Miss Molly Mae turned up her nose and flashed a pouting smile. "Both!"

Opening day of The Hotel Marquesa didn't begin smoothly. Two of Isabel's six employees decided to try the goldfields instead. Then the cook showed up drunk and was fired before any meals were cooked.

At twelve noon a man and woman in their sixties drove a battered but heavily loaded farm wagon up Main Street and parked in front of the hotel. With hat in hand, the white-haired man shuffled into the hotel and over to the counter where Isabel Leon stood. His clothes were extremely faded but clean.

"Would you like a room?" she asked.

He peered down at the battered shoes. "We are a little down on funds right at the moment. I was wonderin' if you knew where folks could get a job in this town?"

"What kind of work are you looking for?" *This man looks like he walked off the stage of a production of* Hard Winter at Broken Arrow Crossing, *Act I, Scene 1.*

"The wife and me operated a restaurant in Omaha. The hotel it was housed in burned to the ground, and all we could save is what we have on that wagon. She's a mighty good cook, and I can do odd jobs if needed."

"You ran a hotel restaurant?"

"For seventeen years. We decided to move out to Boise City to be with her sister, but we ran out of money and resolve a few days ago. Now we just want to settle down."

"Are you nondrinking, God-fearing people?"

"Yes, ma'am."

"I'll hire you both."

The man's eyes lit up, and he looked ten years younger.

"Thank you, ma'am!"

"I'm Isabel Leon. This is my hotel. Most folks call me the Marquesa."

"Ma'am, you won't be sorry. When would you like us to get started?"

Isabel looked over at the oak and cut-glass clock in the lobby. "How about in an hour?"

"Yes, ma'am, eh, Marquesa. That'll give us time to make a camp down in those trees south of town."

"Camp?"

"We need a place to stay until we get paid, I reckon."

"What is your name?"

"Cyrus Woods. My wife is Stella."

"Mr. Woods, I have a small apartment right off the kitchen. I'll allow you to stay there for free if you'll be my night clerk and get up when necessary."

"Marquesa," the older man shook his head and wiped his eyes on his sleeve, "you're surely an answer to prayer." He held out his hand to her.

She shook his strong, callused hand. "There have been some prayers answered today for everyone."

The Marquesa's first break came about 3:00 P.M. She carried a hot cup of coffee up to her suite. She pulled off her lace-up shoes and walked in stocking feet out on the veranda.

Lord, this is even better than I dreamed. The sense of belonging . . . of being somewhere that's mine . . . of having a business to look after . . . and people I belong to.

And, if I were honest, having You to talk to. It's like You've always been a friend, but I've ignored You for years. No more. I like this.

Even the hard parts make sense.

She stood with coffee cup in her hand and watched the Monday stage coach from Billings rumble up Main Street, mud flying from its wheels. The driver, sitting high on the seat above the coach, glanced up and tipped his hat.

"Marquesa, did you open 'er up today?"

"Yes, Mr. Massey, we are open for business."

"You don't mind if we make our stop at the hotel from now on, do ya?"

"Mr. Massey, that will be our privilege."

"Yes, ma'am. I'll let them know up in the camps that you're open."

"Thank you."

Massey swung down off the stage and pulled open the door. "All right, folks. If you're gettin' off at Cantrell, this is your lucky day because The Hotel Marquesa is open, and with any luck you might even get to visit with the Marquesa herself."

The first person off the stage was a short Oriental man.

The second person off the stage was Jacob Hardisty.

He didn't bother looking up at her.

A sense of depression hit Isabel's chest and radiated to every part of her body.

Well, Lord, it was *a great day.*

She pulled on her shoes and abandoned her cup on the veranda railing. Then the Marquesa swooped down the stairs to the lobby just in time to catch Jacob Hardisty talking to clean-shaven Taylor Starr, her newly hired daytime desk clerk.

"Mr. Hardisty wants to rent the nobby suite for a week," Starr reported with a wide smile. "He's paying cash in advance."

"Mr. Hardisty does not rent any rooms at this hotel ever. Nor does he have a meal here nor may he set a foot inside the hotel again. Is that understood, Mr. Starr?"

The middle-aged clerk put on his gold wire-framed glasses and looked more closely at Hardisty. "Yes, ma'am."

"Isabel, I can't believe you would—"

"Mr. Hardisty, would you please leave this building immediately!" she demanded.

"But I've—I've never been kicked out of any hotel in the world," he fumed.

"You have now. If you'll kindly get back on the stage. I believe you left Cantrell last summer with the clear understanding that you are not welcome to return."

"I own a bank in this town!" he asserted.

"And it's being run splendidly by Mr. Milton and Mr. Ostine. I do not know why you came back. You should have known you'd be treated this way."

"You can't deny me a room for the night! Where's your charity?"

"My charity for you, Jacob Hardisty, was emptied violently, painfully, and against my will in a New York hotel room long ago. It was wrung utterly dry when you forced me into a lice-and-rat-infested jail cell while Logan died all alone. Your charity today is that I didn't shoot you on sight, as I have done in the past."

"You've tried to kill him?" Mr. Starr gulped and stepped back from the counter.

"On more than one occasion. Unfortunately, marksmanship is not one of my strengths."

"I will not be bullied by the likes of you!" Hardisty huffed.

Having just adjusted a couple of sticky doors on a downstairs room, Captain Dawson Mandara, carrying a bucket half-filled with nails and a claw hammer, stole up behind Hardisty.

"Captain Mandara, will you please escort Mr. Hardisty out to the stage?"

The captain stuck the handle of the hammer in the man's back. "Throw your hands up, Hardisty."

"You must be kidding," Hardisty sneered. "My word, man, that's only a hammer handle!"

"You ever been whacked in the back of the head with a claw hammer?" the captain growled.

Instantly Hardisty's hands went up.

"What do you want me to do with him, Marquesa?" the captain asked.

"Put him back on the stagecoach."

"Conscious or unconscious?"

"It really doesn't matter to me."

"You heard the lady."

"I've got a bank to look after," Hardisty protested.

"Not today. Not any day. Out the door."

The shoulders of his expensive New York tailor-made suit drooping, Hardisty shuffled out the front doors onto the wide boardwalk. A crowd of prospectors and cowboys had huddled there to observe the commotion.

"Looks like you got the drop on him, Captain," one man called out.

"You going to nail him?" another jibed.

"Hey, mister, there ain't no man in Cantrell better with a hammer than the captain. You'd better take it easy!"

The hoots and laughter from the crowd continued. July Johnson squirmed his way through the throng carrying a double-barreled shotgun. "Hardisty! You ain't welcome in this town!"

Jacob Hardisty held his arrogant head high. "I cannot imagine why everyone is so hostile."

July scratched his bare head. "What are you going to do with him, Captain?"

"The Marquesa wants him on the stagecoach," the captain reported.

"The stage already left town," someone in the crowd shouted.

Suddenly Hardisty yanked a sneak gun out of his coat pocket. He whipped around and pointed it at the captain.

The crowd gasped and scattered.

But the hickory handle of the hammer caught Hardisty's wrist. An explosion of cracking bones silenced the crowd. Hardisty screamed in pain and dropped his gun.

"Get over to your bank, Hardisty. You're going to stay in that building until the stage comes back. I don't want to see you on the street!"

"My wrist is broken!" Hardisty wailed.

The captain prodded him with the hammer. "Put it in a splint and bind it. You'll survive."

"I will not be confined!" Hardisty screamed, holding a limp wrist with his other hand. "By what authority are you doing this?"

The captain appealed to the crowd. "Boys, do I have the authority to do this?"

"As far as we're concerned, you can hang him, Captain," one man shouted.

"Did he really have the Marquesa thrown into jail?" a woman probed.

"Yep."

"Why?"

"Because she tried to kill him," the captain explained.

"Is that a crime?" someone snarled.

Captain Mandara shoved Hardisty toward the street. "It is in Billings."

"It ain't in Cantrell!"

"Hardisty, this is the wrong town to harass a lady in," the captain lectured. "Either stay in the bank, or I'll let the crowd take care of you."

Isabel watched Jacob Hardisty whimper his way across the street toward the bank.

"Ain't you goin' to hang him?" someone shouted from the front porch of the hotel.

"Not unless he comes out of the bank," the captain asserted.

"Get me a doctor!" Hardisty cried.

"If you wanted a doctor, you should have stayed in Billings," July called out as he trailed behind the captain who still continued to keep Hardisty covered with the claw hammer handle.

Mr. Ostine was waiting by the open bank door.

Some words were shouted, but Isabel couldn't make them out. Then the bank door closed, and the crowd slowly dispersed. Isabel watched the captain and July march back across the street to the hotel.

The shotgun was lying across July's thin but muscular shoulders as the two hiked through the hotel and up to where she stood.

"Why didn't you pull your gun on Hardisty?" July asked the captain.

"No reason to pull a gun when a hammer will do."

"I can't believe Hardisty would come to town!" Isabel fumed. "He's brought so much pain into my life, and he wants to inflict more. I don't understand! Why is this happening to me?"

"Looks like you need to promenade," the captain suggested.

"What I need is that man out of my town!" she shouted.

The captain grabbed her hand. "Come on, Marquesa."

"Where do you think we're going?" She jerked her hand back.

"To the veranda for a walk. That's why you built it, wasn't it?"

"Not for when I'm angry. And I'm furious!"

"Then let's keep walking until you're not angry."

She reached out and slipped her long fingers into his. "You promise to behave yourself?"

He pulled her hand up and kissed it. "I promise no such thing."

She gave a big, deep sigh. "Good."

It was on their third stroll around the veranda that she began to talk.

"Captain, I honestly do not know what to do about Jacob Hardisty. I told you what he hired that New York doctor to do to me. You saw how he treated me in Billings. I never, ever in my life wanted any person dead as bad as I want him dead. He brings out the very worst in me. He can have the whole world. I just want Cantrell to myself. I don't know why the Lord is allowing this!" she cried.

"I don't know if I can explain it," the captain began. "But if a certain general showed up, I reckon I'd feel the same way. About like July felt when Rosto Rollins came to town. Everyone seems to have a person or two in life that pushes his virtue to the wall. I reckon how we deal with that one person says a whole lot more about us than how we treat 100 nice folks."

"So what should I do about Hardisty?"

"Quit giving him something to live for," the captain suggested.

"What?"

"Look at him. He lives a totally useless life. He takes his daddy's money and plays around with gold mines and stock speculating. But you've given him a life goal to prove that's he in control in Cantrell, Montana. I'm sure he came back only because he heard Ranahan was out of town. He was going to stay at your hotel, eat at your restaurant, and brag about his conquests. He came because it's the only challenge he has."

"That's a pathetic way of looking at him."

"He's a pathetic man."

"I can't think of one reason on earth why that man is alive!"

The captain slipped his arm around her waist as they continued to stroll. "Hatred for him brought you to Cantrell in the first place. If you hadn't been here, I would never have met you."

"The Lord would have brought us together some way. I just know it!"

"Maybe. But what if Hardisty came to town, and no one cared. No one pitched a fit. No one said anything. What if he was no more important than a fresh pile of horse manure?"

"Jacob likes being at the center of things," she concurred.

"Exactly."

She grasped his arm closer as they continued their stroll. "I don't have to let a pile of fresh horse manure check into my hotel, do I?"

"Nope."

"So we just go on and forget him?"

"Yep. Who cares where he is or what he's doing?"

"That will work as long as I don't see him," she sobbed. "He caused such pain in my life. I can't get it out of my mind. It is because of him that I will never have children!"

"You'll have children," the captain corrected, "in a little more than a week."

"Are you saying I should forgive him?"

"I don't know, Marquesa. I've battled this thing with General Clarkston for years now."

"What did you do?"

"I turned him over to the custody of the Lord."

"What do you mean?"

"Well, in the army we were sometimes called upon to transport dangerous criminals from one fort to another or from one court to another. A lot of these guys didn't deserve to live. I knew that. But it wasn't my job to do anything about it. I delivered them over to a court system that is basically just and then released my responsibility for them."

"Are you saying I should do this with Jacob?"

"Whether he will find forgiveness for his actions or a just and swift punishment, that's up to the Lord. You've got to go about living your life."

"I don't know if I can do that."

"I hope you'll try. I don't want this to keep grinding at you year after year."

"Captain, I think you are asking me for more than I can deliver."

They stopped walking the veranda and glanced across the street at the front of the bank. "Well, let's suppose next fall you're settled right up here," he said. "Next to you is Nellie. She's sitting there embroidering slip cases. Georgia is prowling the rail looking over the crop of thirteen-year-old boys."

"What am I doing?"

"You're barefoot and sipping on a fresh cup of coffee after a successful run of *H.M.S. Pinafore* at the hotel."

"That sounds nice."

"And just suppose me and the boys are fishing in the Yellowstone. Georgia looks down the street and says to you, 'Here comes Mr. Jacob Hardisty.' What I want to know is," the captain pressed, "are you going to pick up a carbine and shoot him on sight?"

"No."

"Good."

"I'm not a very good shot at this distance. I think I'd shoot him point-blank with a handgun instead," she teased. "Actually I'll treat him like a . . . like a pile of fresh horse manure, trying to avoid him whenever I can and scraping him off my boot if I get too close. Is that what you mean?"

"I think that will work." The captain slipped his tough, callused fingers into hers. He glanced down at her. "You know," he said, "I didn't think I'd ever feel something as sweet and peaceful as that ever again. Claire and I used to . . ." His voice trailed off.

"It's all right."

"No, that's not fair. I shouldn't be bringing her name up."

"Captain, for as long as I live I'll never be Claire. I'm not going to try to compete. Your deep love for her is one of your strengths."

"Marquesa, you are my reward in life."

"What do you mean?"

"I've had a number of things go against me. Times when I tried hard to do the right thing, and my world came crashing down anyway. But I kept telling myself that the Lord was in control, and in the long run, there would be rewards for righteousness. You're my reward."

She pulled away from him, her hands on her hips. "Captain Mandara, I have been in hundred of plays . . . maybe thousands. I have heard or memorized almost every line penned for the past 300 years. And you are the smoothest-talking man who ever lived. You ought to be writing plays."

His brown eyes were startled. "You think I'm making this up?"

"No!" She slipped her arms around his neck. "I love you, Captain Mandara!"

He started to respond, but her lips smothered his.

Finally she pulled back. "Do you know what I'm thinking, Captain Mandara?"

"Probably the same thing I'm thinking."

"Hey, good. You two ain't busy." July Johnson burst through the upper parlor doors and out onto the veranda. "Did you see what's happening down there?"

The Marquesa pulled away from the captain. *Excuse me, Mr. Johnson, would you mind dropping off the face of the earth?*

"Did you see that line forming at the bank?"

She and the captain stepped over to the railing and watched as prospector and businessman alike stood in line out on the uncovered porch in front of the Assay Office and Bank. "Are they making a run for their money?"

"Yep," July announced. "Word around town is that Hardisty doesn't deserve their business."

Isabel laid her head on Captain Mandara's strong shoulder. "Poor Mr. Ostine and Milton. They are good men."

"Folks don't like Hardisty," July reported. "So they're pulling out their money."

"But most of them don't even know Hardisty," she pointed out.

"They all know the Marquesa," the captain reminded her.

"What do you mean?"

"The captain's right," July blabbed. "They figure if Hardisty don't treat you right, they don't want their money with him."

"They're doing this because of me?"

"You're the Marquesa," the captain insisted.

"But . . . I'm just . . ."

"You're ever'body's Marquesa," July insisted.

"What do you mean by that?"

"Cantrell has some special people who make it what it is. One is Carolina Parks. She's the queen. We all sort of feel allegiance to her," July explained. "But a queen has got to be, you know, separate from common folks. But you're the member of the royal family that visits with everyone. In a way you sort of belong to everyone. Whether it's the gamblers on Second Street or the store owners or the prospectors, you're our own Marquesa."

"But I'm not even a real Marquesa!" she protested.

"That's where you're wrong," the captain insisted. "It's a title given to you and sustained by your loyal subjects. If we had a vote today, you would receive a unanimous vote to be the Marquesa of Cantrell. Isn't that right, July?"

"Yes, sir. She's the Marquesa, all right."

"Well, that's very exciting. But what will we do about Mr. Ostine and Milton? I don't want them to lose their business. We need them in this town."

"Maybe they can start a new bank," the captain suggested.

"Or maybe . . ." Isabel pondered.

"Looks like Mr. Milton's headed this way!" July called out, waving his arm. "We're up here, Mr. Milton!" July yelled out.

By the time Isaac Milton made it to the veranda, sweat soaked the collar of his white shirt that was neatly tucked under a wool vest and wool suit coat. He loosened his black tie as he approached Isabel.

"Marquesa, I suppose you can see we're having a run."

"Do you have enough money in the safe?" Isabel asked.

"No, some is tied up in construction loans and the like. I was wondering if you could do or say anything to stop this panic," Mr. Milton pleaded.

"I seem to be the cause of it, don't I?"

"Mr. Hardisty stirred it up, but I don't have any choice in the matter. He owns the bank."

"I have a deal for you, Mr. Milton," Isabel suggested. "What if I encourage everyone in town to pull their money out?"

"What? That would break us!"

"Yes, and what do you think the bank would be worth then?"

"Whatever the building and furnishings would bring," he cited.

"When the funds get to zero, offer to buy the building from Mr. Hardisty. If you and Mr. Ostine are the new owners of the bank, I guarantee I'll convince everyone to put their money right back in."

"And you two would own it outright," the captain declared.

Milton squeezed his hands together in front of him. "What if he doesn't want to sell out?"

"I'll build you a new bank," the captain offered.

"Are you kidding?"

She laid her hand on Mr. Milton's sleeve. "The captain doesn't kid. Does he, July?"

"No, ma'am. He doesn't kid."

"So we just let the run go and offer to buy him out?" Milton quizzed.

"July and I won't pull out the Mercantile's money or the hotel's money. That ought to give you some breathing room."

"You'd do that for me?"

"Yes, we would."

"You two are Cantrell pioneers!" July added. "We pioneers stick together."

Isaac Milton wiped his brow and unfastened his tight shirt collar. "Okay, then let the run continue. We'll strip the safe of every penny. Even the backup safe."

The Marquesa released his arm. "Let's try it."

Mr. Milton hustled down the stairs. They watched from the rail as he scooted back into the bank.

The captain turned to July. "Let's spread the word for everyone else to pull out their money. Maybe Hardisty has some cash with him. If so, he'll have to cough it up to keep the bank solvent."

The Marquesa nodded agreement. "Maybe it's a good thing I didn't kill Hardisty. He would have never lived to see this."

"That's right," the captain responded. "Killing him would let him off the hook too easy."

At 8:00 P.M. a dejected Isaac Milton and Theodore Ostine came into the hotel restaurant. The captain and the Marquesa were seated at the round oak table by the box window that allowed them to see everything on the darkened street and in the ballroom/dining room at the same time.

"You men look like you've been busy! Come and join us for dinner," the Marquesa called.

"Thank you, but we can hardly afford it. We dug into our own wallets to pay the last depositor."

"In that case, supper is complimentary. My first day has been quite brisk. Every room is let out except for the Royal Suite. I might have set the price too high on it."

Both men slumped into their chairs. Milton spoke up. "Well, the bank's busted, and Hardisty won't sell."

"What?"

"He's been in our backroom drinking and nursing that broken wrist," Ostine reported. "Said he wouldn't sell, and he'd kill the captain as soon as he sobered up."

"I'm not going back there to sleep tonight," Isaac Milton insisted. "The man's deranged."

"Let him sleep it off tonight and see what he thinks in the morning," the captain suggested.

"How about you taking the Royal Suite tonight?" Isabel offered. "Guests of the house."

"You don't have to do that, Marquesa. You need to turn a profit just like everyone else."

"But I want to say the place was full on opening night. I insist. July was right," the Marquesa affirmed. "You two are pioneers. By tomorrow night we'll have Milton and Ostine's Bank on Main Street."

"Nope," Mr. Milton corrected. "Me and Ted talked it over. If we own the bank, we're calling it the First Bank of Cantrell."

"I like that!" the captain added.

"But Hardisty is mighty dangerous drunk," Ostine reminded them.

"He's not real sweet sober," the Marquesa added. "If you men will excuse me, I'm going to register our guests in the Royal Suite. I don't want anyone else to grab those rooms."

She pranced around her bedroom in a new silk nightgown. She could still feel the captain's hands in hers. She could taste his lips on hers. She could hear his "I love you" in her ears.

I've waited for this day for four months—or maybe a lifetime. The hotel is open! I'm in my suite! My captain is over in his ready-made house waiting for his children and pining for his Marquesa!

Lord, I just don't know how anything could be better.

She looked at the brand-new cotton sheet turned down on the empty bed.

Okay. I do know how it could be better.

But I can wait.

This time I'll wait until everything is perfect.

She plopped down on her back in the middle of the bed. Her eyes were wide open.

Let's see, the night shift is covered. The kitchen is clean. The rooms are full. The staff know their tasks. Mr. and Mrs. Woods gave me a list of supplies I need to order. I don't know if the pantry is large enough, but the captain said he'd make more shelves tomorrow.

She reached over and turned the lamp off.

I'll never get to sleep, of course.

Within three minutes she was sound asleep.

Isabel Leon was twenty-one years old in 1876 and living in New York City. The name of the musical play was *Old Glory Forever.* She played the part of Miss Liberty, and her costume barely hung to her knees. The finale included her standing on the shoulders of two strong men where she waved a brand-new thirty-eight-star flag while she sang a stirring rendition of "This Lovely Land!" At the end of the song, with audience standing and cheering, they set off a small anvil cannon backstage. The cannon boomed, smoke swirled, and the audience roared with approval.

No one in the cast knew exactly how loud the cannon would sound, since they didn't want to waste powder during rehearsals. On the night the play opened, everything went fine until it was time for the cannon. The blast echoed through the theater much more loudly than anyone had expected.

The two men holding her up above the set jumped at the sound of the blast. She tumbled off their shoulders and into the arms of the play's hero. Isabel had been so relieved not to fall on her neck that she had flung her arms around the man and kissed him.

On the lips.

The audience gave the cast a thunderous ovation that lasted over twenty minutes.

After that the tumble and the kiss were written into the script and repeated every night. It also began a short-lived but wild and hilarious romance between Isabel Leon and the play's hero.

As a result of an eight-week run of that play, any explosion in the night caused Isabel to relive that scene.

This time when the blast boomed from across the street, Isabel sat straight up, hugged her pillow, and kissed it right on the . . . embroidered butterfly on the slip case.

Was that thunder? Someone shooting?

She tugged on her green silk robe and scooted barefoot toward the double doors that led out to the veranda. By the time she reached the railing on Main Street, several other hotel guests stood alongside her. With the sky turning morning-gray in the east, a number of men gathered in the street around the front of the bank.

From her vantage point on the second-story veranda, she could see Captain Mandara trotting down the hillside from his house. Even in the dim light it looked like he was carrying a rifle or a carbine.

She looked down and shouted at another man carrying a gun.

A young man.

"July, what's happening down there?"

"Someone set off some dynamite in the bank, I reckon. It knocked a whole shelf of air-tights off the wall at the store," he reported.

"Is Hardisty still in there?"

"I suppose so."

"What's he trying?"

"I don't know." July surveyed the now-crowded hotel balcony. "Is the captain up there with you?"

"Of course not!" *Relax, Marquesa, he didn't mean anything by that.* "He's around by the side door of the bank."

She watched July cut through the crowd to the side of the bank where the captain was instructing someone to lead off two horses tied in the alley. She saw the captain put July and two other armed men behind a wagon with their guns pointed at the bank's side door. Then the captain hiked around to the crowd in front of the bank and shouted orders.

"You two men with carbines take cover at the cafe behind that freight wagon. The other two with rifles hustle up there on the veranda of the hotel next to the Marquesa. Turn those benches on their side and use them for cover. They're heavy. I know—I made them. Now the rest of you get back out of bullet range. We've got a couple of *hombres malo* in the bank. And if they come blasting out of there, I don't want any of you hurt."

The entire crowd scurried for safer quarters, and the marksmen sprinted to their positions.

"Captain," she called down, "what's happening?"

"Those ponies belong to Cigar DuBois and Rosto Rollins. July and I were trailing those horses the other day."

"You think they tried to rob the bank?"

"I reckon so."

"But there's no money in the bank."

"I reckon that was a surprise."

"What about Jacob?"

"That's a good question." Captain Mandara cupped his hands over his mouth. "Men, if they come out shooting, gun them down right where they stand. If they surrender, keep them in your sights until I disarm them and get them tied up."

"Be careful," she hollered down.

Be careful? Did I say that? What I meant to say was, don't you dare get yourself killed, Captain Mandara. If anything happens to you now, I would absolutely go mad.

The two men with rifles crouched down beside her behind the

benches on the veranda as the rest of the guests withdrew into the building.

"You better get inside, Marquesa," one of the men insisted.

"Boys, my entire life stands inside those black polished military boots down there. There's no way on earth I'm not going to watch this."

The captain, with .45 army Colt drawn, trotted over to the Mercantile and then along the covered porch until he was next to the bank, well out of sight of its windows and doors.

"DuBois! Rollins! Toss those guns out ahead of you. Come out on the porch with your hands above your heads."

The front door of the bank opened a crack, but no one appeared. Thick gray smoke filtered out into the cool spring air.

"Says who?"

"The citizens of Cantrell!" the captain yelled.

"And what if we don't?"

"You'll get mighty hungry sooner or later! Toss the guns out on the porch."

"Come in and try to get 'em!"

"Why would we want to do that? There's absolutely nothing in there we want. We took our money out yesterday. I guess you could steal the wall clock or something. If you walk out of there with your hands on your guns, you'll get shot down on the porch. What's it going to be?"

"We ain't makin' no deals. We aim to kill ever'one of you!"

"You've got about as much chance of that as James and Youngers in Northfield."

"We ain't comin' out."

"That's fine," the captain yelled. "We'll wait. We'll take shifts. Some of us will be eatin' biscuits and gravy; others will be waitin' to shoot the first one out the door."

"You ain't scarin' us."

"Rollins, is that you?"

"So what?"

"It would be better for you to surrender out the front door. I've got a kid at the side door with a shotgun. Said he watched you and your men gun down his folks in Custer City. He'll blow you in half if you go out the side door for sure. He doesn't aim to let you surrender."

"You ain't scarin' us!"

"I didn't mean it as a scare. It was an act of kindness. Folks around here are mighty fed up with you and DuBois. I don't know if I can keep them from gunnin' you down, no matter what. All I know is the longer the day goes on, the more impatient they will be."

"Give us back our horses and pull the men away from the side door. We'll mount and ride off."

"Nope. We let you ride off before. That didn't work! Come out unarmed now!" the captain pressured.

"We ain't going to do it!"

"It will be a mighty sad line in the history of outlaws. The fearsome Cigar DuBois and Rosto Rollins broke into an empty bank and got shot down by the women and kids of Cantrell, Montana. That will add a little humor to a gruesome subject."

"You can go to Hades!"

"Glad to hear you boys are thinking about eternity. I'll see that the Bible gets read over you. 'Course, before they let me bury you, they'll want to put your bodies on display."

Several shots were fired wildly out the front door. As far as Isabel could tell, they hit nothing.

"How do we know you got guns out there?"

"That's simple to prove," the captain hollered. "One of you just walk out on the porch with your gun still in your hand. The other one can count the bullets that tear into his body. Which one of you wants to try it?"

"Ain't nobody bluffin' Rosto Rollins."

"You're right," the captain hollered. "No one out here's bluffing. Rosto, I'm gettin' a little bored with this. I'm going over to the cafe and get some eggs and ham."

"Wait!"

Even from across the street on the hotel veranda, Isabel could hear shouts and scuffling inside the bank.

"We'll make a deal with you!" a voice finally shouted from the bank.

"You going to surrender?" the captain called.

"You bring us horses and $500, and we let Hardisty go."

"Hardisty?"

"We've got Jacob Hardisty here at gunpoint."

"You can have him," the captain yelled.

"What?"

"There isn't anyone out here that gives two bits whether he lives or dies. We were thinking about lynchin' him last night ourselves. You boys will have to come up with something better than that."

"We ain't bluffin'. We'll shoot him."

"Go ahead," the captain called back.

A coatless and shaken Jacob Hardisty appeared at the door of the bank. The hand of an unseen bank robber held a gun to his head. "My word . . . do something to help me!" he pleaded.

"We'll kill him!" Rollins threatened for the second time.

"Hardisty is worthless. He probably doesn't deserve to live. But if you do shoot him, you understand there won't be any chance of surrender after that. We'll cut you down no matter what."

"Wait!" Hardisty pleaded. "You can't let them do this. In the name of decency, you must do something!"

"What decent thing did you ever do, Hardisty?" the captain challenged.

"Marquesa!" Hardisty cried. "In God's name, Marquesa, don't let them do this!"

I can't believe he would appeal to me. I've wanted him dead for years. This isn't fair.

"Marquesa! Please!" Hardisty begged.

She turned to the two gunmen next to her. "Pitiful, isn't he? Boys, when Hardisty drops to his knees, fire several shots halfway up that door. That should keep them away from the opening. Maybe he can crawl away."

"You think that will work?"

"I hope so. Anyway . . . I think I hope so."

"Marquesa!" Hardisty screamed again.

She cupped her hands to her mouth and shouted, "I can't do a thing for you, Jacob. You'd better make your peace with God!"

Hardisty collapsed to his knees. The riflemen next to her let fly with a barrage of bullets into the bank door. Her hands went over her ears at the first explosion. The gun smoke from the shots almost blocked her view.

Jacob March Hardisty crawled across the porch toward the Mercantile. Then the captain leaped over the railing of the porch, grabbed Hardisty by the arm, and dragged him out of the line of fire. Several more shots were fired aimlessly from inside the bank.

"Marquesa, how did you know Hardisty was going to drop to his knees?" one of the men next to her asked.

"When he gets scared enough, he either falls to his knees or wets his trousers. I was hoping for the former."

Back in the security of the front porch of the Mercantile, the captain shouted again, "That was a dumb move, boys. You made folks out here mighty mad. I don't think they'll let you surrender now. They're sending the kids home to get the spare guns. It seems like everyone in town wants to take part in this. You'll have so much lead in you, we'll be able to dump you out in the middle of the river and just let you sink."

"This whole town's crazy!"

"I'm going to get my breakfast now. I've left word to shoot you if you come out. The others refuse to talk to you, so if you've got any last requests or anything, better tell me now. I'm hungry."

"Wait, mister . . . wait a minute!"

Isabel peeked over the railing of the veranda. Long beams of the rising sun splashed down Main Street like jagged daggers. She could see the captain squatting on the Mercantile porch, his hand-gun trained on the front door of the bank. Sitting on the porch with his back against the wall and nursing his right wrist was Jacob Hardisty. The door to the bank was mostly open, but blackness and gun smoke were the only things she could spot inside.

"How do we know you won't shoot us anyway?"

"You've got my word on it."

"We don't know you. How do we know we can we count on you?"

"You can't. But here's what I want. Toss all five guns out on the street. Not on the porch but out to the dirt."

"We've only got two guns!"

"You've got at least two each, counting the ones hidden in your belts. And there's Hardisty's sneak gun from his boot. That makes five. Surely you found that one. If I don't see five guns tossed out, the deal's off. Then you come crawling out on your bellies on the porch with your arms and legs spread-eagle out."

"I ain't crawlin' for nobody!"

"I'm through talking," the captain concluded.

"I'm comin' out, but I ain't crawlin'! Do you hear me? I said, I'm comin' out! You promise you won't shoot?"

The Marquesa peeked over the bench and watched as five guns were tossed out the front door of the bank. The final one hit the edge of the porch and toppled into the mud and dirt.

"Don't shoot. We're comin' out, but we ain't crawlin'! Mister, are you still there?"

The streets of Cantrell were perfectly quiet. It was as if every bird stopped its spring songs at the same time.

Then Isabel saw it.

First DuBois.

Then Rollins.

They crawled on their bellies out onto the middle of the bank porch and spread their arms and legs wide.

"All of that business with Jacob Hardisty seems so long ago. I wouldn't care if he walked up to me right now. It wouldn't phase me one bit! I have more important things on my mind. Captain, what do you think?"

"Marquesa, I think you're a little nervous."

"I'll tell you who was nervous. It was that Lieutenant Sarret when you turned DuBois and Rollins over to him. You think he'll make it back to Dakota with them?" She paced back and forth.

"The sergeant will see to it that they make it. Now would you stop pacing. You'll wear a rut in the floor."

"Yes, well, at least Hardisty did sell the building to Milton and Ostine. So I guess that turned out all right. Did you hear someone else is thinking of starting a bank? Two banks in Cantrell. It's hard to believe."

"Do you always babble on when you're jittery?"

"Yes. And I've barely begun!" The Marquesa stopped and glanced at her reflection in the glass window on the south side of the Billings train depot. The splash of green in the new dress gave her outfit some spirit. At least she thought it did.

"Do you think I should have put my hair up and worn a hat? Will they expect me to wear a hat? They will, won't they?"

Captain Dawson Mandara sat on the polished oak depot bench, his suit coat buttoned at the top, his arms folded across his chest, his hat pulled down low on his mostly gray hair, his long legs stretched out in front of him, and his fifteen-inch stovepipe-top boots polished to a glistening black.

"Marquesa, would you just sit down and relax? I told you, you don't need a hat. Your hair is absolutely gorgeous, and there's no reason to hide it."

"Most women wear hats."

"Most women do not have beautiful naturally wavy hair."

"You think I look all right?"

"All right? I think you are truly one of the most beautiful women ever to walk on the face of the earth. You know that."

"You're not kidding me? I mean, no . . . you aren't. You never kid."

He pushed his new wide-brimmed black hat to the back of his head. "Everything will be fine. Don't be so nervous."

"Don't be nervous? Dropped into a cistern full of poisonous snakes—that would be less stressful compared to what I feel now. Falling out of a hot air balloon while crossing shark-infested waters off the coast of Australia—that would make me only a little jittery. Showing up at the queen's coronation wearing nothing but a smile—that would make me nervous. But at the moment I'm on the verge of total, complete, irreversible physical, intellectual, and emotional collapse!"

"Oh," he mumbled.

"I feel like I'm about to audition for a part in a play that will drastically change my entire life forever. And it's a part that I've never played."

His voice was powerful, yet peaceful. "Marquesa, I love you."

"It's a part I don't even know I can pull off—a part that I know I don't deserve."

"Did you hear me? I said, I love you!"

"There must be hundreds of women all over the country who are better qualified." She folded her arms across her chest and continued to pace.

"I love you, darlin'."

"Why in the world did I ever think I could do this? Those children deserve someone a whole lot better than . . ." She plopped down on the wooden bench next to him. "What did you say?"

"I said, I love you, Isabel Leon. You've already got the part if you choose to take it."

"What if they hate me?"

"They were raised better than that. They know how to give and receive love. All you have to do is show them that you love them, and they'll adore you forever."

A distant rumble drifted into the depot. The Marquesa leaped to her feet. "Is that it? Is that their train?"

The captain stood beside her and took her arm. "This is Billings, not New York. There's only one train from the East. That's their train."

"Oh, please, dear Lord, don't let me faint!" she mumbled.

"What?"

"Wait. I said, can we go wait on the platform?"

He led her out of the depot to the covered wooden platform that stood next to the Northern Pacific tracks. She gazed east at the column of smoke as the engine slowed and chugged its way into the station.

The Marquesa slipped her white-gloved hand into his and squeezed it hard. She took a deep breath and let it out slowly. *Lord, You have been so incredibly good to me. Just this one more thing.*

She watched as the engine rolled slowly past them.

Give me the courage and the grace to accept Your will in this. Please . . . please . . . may it be Your will that they like me!

The first passenger car stopped about ten feet in front of them. She turned to look up at the captain. "Dawson, I just want you to know that even if your children hate me and won't let you marry me, I'll love you forever!"

His lips on hers were warm and slightly chapped. The arm around her was confident but gentle. His chest, pressed against hers, felt extremely comfortable and thrilling all at the same time.

"Well, I certainly hope this is your captain!" the woman's voice teased.

Isabel blinked her eyes open and pulled back. "Carolina! Ranahan! But . . . I didn't . . ."

Carolina Cantrell Parks was the most naturally regal woman Isabel had ever met, always a woman of charm and grace, the kind men trip over themselves offering to assist. Her brown hair was immaculately pinned into her stylish hat.

"You must be the Parkses." The captain reached out his hand to Ranahan. "I'm Dawson Mandara, but I still seem to be called Captain Mandara."

"Thank you for taking care of our Marquesa." Carolina flashed her light-up-the-whole-room smile.

"I intend to take care of her for a long, long time!" Captain Mandara added.

"And here's our little David!" Carolina rolled the brown blanket from the bundle in her arms.

"He's beautiful!" Isabel cooed.

"Fortunately, he gets that from his mama." Ranahan grinned. "The only thing he got from his daddy is bowed legs."

With her free hand, Carolina reached out and held the Marquesa's arm. She leaned forward and whispered. "I like him!"

Isabel nodded. "The Lord has been very good to me."

"When you wrote about your trust in Jesus, I broke down and cried," Carolina admitted. "It will take us weeks to get caught up."

"The captain's so strong and yet gentle, Carolina. You know what I mean?" Isabel whispered.

"I most certainly do! But you didn't know we were going to be on this train. What are you doing here? You aren't slipping out of town, are you?"

Isabel gazed across the platform as four children scampered toward Captain Mandara. "Oh my, we'll talk later. Pray for me!"

Isabel stood back from the captain several feet and watched as the second-tallest girl raced ahead of the others. She leaped into his arms, threw her hands around his neck so wildly that his hat tumbled to the platform, and kissed him on the lips.

The tallest boy retrieved the hat and put it on his own head, letting it droop down past his ears. The captain squatted down and hugged both boys at the same time.

"Hello, Marquesa, I'm Nellie."

Isabel was startled to see the oldest girl bypass her father and come straight over to her. Isabel reached out her gloved hand.

Nellie didn't take her hand. Instead she stepped closer and gave Isabel a big hug. "We're kind of a hugging family," Nellie explained.

"I like that!"

"Do you love my daddy?"

"I love him dearly. He is a wonderful, wonderful man."

"Yes, he is, isn't he?" Nellie slipped her gloved hand into Isabel's and tugged her toward the others. "Do you sew?"

"No, not really," the Marquesa admitted.

"Don't worry, I'll teach you," Nellie replied. Then she turned to the other children. "Hey, everyone, this is our very own Marquesa!"

There were several moments of hugs, tears, and more hugs.

Finally, the captain led the procession to the baggage room. As they passed the dark-blue-uniformed conductor, he reached out and handed Grant a coin.

"What was that about?" the captain asked.

"Oh!" Grant beamed. "I bet the conductor a nickel that our Marquesa was the prettiest woman in Montana." He grabbed Isabel's free hand and looked up at her. "I won!"

She looked down at Grant's dancing, joyful brown eyes.

Young man, I'm the one who won.

Oh, sweet Lord, did I ever win!

Look for book #3 in the

Heroines of the Golden West Series

by Stephen Bly

Images of
Oliole

Follow Oliole Fontenot in her quest
to photograph women of the
West in Montana Territory.

For a list of other books by
Stephen Bly
or information
regarding speaking engagements
write:

Stephen Bly
Winchester, Idaho 83555